PRAISE FOR *WE'RE ALL LYING*

I love a twisty, turny thriller and this was exactly that. A gripping, empathetic read and a wonderful debut.

-John Marrs, bestselling author of *The One*

Full of twists and turns, *We're All Lying* lives up to its title and then some. This debut is a domestic thriller with plenty of surprises, keeping you guessing all the way through to the shocking end. I loved it.

-Kaira Road, USA Today and Amazon Charts bestselling author of *Somebody's Home* and *Best Day Ever*

Marie Still's WE'RE ALL LYING is the delightfully dark thriller you've been waiting to sink your teeth into. A cast of characters you know better than to trust, a twist you never saw coming, and an utterly satisfying ending. Still's debut will leave you breathless.

-Jessica Payne, international bestselling author of *Make Me Disappear and The Lucky One*

WE'RE ALL LYING

MARIE STILL

Text copyright © 2022 by **Marie Still**

All rights reserved. For information regarding reproduction in total or in part, contact Rising Action Publishing Co. at risingactionpublishingco.com

Cover illustration © Nat Mack

ISBN 978-1-990253-31-7

FIC031000 FICTION / Thrillers / General

FIC031080 FICTION / Thrillers / Psychological

FIC030000 FICTION / Thrillers / Suspense

Follow Rising Action on our socials!

Twitter: @RAPubCollective

Instagram: @risingactionpublishingco

Tiktok: @risingactionpublishingco

RISING ACTION

WE'RE ALL *LYING*

For all the women (and men) who have been scorned and wanted to do bad bad things.

And my husband for being hot, funny, and my biggest fan. Love you forever.

PRESENT

CASS

EMMA HAS RUN AWAY, perhaps into the arms of another married man. Or maybe she's floating beneath the glassy waters of the Everglades, slowly spinning in an eternal death waltz with the seagrass. Is her willowy body bloated, her porcelain skin gray and mottled? Has her shiny black hair now knotted around the roots of the cypress trees?

For some reason, the police officer who has rudely interrupted my evening is sitting in the living room in our temporary rental asking me to help find her—the woman who slept with my husband and ruined my life.

"Mrs. Mitchell?" Officer Daley says.

"Cass," I say. "Haven't we known each other long enough to lose the formalities? Call me Cass."

My eyes shift from Officer Daley to Ethan, my once faithful and adoring husband. At least, the man I believed to be those things. I'm not so sure anymore. Our entire life may be a lie. He's sitting here with me now, and she's—well, who knows where she is, but is he *really* here? All of him? I squeeze my phone, a substitute for his neck.

Emma's disappearance isn't news. Hell, I was the one who tipped off the police in the first place. I want her found more than anyone. We deserve justice for what she's done. However, Officer Daley showing up at the house unannounced tonight *is* a surprise, and I don't like surprises.

This isn't the first time we've sat with him, but on this night, it's different. A weird energy crackles in the room. He's asking me questions he already has the answers to. He should be out there instead, hunting her down. Doing whatever it takes to arrest her.

I inspect his movements, overanalyze every shift of his body and each twitch on his face. The belt around his waist holding his pistol, handcuffs, and other items looks foreign on him—too big and clunky for his tall, skinny frame. He fiddles with his belt, unable to find a comfortable position in the armchair, then clears his throat.

"There have been recent developments. I need to ensure we haven't missed anything that will help us find Emma."

I shudder when he looks at me. It's like acrylic nails are scraping down my spine. He hasn't learned how to hide his intentions and feelings behind a stony expression yet, like a more seasoned police officer would. Or like I do. It may be a skill he'll never hone. This ability to morph and mold oneself into whichever persona is needed takes years of experience. When you grew up like I did, clawing your way out of the trailer park, swimming through a sea of syringes and shit, you become adept at these things. You know which occasions require which masks. You can become someone else, the person you want to be, rather than the person you are.

"Cass, you're pale. Are you okay? Can I get you a drink?" Ethan's blue eyes swim with concern as his eyebrows meet at the bridge of his nose. I wish I could smack the worried look off his handsome face. Yes, my mouth *is* dry, and my throat feels coated in sandpaper, but I don't need my husband pointing out how bad I look in a police officer's presence. He wasn't always this stupid. Or maybe he has been, and I didn't hate him enough to notice.

"I'm fine. But why don't you get *all* of us some ice water?" I turn my head, unable to stand looking at him a second longer. He stands and walks to the kitchen.

My reflection stares back at me from the television hanging on the wall. I'm wearing navy blue leggings and an oversized knit sweater despite Florida's scorching heat simmering outside. With my blonde hair framing my makeup-free face, I look like an innocent forty-year-old mom; the best look for this occasion. "Powerful advertising executive" may elicit the wrong assumptions. And right now, I don't need any incorrect conjecture from our unwelcome visitor.

Emma has a mom, a distraught mom most likely. My daughter's face flashes in my mind. I can't imagine what the not knowing must be like. *If Aubrey ever disappeared—no, I can't think like that.*

I shake my head and turn my attention back to Officer Daley. "What developments? You've been working *my* case for months now with zero progress." I emphasize 'my' to remind him who the first victim was. *Victim,* the word is being thrown around so flippantly. Emma has probably run away, too afraid to face the consequences of her crimes. Of course, she did, she's a child—much like my man-child of a husband who couldn't keep it in his pants. His lack of self-control has left a wake of victims. His wife, his daughter, his son, and even Emma if I dig deep enough, past my anger, and really think about it.

"Let's try starting from the beginning. Even the smallest detail may help. I know you want her found, too," Officer Daley replies. He's trying to establish trust, to come across as empathetic. He doesn't realize the spaces surrounding his words are so revealing. I can't trust him. Not anymore. Once again, I've put my trust in the hands of the wrong man.

Ethan rejoins us with my water, which I ignore. I sigh and glance from Daley to Ethan and back again. What a group we make. The cheating husband, the trustworthy police officer, who may not be so trustworthy after all, and me, the scorned wife with secrets of her own.

"You know about Emma and Ethan. And what Emma did to us. I'm trying to move on with my life, put her and all of it behind me. Is all this necessary?" I wish he'd fold shut the stupid little notebook his pen is hovering over, apologize for interrupting our evening, and leave. Aubrey's face returns. I hate myself for the guilt souring my stomach, almost as much as I hate Ethan.

"I know this is hard—" he starts.

"No," I interrupt him, leaning forward to meet his stare. "With all due respect, none of you knows how *hard* this is." I wave my hand dramatically between them. How could they even pretend to know? No one knows what hell my life has been because of the affair and Emma's persistent stalking.

After an awkward pause, he continues, "We simply want to find Emma. Her family is worried."

"Then you should ask my dumbass husband where she is," I say.

"Huh?" Ethan asks.

Oh shit, did I say that out loud?

I spin my wedding band around my finger to keep my thoughts from tumbling from my mouth. Ethan reaches for my hand. Now he wants to play the part of the caring husband. I pick up my glass and wrap both hands around it. He has the audacity to appear hurt. *Does he not understand the gravity of our current situation?* Officer Daley jots something down in his notebook. Fucking Ethan, always getting me in trouble. His myopic view that the world revolves around his need for affection and admiration got us into this mess, and now I'll have to get us out of it.

"Fine," I relent, knowing if I don't give Daley something, he'll sit here staring at me all night with that notebook of his. "Am I correct in assuming that when you find her, she'll be prosecuted?"

"Yes, your case is still open and active. If it's proven she was involved, we'll move forward with charges."

If. When did her guilt come into question? I let my vision blur, then tell my story. At least the parts I'm willing to share.

We're all liars, after all.

TWO

CASS

THE MORNING my life imploded started like any other. I waited in my kitchen for the kids to get ready for school. In six months Aubrey would have her driver's license. The paralyzing fear produced by thinking of her as a teen driver didn't stand a chance against the freedom—my freedom—this privilege would deliver. I could put in my notice, hand over the keys, and retire from my side job as a personal driver. I couldn't wait.

I placed a finger on my MacBook's touchpad to unlock the screen. As it came to life, I surveyed my nails and resisted the urge to pick at the chipped polish. I noted the need to fit in a trip to the nail salon, knowing full well I'd ignore it for at least two more weeks.

A photo from our last family vacation filled the screen before me. Ben and Aubrey smiled at me, their arms flung around each other's shoulders, hair dripping with the water from the lake behind them.

Ben was a year younger but already a foot taller than his sister—height he got from his father. The rest of his looks were all me: blond hair, blue eyes, and pale skin that, despite copious amounts of seventy SPF sunscreen reapplied every hour, turns an angry pink with the slightest exposure to sun. An inconvenience when you live in Florida. Aubrey, the opposite of her brother, shared my lack of height and resembled her dad in all other physical aspects—chestnut hair, olive skin, and blue eyes that have always reminded me of the water lapping the shores of our local Tampa Bay beaches—my favorite color. Despite being the female twin of her father, her personality mirrors my own—the good, the bad, and the ugly. If I still had a mother, she'd tell me Aubrey's antics and outbursts were payback for all the trouble I caused as a teen. But I don't have one. I've suffered alone through the 'I hate you's' and the door slams. The photo captured a rare moment, their faces weren't buried in their phones, and their love for each other, often hidden behind bickering, shone brightly.

With an elbow on my white marble countertop, head supported in my hand, I mindlessly scrolled Facebook. Typical stuff filled my feed, political fights and memes—an occasional funny one—but most posts were people hiding their boring, meaningless lives behind utter bullshit. There was a smiling family photo from one friend who, just last week, had been in hysterics over her husband's drinking and the constant fighting it caused. Next up, a scenic view from an all-inclusive luxury resort from another friend who was always complaining about her gobs of debt. I rolled my eyes, though I've been hiding those same rotten bits of my life behind a shiny exterior, too.

If I could have somehow changed how time works,

frozen myself in that moment on my computer's background, I could have lived in a blissful state of ignorance forever.

The empty stairs were tempting me to yell at the kids for the third—or was it fourth?—time. I sighed. *What good would it do?* They'd spent years perfecting the art of tuning me out. I could lead my advertising agency to meet our clients' ever-changing and unrealistic demands, but I still hadn't figured out how to leverage my logistical prowess to manage my own household.

Done with social media, I clicked into my personal email. A subject line made me pause: *CASS RU LISTENING.* Working in advertising, I'd seen plenty of pitch concepts for click-bait email tactics. I hated them, and they never made the cut for campaigns. But curiosity, the one who always killed the cat, got the best of me.

I stood in my kitchen reading those vile words, gaping at a photo of my husband with another woman, while my stomach plummeted into an abyss.

The blood rushing through my ears drowned out all sounds, including Ben's arrival. When he appeared in front of me, my hand slammed down the laptop's lid, and I plastered a smile on my face.

"Ma, you okay?" he asked.

"Yes. I'm fine. We're going to be late. Where's your sister?"

My life played out behind my eyes like an old projector film, choppy and in black and white: our first date; our wedding day; Ethan bringing a bag of McDonald's into the delivery room when I was in my eighteenth hour of labor, then laughing when I threatened divorce; the inside jokes; the tears of joy, frustration, and sadness ... all of it. Ethan worshiped me ... no, we worshiped each other, in our own ways. He'd always been there for me, and I assumed he always would be. Once again, I'd gotten it all so very wrong.

"Your face looks funny. Your voice is weird, too." Ben flipped his hair from his eyes and squinted at me. His voice bumped me from my thoughts and back into our kitchen.

"You always give the best compliments." I stepped around the counter and tousled his hair, hoping he wouldn't notice my shaking hand.

"The hair!" His hands rose in defense. My distraction was successful. Ben ran to the bathroom to undo the damage my hand had inflicted.

Holding myself up by the kitchen table, I forced deep breaths in and out. I couldn't think about Ethan now, despite my mind wanting to evaluate every moment of our courtship and nineteen-year marriage. The inanimate objects of my life filled my kitchen. White marble countertops—an image of Ethan bending a woman over—*no, Cass, stop*. I dug the heels of my palms into my eyelids and focused on the lights exploding behind my eyes instead.

A lump formed in my throat. I attempted to massage it away, but it metastasized like a cancerous cell. I forced my racing mind to center on how to survive the next hour. *Get the kids to school, get to work, potentially plan a murder or two*. The women on *Dateline*, the ones whose pain fed by betrayal drove them to murder, became relatable.

"Can I drive?" Aubrey asked, not looking up from her phone as she entered the kitchen. A third sneak attack. The email, Ben, and Aubrey. Remaining present was proving to be an arduous task. It would be a long day, a long night—a long everything.

I wouldn't have to continue pleading with the kids to get

moving, though. At least one thing was going my way. They didn't deserve my wrath, and I was certain if I had to keep begging them to get moving, I wouldn't be capable of keeping my words from turning into knives.

"Sure," I replied, forcing another teeth-gritting smile onto my face.

In the earth's history, the earthquake with the highest magnitude registered a whopping nine point five. My composure, comparatively, was at a twelve. As the seconds ticked on, it became harder to hide my unraveling. The familiar claws of a panic attack were snaking their way from my stomach into my chest and up through my throat, squeezing every organ on its way. I wiped the sweat beading my forehead with a slow swipe of my hand.

Aubrey cocked an eyebrow. She'd always been able to read things in my expressions even Ethan would miss. I watched her lift her phone and turn her attention back to shooting the perfect selfie before I allowed myself to release the air burning in my lungs.

I checked my phone's calendar app. With no meetings before one, I had five hours to process what I'd learned and begin my investigation. I mentally started my checklist. Facts: Ethan was a cheater. Still unknown: who he was cheating with. Not knowing the identity of my enemy was unnerving. I needed every piece of data, every dirty detail. I also needed to fully prepare for the confrontation with Ethan. The one barreling toward him while he sat at work unaware.

The morning's activities turned blotchy. I was in the kitchen then, *blink*, sitting in the car's passenger seat, *blink again*, Aubrey pulled into the high school's carline. The car stopped, but my next step wasn't registering. I stared out the windshield with unfocused eyes while a thousand questions screamed through my mind. *Who was the woman? How had this happened without me realizing it? Who was this man I married?* The questions tumbled and tripped over themselves, demanding their answers. I put my fingers in my ears to quiet them so I could stop losing time.

"Mom, hello?" Aubrey waved her hand in my face. "You can sit here all day like a weirdo, or you can get in the driver's seat and leave like a normal person." Aubrey jogged from the car toward the school after muttering something about *embarrassing* under her breath. With a reliance on muscle memory, I unbuckled the seatbelt, walked around the car, got behind the wheel, and somehow drove myself to work.

Easing my Range Rover into my assigned spot, I looked up at the stand-alone building. A wall of glass glittered in the morning sun. Since reading the email, everything seemed off, including the once welcoming but now menacing office looming over me. The palm trees lining the parking lot quivered in the breeze like they were laughing at me.

While my hands gripped the steering wheel even tighter, I tried to remember the breathing exercises they were always droning on about in yoga class. *Deep breath in, exhale the bad.*

Unfortunately, no matter how many cleansing breaths I forcefully pushed out, the tension wouldn't lift from my chest. *Ugh, I should have focused more on the breathing and advice in yoga, and less on trying not to fart or fall asleep.*

"Well, you can't spend the day sitting in your car. Get your shit together, go in there and get to work," I said to myself. A Sandhill Crane meandered by on the sidewalk; I'd always found its long, curved neck and the red mask rimming its eyes to be beautiful. I slipped on my own mask, the one I used to cover my shame and anger, then stepped out of the car into the morning's muggy air.

Head tucked down, I walked with long, fast strides through the halls of Mitchell & Parker Advertising Agency. My stilettos clicked on the marble floor and echoed through the modern open office. Most mornings, I'd make it a point to walk around and greet everyone on my way in. I'd ask about their lives, their boyfriends, girlfriends, spouses, kids, or whatever personal details I'd committed to memory. It was important to me they felt valued as humans and not just employees. As such, it was unusual for me to bolt past them, and I hoped it didn't raise any suspicions. *Life is fine, everything is great, no, my husband isn't a cheating bastard.* If I could convince myself, even for the few minutes it took to run to my office, then I could convince the staff. Maybe.

Alice, my assistant, scurried toward me as fast as her loafers would carry her, foiling my plan to sneak in unnoticed.

"Mrs. Mitchell!" She waved her hand above her head. The stack of folders she carried in the other threatened to fall.

I cringed, then forced a smile. "Alice, good morning." My jaw hurt from a morning of clenched teeth and fake smiles. I resisted the urge to reach up and massage the aching away.

Alice caught her breath and straightened before pushing her glasses up her nose. "You look beautiful as always. I simply love that blouse! Where'd you get it? I'd buy one for myself, but it wouldn't look as good on me." She looked down at her nondescript white cotton button-up with a slight frown. I cracked my knuckles to hide my impatience. Although my bruised ego *could* use a few compliments, that morning I was in a rush. She shook off her frown, straightened her back—all business—and continued, "You have the Blaxten presentation today at one. I'll have coffee and light snacks set up in the boardroom by twelve-forty. I've made copies of the presentation for everyone. Is there anything else you need from me?"

I stepped around her and walked toward my office. She followed behind, notebook open, pen poised ready to record any last-minute instructions, of which there'd be none.

"You've been my assistant for ten years and have never forgotten so much as a pen. You know better than I do what's needed. I trust everything will be perfect. It always is in your capable hands."

"Your trust is appreciated, Mrs. Mitchell. I can assure you everything will be up to your standards. Thankfully, you have no other meetings scheduled today. If you decide to make any changes to the presentation, I'll need them by eleven in order to have enough time to re-print. But of course, if they come in after that, you know your wish is my command."

We arrived at my office. I turned and my face relaxed into its first genuine smile of the day.

"I'm sure that won't be necessary."

Alice was one of our first hires, second only to Carla, the office manager, head of HR, and other many hats she wore. Initially, Alice supported both Julie, my best friend and business partner, and me. But as the agency grew, we both needed our own assistants. Julie, despite being against the idea, relented. I took Alice and she hired a new assistant, then another, and yet another after that. I couldn't blame the poor assistants for the revolving door—Julie was an acquired taste. You had to learn to not take her sharp tongue personally and how to push back. Her bark is much worse than her bite.

Alice gave a curt nod, pushed her glasses up her nose again, and began to take her leave.

"Alice, one more thing. Please hold all my calls. Tell them ... I'm busy, or out of the office, or whatever." She turned and looked at me quizzically. "I just want to ensure I'm ready to nail this presentation and secure this account."

"Yes, of course, Mrs. Mitchell, not that you need the extra time; there is no one better than you. Shall I order your usual salad from Café Ponte for lunch and bring it to your office?"

"That would be wonderful. Thank you."

Alice retreated to her desk, a large double cubicle with multiple monitors. She could have as much space and as many monitors as she needed. *Without her, my life would be in shambles. Not that it isn't, but before this morning it has been relatively shamble-free.* Based on her employee file, I knew she was forty-five, only five years older than me, but she had the aura of an older woman, an old soul I suppose. Order and predictability oozed into every area of her life, including her work, mannerisms, and wardrobe. I imagined her closet, a row of neatly pressed ankle-length skirts, white blouses, and cardigans. The same three articles of clothing multiplied in various neutral shades. She always styled her brown hair in a neat bun at the nape of her neck, the same hairstyle every day for ten years. She never got sick and rarely took time off. When she did, it was only because I'd forced a vacation day on her. I did, however, like to imagine her taking that bun down, shaking her hair loose, and hitting the bars, dancing like no one was looking. No one should suffer through being *that* buttoned-up all the time. But I had too much going on to concern myself with Alice finding joy from something other than a new file organization system.

THREE

CASS

I STOOD LOOKING at my office door, thinking about how satisfying it would be to slam it shut. *No need to cause a scene, Cass.* I eased it shut. Once closed, I pressed my back against it, dropped my purse and briefcase, closed my eyes, and sank to the floor. I wrapped my arms around my knees and lowered my head between them. In twenty-four hours, everything had changed. One day I was living my mostly perfect life, in my mostly perfect marriage, with my mostly perfect family ... then, I wasn't.

A checklist. Make your list. Cross off each item one by one.

My head lifted. I looked at my desk. Five steps. I commanded my legs to stand and bring me there. They obeyed.

After collapsing into my chair, and flinging my purse on the credenza behind me, I ripped my computer from its briefcase and slammed it onto the stand. The tremor in my hand made it hard to connect the monitor's plug into the small port on the side of my laptop. Finally able to jam it in, I pressed my finger with more force than necessary to unlock it. My sweet, innocent children smiled back from the monitor. The cool gray wood of my desk seemed to pulse under my splayed hands. Looking at their faces, a watery haze filmed my eyes, turning the picture into a soft watercolor painting. I rubbed my eyes with clenched fists. He couldn't have my tears, not yet. An unsteady hand moved to the mouse.

I should delete the email, pretend I never saw it.

There would be no pretending. Far too late for that.

My finger tapped nervously on the mouse's button, not depressing it fully. *It's like a Band-Aid; you have to rip it off.* With one click, I opened the life-shattering email and re-read it, this time looking for clues of the sender's identity.

Cass,
You don't know me, but I know your husband. We've been sleeping together for six months. Your perfect Ethan, not so perfect, is he? Surprise! It's not just sex either. He loves me. The only reason he hasn't left you is the kids. Ha! Such a cliché. But whatever. Your life is about to fall apart and mine is about to begin. Everything's always so easy for you, isn't it? Well, it's about to get a tad more difficult. In case you don't believe me, I've attached a few photos. Enjoy!
XOXO,
The Future Mrs. Mitchell

I re-downloaded the first one now that I had time to examine it properly. Ethan stood with his arm looped intimately around a microscopic waist. I leaned in, trying to grasp onto anything I recognized about her. She had colored over her face with black—*tricky little thing.*

I tucked my hair behind my ears and cataloged our differences. Jet black waves cascaded down her shoulders, and she had the body most women slaved hours at the gym for. Her delicate frame suggested she achieved that body by eating whatever she wanted and laughing about how no matter how hard she tried, she just couldn't gain a pound. *Bitch.* At forty, I'd finally reached a point where I loved and accepted my body—the stretch marks, extra pounds, wrinkles, and all. But those old insecurities were rearing their ugly heads. Guilt turned my stomach for being so bitchy, the exact thing I accused her of in my head. I took great pride in supporting women, never judging them for their looks. Despite the nasty email, it wasn't her fault, not entirely.

I could kill Ethan.

Unable to stand the proud smile on my husband's face, I angrily clicked my mouse to close the photo. There hadn't been time to open all the attachments earlier. If I'd known the filth awaiting me, maybe I would have skipped them completely. Probably not though, I know myself better than that.

The same woman was in bed with Ethan. Both were naked, hair tousled from sex, posing for a selfie. She'd blacked out her face again. I opened the last attachment. An image of Ethan's face buried between a pair of milky legs filled the screen; he was too busy to smile for the camera. I'd seen that angle enough to recognize the top of his head. I imagined the motion of his tongue.

My hand shot out for my trash can. I had it between my knees with my face hovered over it in time to vomit. That was *my* pleasure, I *owned* it.

"Knock, knock. Good morn—" Julie halted halfway in my office. "Cass, what the hell? Are you okay?"

I lifted my head. Snot dripped from my nose and tears streamed down my face. One look at Julie and the dam crumbled. I didn't realize how much I needed my best friend until she was standing in front of me. Julie slammed the door, which, despite my condition, I wished I could stand and slam for myself—over and over again. She ran to me and crouched down, grabbing my shoulders. Her brown eyes danced in their sockets searching my face.

"What's going on?" she gasped.

I pointed to my monitor. If I had to say the words out loud, I'd puke them into the trash can on top of that morning's coffee and stomach bile. Julie's gaze followed my finger, and she recoiled.

"What the—?" She leaned closer to the monitor while her finger frantically clicked the mouse. Her eyes darted side to side reading the email, then bulged when she flipped through the photos. Her dark hair, slicked back in its signature high ponytail, swung back and forth with each shake of her head.

Julie whipped her head from the screen. "Bastard. I'll kill him."

"I don't understand," I stuttered, finding my voice. "How could he do this to me? To the kids? And she says he's leaving me for her, that he *loves* her. Do you think that's true?" I searched my mind for any signs I'd missed. A faint smell of an unknown perfume wafting up from a basket of dirty laundry. A credit card receipt for a piece of jewelry I never received. A sudden increase in business trips and work-related dinners or evening outings. Our sex life was great, better than most. We had raised kids together, and barely fought. We still made each other laugh, even his ridiculous dad jokes and random ass slaps followed by 'good game.'

None of it made sense. I clutched at my chest; it was as if my heart had been raked by a cheese grater.

Julie grabbed the photo of Ethan and me off my desk, opened a desk drawer, and threw it in.

The drawer crashing made me jump. From her angry eyes I expected her to follow it up with a few good kicks. I looked at the closed drawer and envisioned the photo of the two of us standing on a white sandy beach. My arms wrapped around Ethan's tanned six-pack, my gaze locked only on him. And Ethan looking at the camera, face filled with that knee-weakening smile. The truth hit me like a smack to the skull with a hammer—the affair had already started when the photo was taken three months before. I slid the drawer open, picked up the frame, then slammed it against the edge of my desk until the glass shattered and the frame lay scattered in pieces.

"Feel better?" Julie deadpanned.

A buzz sounded from my desk. Both our gazes locked on my phone.

"A text. You don't think it's him, do you?" I asked.

"Could be. Read it," Julie encouraged, nodding toward it.

I wiped my sweaty hands on my navy slacks, picked up the phone, then with a shaking voice, read the text out loud. "Hey babe, hope the kids weren't a pain this morning. Don't wait on me for dinner. Work stuff." My shoulders slumped.

"Work stuff, ha! He's something, isn't he? Of all the men, I'd never expected this from him. What a dick. What a disgusting dick." She gazed out the window. I wondered what thoughts were somersaulting through her mind. An uncontrollable wince pulled every part of my face inward. Ethan had committed the ultimate act of betrayal, yet a small part of me wanted to defend him. I wanted to punch that part in the mouth.

"Write him back right now and tell him you're on to him." She jammed her finger at the phone.

My fingers hovered over the keyboard. I changed my mind and placed it face down on my desk.

"Nineteen years, Julie. We've been married nineteen years. How can the person you think you know better than anyone in the world turn into a complete stranger in seconds?" I asked, an obnoxious whine raising my voice. "You knew everything about our marriage. Would you ever have imagined it would come to this?"

"No. But fuck him." Julie's frown deepened.

I puffed my cheeks like a blowfish and let the air leak out. "I can feel my eyes swelling shut. Blaxten will be here in a few hours. The most important pitch of the year and this happens." My fingers delicately tapped under my eyes.

"I have a makeup bag in my office. Want me to grab it?" Julie asked.

"Nah, I think I have some concealer." I looked back at my purse, but my arms felt too heavy to reach for it.

"You better talk to him tonight. No sitting around planning and practicing your speech until you've memorized every word. And do *not* let him off easy. He's a charming fucker; don't let that smile of his fool you. You better not fall for his shit and cave. He's always been your weakness, and all this time, I thought he was worthy of being that." I ignored the dig—*weakness, my ass.*

"I'm waiting up for him so I can get this over with tonight. Who do you think she is?" I asked. Half-moons were forming in my palms from my nails.

"Probably some young naïve idiot half his age from the

looks of those photos." Julie sneered. "Typical. Pigs, the lot of them. You should give up on men. I have tons of single girlfriends I can hook you up with."

"Don't be silly. Women cheat, too."

Images of every woman I'd ever met rotated through my head. There's no way that long black hair wouldn't have made an impression. Once my mind wrapped its tendrils around a problem, it wouldn't let go until I found the solution. Right then, the need to identify her suffocated me. A face. A name. An address.

"Have you looked through his social media yet?" Julie asked.

"No, I was planning on it but got distracted by the projectile vomiting."

"Well, if she's there, you'll find her. No one's a better internet stalker than you. FBI level skills."

"The thought of him saying I love you to someone else is almost worse than those photos."

"Leave his ass. Kick him out tonight. You don't need him or any of this shit," Julie said.

I looked at the photo of us now sitting on the floor next to my chair. *Leave him.* I rolled the idea around my mouth. It tasted like sour milk.

Julie checked her phone. "Shit, I have to run. Meeting." She stood to leave, her face and voice softened. "You going to be okay?"

"No." I snorted. "But you don't need to sit here and watch me cry. Go. I'm going to see if I can figure out who she is. I'll let you know if I find anything. I also need to review my presentation. This deal is too big to screw up."

"Never. You could do that presentation in your sleep. No way we don't win the account."

I struggled to wrap myself in her confidence like a blanket.

"I hope you're right. Or I'll burst into tears in the middle of the meeting and humiliate myself." I laughed dryly.

"I should have IT record it just in case." Julie half-smiled.

"Funny. And IT is James. It's one person, and he has a name. Fuck's sake, Julie. I'm giving you an org chart and making you study it until you've learned everyone's name."

"Yeah, yeah." Julie sobered. "We'll get through this, Cass, I promise. We'll figure it out, okay?"

"I hope—" My voice trailed off. I tilted my face to the ceiling to keep more treacherous tears from falling. I had broken my cardinal rule of never crying at work more times in one day than I had in my entire career. She closed the door with less ceremony than she'd entered.

"Where do I even start?" I asked the now empty room. *Work the problem. All problems have solutions. I just needed to break it down into smaller chunks. Make a list and cross each task off until they're all complete.* I picked up my phone and returned Ethan's text: *K. We need to talk tonight.*

Sick of watching the blinking dots at the bottom of our exchange, I slammed it face down on the desk. Then picked it back up and spun it over to check if the screen had shattered. There was nothing more to discuss over text anyway, as what I had to say required a face-to-face discussion. I needed to see his reactions, analyze his facial expressions, and observe his body language. It was too easy to slip a lie through a text. And Ethan, it turns out, was a very capable liar. I also liked the idea of him spending the day wondering and worrying if I'd discovered his little secret.

Social media, bank statements, phone records, and

Google were all dead ends. I slouched back in my chair and steepled my fingers under my chin. Only one option remained. Take my investigation to the source, my cheating husband.

A low growl vibrated from the depths of my mind. *Who is she?* it whispered, until its screech reverberated within my skull. I opened the Blaxten presentation to rehearse the pitch and ignore the monster before it took over. After reading the first bullet point for the twentieth time, I rocked back and rubbed my temples.

Desperate times and all that. I dug through the junk in my purse and found a bottle of magical football-shaped pills. Shaking it, I sighed with relief as clacking resounded from inside. I popped the top open and swallowed a Xanax dry. Hand paused with the bottle top partially turned back in place, I stopped. This was an emergency. A second pill followed the first down my throat.

Helpful, but not enough. I pretended to read my phone and rushed through the bright halls to the back staircase. Our open floor layout allowed every employee to observe my escape, so I hoped they'd assume I was running around working on final preparations for the afternoon's guests. Blaxten would be a huge win for the agency.

Down the back staircase, I pushed open the door leading outside to the alleyway. The sharp smell of smoke hit me. My jaw unclenched at the sight of the small, huddled group.

"Anyone have one I could bum?" I asked.

Jim, the director of business development, HR head and office manager Carla, and Alec, one of our graphic designers, stared at me with matching saucer-shaped eyes.

"Bad day?" Jim asked.

"You could say," I answered.

"Sorry, none here. Unless you want a puff of this," Alec replied, holding up his e-cig. I shook my head. I needed the real deal, the sharp pang of nicotine-filled smoke in my lungs.

"Here you go, love," Carla said, handing me a Marlboro Light. My brand.

"Thank you," I cooed, grabbing the cigarette. After several attempts, the lighter flicked to life. The cigarette's end turned red and crackled as I inhaled the first drag. After handing the lighter back to Carla, I walked a few steps away and exhaled smoke, letting it curl from my mouth, then leaned against the concrete wall of the building's ugly rear foundation. The group resumed their hushed conversation while the Xanax and cigarette lightened my head. My rage was now less likely to explode. It simmered below a dulled surface. After a few drags of the cigarette, I stomped it out with the toe of my Louboutin, red sole be damned. The black marks would be a fitting complement to my now tarnished life.

Everything angered me, including my designer shoes. For two thousand dollars, my feet shouldn't hurt after an hour. If I had my way, I'd show up to work in ripped jeans and a hoodie, or even sweats to truly put the casual in casual Friday. But Julie had always insisted that appearances matter. I'd debated her, claimed a sharp outfit didn't make my work any better or worse. I was full of shit. I'd been using appearances—clothing, facial expressions, body language, all of it—to my advantage long before meeting Julie. Appearances *did* matter, and today I was thankful for my Louboutin heels, Armani slacks, and Valentino blouse. I looked much more confident than I felt.

Julie had her reasons, ones she'd only confided in the two

people closest to her, me and her wife, Victoria. "There are two things this industry holds against me," she told us once when we were first starting the agency, "a vagina and a spouse with a vagina. I'll be damned if I give them anything else. Not only will we be the best fucking agency on the east coast, maybe the entire country, but we'll look good doing it."

Back in the safety of my office, I stared out the window into the parking lot mentally rehearsing what I'd say to Ethan.

'What are you talking about Cass?' 'What affair?' In any argument, he always started with denial, then would flash the smile that crinkled the edges of his eyes and charm his way out of whatever mess he'd gotten himself into. It always worked. His smile would melt me like butter in a heated pan. My fists clenched at his imaginary responses, and I slammed them on the desk. He would not be sliding through this fight unbruised. The more I pictured his grinning face, the angrier I got. That was *my* smile. Those were *my* crinkled eyes. I grabbed the closest thing to me, a stapler, and threw it against the wall. Two people walking by turned their heads. I smiled at them through the glass window and shrugged, inwardly thanking Alice for her extended cubicle and the geographic convenience of my corner office blocking me from more potential curious stares. The chitter-chatter of the imagined gossip tickled my neck. It wouldn't be long before people knew, before everyone knew. Those things always had a way of getting out. I smoothed my hair and the front of my blouse and remembered my breathing. There was no sense in getting worked up over a made-up conversation.

What I wanted—more than anything—was to drive

home, tell Alexa to play every Adele album, and cry myself to sleep. But there'd be plenty of time for more tears and Adele later.

Who is she? the relentless voice returned.

"Mrs. Mitchell?" Alice's head peeked into my office.

"Yes, Alice?" I asked, too tired to disguise my annoyance.

"Everything okay?"

I sat up a little straighter. "Everything is fine. I was lost in my thoughts, running through this afternoon's presentation."

Alice opened the door fully.

"Okay, here's your lunch." She placed the Styrofoam takeout container on my desk. She started to leave and paused at the door. "You aren't stressed about the presentation, are you?" She wrung her hands; it made her look like a child who'd done something wrong, or perhaps a concerned mother. Not that I'd had any first-hand experience with the latter from my childhood.

"No." I smiled. "I'm surprised it's lunchtime already, is all. The day has flown by." My voice sounded false, overly cheery. Now I was the guilty child.

Her head tilted sideways. She eyed me quizzically. I busied myself with unwrapping my utensils and concentrated on my grilled chicken salad like it was the most captivating creation I'd ever encountered.

She nodded curtly and told me she'd let me know when Blaxten arrived and settled in the boardroom. She shut the door behind her. I threw the salad in the trash and tucked my lowered head into my folded arms.

FOUR

ALICE

MY KNEE SHOOK beneath my desk. Something was amiss. It was my job to know when things weren't going as expected. It had been my responsibility for almost a decade, and I was very good at my job. I chewed my fingernails. *It's not the presentation. Work doesn't make her nervous. She's too brilliant to be nervous.* She was confident, sometimes too confident and too sure. But that always worked for her and for us. I could count on one hand, with only three fingers, the number of large clients we didn't get after one of Cass's pitches. Those three were easy to remember.

She had many strengths but handling rejection wasn't one of them. Much like those athletes who moan and pout when they've lost one of their games, after each loss Cass would do the same. It would take weeks of extra compliments, tiptoeing around her feelings, and an extra bit of coddling to raise her spirits lifted and get her grumpies gone. I had never minded. I would have done anything for

Cass. I knew she'd do anything for me, too. She didn't always show it the way I did, though. She was a very busy woman, so it was to be expected. There's only so much one could expect from a person in a position such as hers.

I snuck a glance at Cass's office. Julie was in there with her. I was desperate to know what all the yelling and clamor was about. I had to be careful, though. Getting caught snooping would not fare well for me. They were too entrenched in whatever had them so worked up to notice anything, much less me. I stood and pretended to stretch. Moving regularly is imperative to spine health. Proper posture too. So many people sit slumped over their computers for hours every day, then complain about their chronic back pain. Not me. Every twenty-five minutes on the dot, I am up and going for a walk and doing my stretches. It comes in handy in situations like the one I was in. I stopped in front of her office and bent to pick up a non-existent piece of trash on the floor, leaning toward her door. If either of them came out, my presence would be nothing out of the ordinary. Just me, taking my regular walk, preventative health and all that.

Ethan's name is being said quite a lot. Interesting. Not work then, it seems.

I straightened and rolled my shoulders back, giving them their perceived privacy. It was imperative for me to find out whatever was going on, even if it involved Cass's personal life. I needed to know. I needed Cass to depend on me. Much depended on this.

In the past, I'd been told I get too attached to people, things, ideas, and situations. Teenage girls are harsh, so their opinions are of no consequence to me—not now anyway. Little hawks, always circling around, watching and waiting for you to screw up. 'You're too much, Alice' 'You're not my only friend, Alice' 'Stop stalking me, Alice.' I never 'stalked' anyone. What a preposterous idea. I was simply fiercely loyal to the few friends I had. Cass appreciates my loyalty. All those so called 'annoyances' became my greatest assets. I was invaluable to Cass because of them.

Maybe if things had been different—

I walked into the bathroom and sat in a stall on top of a closed toilet seat. This is where I go when my mind did that thing it liked to do sometimes. I called it my "what ifs." I had no room for them in this life. The past was the past, and it needed to stay there. I reminded myself to focus on what I could control, not on things that could not be changed. Ten years I'd spent working to get to this position, and the time prepping for it, of course. I couldn't let those nasty girls from the past ruin it for me. I'd come too close to finally getting what I wanted. I was almost there. A bit more time and everything would fall perfectly into place. I rolled up my sleeve and began tracing Cass's name in my arm with my fingernail, light at first then harder.

The door squeaked open, my head lifted and I flushed the toilet. By the time I opened the door, whoever had come in was already in the privacy of their own stall. I washed my hands, dried them thoroughly, and walked out.

I glanced back toward Cass's office. The door was still closed. Despite my burning desire to stand next to it and find out exactly what all the fuss was about, I took a stroll around the office instead. My steps slowed as I passed by the cluster of cubes where the account managers sat. Not that these junior employees would ever be in possession of more information about Cass than I was. I still listened for her name among the meaningless chatter and gossip. Of all the departments, the account managers were the breeding ground for office rumors, so they did come in handy on occasion. They were all still very young, comparatively. It was the first step into a career in advertising for most, and several of the team were fresh out of college. They hadn't learned the power of knowledge, especially when you're the only one who possesses that knowledge. They handed out their secrets for free.

"Hi Alice," Delaney said, much louder than necessary. A warning to her friends. Whatever they were talking about, they didn't want me to find out.

"Hello, Delaney. I hope this chitchat is all work related."

One girl to my right rolled her eyes. I turned my head and stared just long enough to make her face redden. She quickly tucked her chin and became very interested in her keyboard.

Delaney's lips formed a wry smile. "Of course, everyone is so excited to see what happens today. You must be pretty busy getting ready for the big meeting and all."

My eyebrows rose. "I'm not sure why you would think that. Everything is and has been taken care of for quite some time," I replied, my tone sharp. "You'd best learn," I said, swiveling my head to imply I was imparting this wisdom on the entire group, "that waiting until the last minute is exactly how you run into issues. The most effective approach to any task is to tackle it proactively and efficiently. Procrastination leads to mistakes. Have you learned nothing by watching Cass?"

A snorting sounded from one of the farther cubes. I didn't give the offender the satisfaction of trying to identify who made the appalling noise. "Well. I think that's enough for now. Back to work all of you."

I ignored the stifled giggles and the rising blood pressure they conjured. Resisting the urge to turn back and do something shocking, or worse, I continued to the boardroom, where I found Carla cleaning the table.

"Ms. Diaz, thank you for doing this. Cass will be so pleased."

"Oh, hello darling. I'm almost done in here. I'll be up front waiting to greet our guests. You give me a shout if you need anything, okay?" She threw the dirty paper towel in the trash can and walked out. My face fell into a frown. I had to be nice to Carla as Cass thought she walked on water. I didn't trust her. That sweet old lady act was nothing *but* an act. She wasn't fooling me. Julie either.

Two problems for another day.

FIVE

CASS

"HELLO, TARA, HERB, ASHLEY," I called, strutting into the boardroom. Hand outstretched, we exchanged shakes, greetings, and small talk. "The kids are great." "How's your Amelia?" "So sorry to hear your mother's not feeling well." "A European vacation?" "How amazing, much deserved."

"And how about you, Cass? How are Ethan and the kids?" Tara asked.

I managed not to wince, but my smile spread a bit too far and my eyes opened a bit too wide. "Great, great. Everyone is great," I replied.

Alice, the director of ceremonies, ushered everyone into their seats. Drink orders were taken, coffee preferences noted, and padfolios, eNotebooks, and laptops placed on the boardroom table. I stepped to the front of the room—my stage—ready to give the performance of a lifetime, hoping my acting skills would suffice.

Alice handed me a water bottle. The liquid quivered

from my shaking hand and a foreign feeling of self-doubt clawed its way in. I angled the bottle wrong, and water spilled down the front of my blouse. My cheeks burned, and I laughed awkwardly. No one joined in.

"Can I get anyone anything else?" Alice stepped in front of me, creating a much-needed diversion while I pulled myself together. I considered how big her raise should be after this. I'd give her my entire annual salary if I somehow made it through the presentation.

Instinct took over and I pushed thoughts of Ethan to the side. I breezed through the deck and answered their questions with the authority of a woman who knew what she was doing and not one whose life was floating around her in pieces. At least I think that's how it went. By the time it was over I recalled little of what I had said. I was usually so in tune with the room, able to course-correct based on my observations. There was no room reading on that day. It took all my concentration to get through the hour without passing out.

I walked robotically back to my office and packed my things to go home. Disappointment followed me out the door.

I rode home in silence, unable to bear the sound of even the radio. I needed the surrounding air to be as dull and colorless as I felt. After walking into my house, I called out to the kids. My greeting's echo was the only reply. An empty house. This is what I needed, space to think, to fall apart, to let my stretched skin rupture and release my agony. The room tilted. I placed my hands on the sofa to brace myself. The walls seemed to expand then contract around me as the reality of my situation fully sunk in.

What the fuck am I going to do?

My phone sat buried in my purse where I'd successfully ignored it for the second half of the day. I had been wavering between wanting a reply from Ethan and afraid of what his reply might be. I disregarded the pit in my stomach and dug the phone out. I had kids to think of. Kids who were more important than whatever Ethan needed, cared about, or anything Ethan related.

My bastard husband had nothing to say, but I had the gift of time. Aubrey went to the mall with friends and wouldn't be home for dinner. Ben was studying at a friend's.

I walked upstairs to my bedroom. One step in, and I gagged. I had to grab onto the doorjamb to keep from falling. Reminders of Ethan surrounded me: his side of the bed, the indent from his head still visible on his pillow; a worn copy of *The Old Man and the Sea* with a pair of readers sitting on top of it; his gym bag was in the corner with a heating pad, rollers, and the pile of contraptions needed for post-workout recovery growing larger with each year; a pile of sun-repellent shirts for long days on the boat sat neatly folded and stacked next to the custom case I had built for his fortieth birthday to hold his fly reels and fishing rods. Everywhere I looked, pieces of him assaulted me. Even his woodsy smell hung in the air melting with notes of amber and vanilla from my perfume. Our smell. But nothing would be *ours* anymore. He'd destroyed that. With my fingers clawed, I screamed until my raw throat burned. I was a geyser whose chambers couldn't hold the trapped steam any longer. The expulsion of agony finally released.

Collapsing to my knees, I covered my face with my palms and cried. The emotions came with such force I wasn't even sure what I was crying over. The hurt, embarrassment,

anger, jealousy. All of it. When there were no more tears to
cry, I rolled onto my back and studied the ceiling.

Words and feelings departed. Exhausted, I fell asleep on
the floor. Sleep was good. Pain couldn't reach me there.

THE WHIRRING of the garage door opening jerked me
awake. For one confused second, I forgot where I was. I felt
nothing. It was bliss. I sat up and rubbed my face. As the fog
lifted, I remembered Ethan, the email, the affair—the
pressure returned. The air became two enormous hands
clasped around my body. I was in a vice being crushed,
where any turn of the handle could be the one that killed
me, but I had no way of knowing which one.

"Ma?" Ben called from downstairs. His feet pounded up
the steps, and I sprang into action. He couldn't see me in the
state I was in. I had to insulate the kids from Ethan's mistake
as long as possible. If they experienced even a fraction of the
pain consuming me, I'm not sure I'd have found the strength
to go on. But moms tend to surprise ourselves when it comes
to our kids. You learn just how unbreakable you are when
put in situations where you're forced to protect your
children, both from the seen and unseen.

I bolted to the bedroom door, locked it, and yelled, "I'm
in here, Boo. Gonna take a quick shower, then I'll get dinner
together, 'kay?"

Already walking toward my bathroom, I couldn't make
out his muffled reply.

As the freezing water poured over me, I wished feelings
were tangible things so I could pluck mine out and send
them swirling down the drain with the icy water.

Clutching at my chest, my hands scraped at my skin. If I couldn't rip out my feelings, my heart would do. The physical pain throbbing with each beat was indescribable. I couldn't believe it was still functioning—how it managed to pump blood through my body and keep me alive when it was so obviously damaged. *Maybe it will stop, give up? It has to know this is too much and we can't live like this?* Eyes closed, I held my face in the spray while the water heated, and I silently begged for something, anything, to free me from the torment.

After finishing, I dried off, slipped into my softest sweater, and pulled on a pair of leggings, searching for comfort anywhere. With my wet hair clipped back, I leaned toward the bathroom mirror and wiped a streak through the condensation to inspect my reflection. A woman ten years older than me stared back with red puffy eyes. No makeup artistry could conceal my secrets. I tried to think of a lie to tell Ben to explain away the state of my face. Lies to cover lies to cover lies. *This is what we've become—a family of liars.*

Ethan was foolish enough to cheat, but surely, he had the good sense not to stay out all night. My stomach clenched. The thought of having to face him made me want to pack a bag and run away, to avoid the situation entirely. Make it all just ... go away. There were at least one or two friends who would take the kids and me in, especially if I told them what he'd done. But that would require telling people, which was worse than facing Ethan. Julie already knew, so her house was an option. I pressed the heels of my hands into my eyes. I needed to talk, yell, and scream at Ethan. As uncomfortable as it would be to form the words *you had an affair*, and to hear him finally confirm my greatest fears, I wouldn't let him off so easily. There was no reason to fear Ethan. He, on the other hand, should have been terrified. The rage I'd been holding in all day was waiting for its victim. A few more hours, and it would have its chance.

Bass thudded down the hallway from Ben's room. I walked on my toes down the hall and down the stairs. The longer I had alone, the better. I gently touched my eyes and willed the swelling and redness away. In the kitchen, I opened the freezer and enjoyed the cold puff of air on my face while I attempted to transform the ingredients filling the shelves into a meal. *Not happening. Pizza it is.*

After ordering, my body took over for my exhausted mind, and my legs brought me to the living room where I collapsed on the couch. The doorbell released me from my daze. *How long have I been staring at the wall?* Ben's footsteps hammered down the stairs, and he answered the door.

"Pizza's here," he called over his shoulder on the way to the kitchen. Two grease-stained boxes balanced on one hand bobbed above his head.

I entered the kitchen to find Ben leaning on the counter, not bothering with a plate. He paused mid-chew.

"You look like shit, Mom," he said through a mouthful of food.

"Language. And don't talk with your mouth full."

He swallowed. "Really, though. Are you okay? You look sick."

"Yeah, I don't feel good. I think I've caught something. There was a nasty bug going around the office." I shrugged a shoulder.

"Gah, don't come near me. I don't want to catch it."

"Gee Ben, love you, too, kiddo." I forced a laugh. My

renegade thoughts wanted to wander back to Ethan, the affair, the photos, the woman. But I fought to stay present.

He laughed. "I'm just saying. I have plans. I don't have time to be sick."

"Oh yes," I replied. "My calendar is wide open. Tons of time for lying around doing nothing."

The sound of a car pulling into the driveway snipped my laugh short. Those invisible hands returned and were squeezing my heart in their icy grip. I was already doing a terrible job of hiding my feelings, so to avoid further speculation, I busied myself with getting a glass and filling it with ice and water. With my back to Ben, he wouldn't notice my paled face and the panic storming in my blue eyes.

"I smell pizza!" Aubrey's sing-song voice called. I released a puff of air. Not Ethan.

She bounded into the kitchen, threw her backpack down, then grabbed a slice of pizza before leaning against the counter next to her brother.

"Don't go near Mom," Ben said.

"Huh, why?" Aubrey asked.

"She's sick. Look at her." Ben pointed at me with his pizza.

I hid my face with my glass and took a sip of water. The diamond on my left hand caught the light, and I choked, causing a fit of coughing. Turning my back to the kids, I leaned on the counter to recover.

"'Fraid so," I croaked, turning back around. "I'll probably call out of work tomorrow. I have a terrible headache and feel like crap."

Aubrey narrowed her eyes. "You've been crying."

"I'm sick. I haven't been crying." The conviction behind my words was gone. Let them find out and show Ethan the full depth of his betrayal through their broken hearts. Another piece of my heart chipped off and fell into the cavity of my chest. What mother wishes that on her kids? It wasn't their fault. I wanted Ethan to pay, but not at their expense. I would need to keep reminding myself of that. Not let my anger get carried away. My kids were more important than Ethan and more important than me.

"This idiot may buy that," Aubrey said, pointing at her brother with her thumb. "But I don't. Something's wrong. You've been crying."

I sighed. She knew my face too well. They'd both be so disappointed when they found out. They only get one dad. It's not their fault they ended up with a deceitful, selfish asshole. Anger aside, Ethan *was* a good dad. But I knew better than anyone how the bitterness of parental failure can poison a child's heart. My mother was nothing but disappointment. I'd been living with a wilted heart because of her my entire life.

"Aubs, I haven't been crying, swear. I'm not feeling well. I need to lie down. Your dad is going to drive you two to school tomorrow; I'm staying home."

"Mhm," Aubrey said, her eyes boring into mine. I felt her trying to crack open my head, dig around, and find out what I wasn't telling her. Ben looked from me to his sister. Vomit burned at my throat, and it felt like an ice pick was piercing through my skull. Technically, the 'illness' wasn't a complete lie. I was always very good at justifying deceit, or my own at least. I shuffled back upstairs, the ice tinkling in my glass with each step.

Back in my bedroom, I wrapped myself in a knitted blanket and sat in the armchair facing the door with my legs tucked beneath me. While waiting on Ethan, my eyelids became too heavy to hold open, and I fell asleep in the chair.

THE BEDROOM DOOR creaking woke me. A stranger wearing my husband's clothes and face walked in.

"Who is she?" My growl wasn't much louder than a whisper.

Ethan froze. His mouth flopped open and closed like a stupid goldfish.

"Who the fuck is she?" My voice grew louder, and I leaned forward. I was losing control too soon. Hate and love mixed inside me, creating a poisonous gas so real I expected to see it seeping out through my skin in black wisps.

"I—What's going on here, babe?" Ethan stuttered. His denial was gasoline being poured on an already raging fire.

"Oh, Ethan, are we going to play this game? Are you going to make me say it out loud?" I was unable to keep the sarcasm from varnishing my words.

"I was at a work dinner. Since when are you the jealous type?" He laughed nervously, and shut the door, taking a few cautious steps into the room. I could have smacked the phony confused expression off his face. I should have printed the email. It would have given me something to throw at him. I glanced at the round table between the chairs and considered the candle and glass statue of a couple embracing —both were viable options. The figurine would be more fitting for the situation. I pictured it denting his skull before he crumpled to the floor.

"One more chance, Ethan. Who is she?" I asked through gritted teeth.

"I don't know who we're talking about." He took another tentative step toward me. The creases in his forehead deepened. Right then, I understood how I'd missed it.

"Your mistress sent me an email today. It was super informative. Had pictures attached and everything." I said the words out loud, the ones that would seismically change the course of our lives. His secret was out. For a moment, I wanted to grab those words and stuff them back where they came from. Pretend it wasn't true, pretended everything was okay. I covered my mouth with my hands as if it would make a difference.

His shoulders drooped, and his chin dropped to his chest. There was never a question of the email's authenticity. I'd seen the photos, but watching his body admit guilt was too visceral. I gasped and wondered again how my heart continued beating.

"How could you?" I whispered. A thick sadness filled my lungs, replacing my rage, leaving no room for oxygen. The abrupt shifting of emotions was hard to keep up with; they were a tornado spinning through my chest. Tears streamed down my face.

"Nineteen years, Ethan. And you've thrown it all away, for what? A piece of ass? Wasn't I enough? Wasn't your family enough?"

He stood there staring at me, shock twisted his face, making him almost unrecognizable. His silence was infuriating.

"Do you love her?" I had so many questions and no answers. Each time I pummeled him with one, my voice rose in volume.

"Okay. Let's calm down or the kids will hear." How did

a grown man not know that telling someone to calm down will cause the exact opposite reaction?

"Don't tell me what to do concerning my kids!" I jumped to my feet and took a threatening step toward him. "You want to talk about the kids? You didn't seem too bothered about them when you fucked someone else ... for *six months.*"

I stood and walked into the bathroom, needing a minute. My hands on the vanity, I stared at myself in the mirror, then swept the entire contents to the floor and screamed. No words, just a guttural, animal scream. The vision of him thrusting over some other woman with black hair seared into my brain. He walked in. I stood panting, glaring at him; creams, toothbrushes, toothpaste, tubes of mascara, and lipstick all rolled around my feet.

"Cass, the kids," he whispered, looking around the floor with bulging eyes.

"Everyone is going to know, including them. You've humiliated me. Do you even care?" I imagined our friends finding out. Our colleagues. The murmurs behind my back. I'd never be able to walk into a room without wondering if I was the topic of everyone's conversations before my arrival. The thought made me sob. I stormed from the bathroom back into the bedroom, furious at Ethan, but also furious at myself for caring what people thought of me.

Ethan followed me. "I fucked up, and I'm sorry for everything. Please believe me." He sat on the bed, and I stood over him, my entire body shook. Ice water flowed through my veins while my pain morphed into rage and back into pain.

"Sit down. Can we talk, please?"

"How are you so calm?" I asked, pacing. "I don't understand. Don't you love me?"

"I do. I love you more than anything. It wasn't you. I'm an idiot." *Finally, something we agree on.* The tears made his blue eyes—my favorite part of his face—sparkle. It made me hate him even more.

I put my hands on my hips. "Then explain yourself. And it better include telling me who the fuck she is."

"It was a mistake, a terrible—"

"That's putting it lightly," I interrupted. A manic, too high, strangled laugh escaped my lips.

Ethan put his face in his hands. When he looked up again, the tears that had shone his eyes streamed down his cheeks.

"I know. I've apologized. I love you. But—"

"But. What?"

A silence blanketed the room. My pulse drummed in my ears along with the ragged sounds of my breathing.

He dared to sigh.

I jerked back and swayed. "You're disgusting."

I was looking at a man who I was madly in love with, but who I also wanted to murder. I could wrap my hands around his neck and choke the life from him. It would feel so good.

I didn't know it was possible to hate and love someone at the same time. I hadn't loved many people in my life, and none as fiercely as Ethan. It wasn't the type of love I could switch off like a light. This is the thing people who haven't been in my situation don't understand. It's so fucking confusing. But hate and love are so closely related. You can't hate someone you don't care about. Not that kind of hate. And when you love someone and they do something so horrible and terrible, the hatred infects every cell of your body and melts into you. It becomes you.

His tears stopped, and anger flashed across his face. "That's exactly what I mean, Cass. I couldn't do it anymore. It wasn't right, but it happened. Someone showed me the affection I've craved from you our entire marriage, that I've been begging for, and I caved to it. You never have time for me; you're always working."

"Who is she, Ethan?" I asked, ignoring his awful excuses.

"She's no one. Just some girl," he said, his voice softening. "And it's over. I cut things off. I told her the whole thing was a mistake, which is probably why she emailed you. She's angry. It's a desperate attempt to break us up. But I don't want that. I'm sorry for what I said and sorry for the affair. Please, give me a chance. We can fix us. I'm begging you."

He's deflecting, but why? Our entire marriage, I thought Ethan was an open book, and I was the pretender. Our roles had reversed so quick it made me dizzy.

"Funny, because she claims you love her and are leaving me for her. I think her exact words were something like, 'hadn't done it yet because of the kids.' And I'm glad she emailed me, since you didn't seem too inclined to fill me in."

I crumpled into the chair. Talking about her made the entire situation too tangible, like a boulder sitting on my chest. The walls started closing in again. My desperate need to learn her identity was gone. Him sitting there begging for forgiveness was suffocating, he needed to go.

Am I ready to watch his lips form her name? The same lips that have, for nineteen years, revealed his feelings for me through words and kisses?

I wasn't. My heart, once a solid mass feeding my body

with life, was now a shredded mess of spindly fibers floating aimlessly within my chest. I needed her name. But not that night. I decided she'd remain a faceless stranger. I feared the next blow, her name, would be the fatal one. I also feared what I was capable of.

"I can't do this anymore tonight. Go sleep in the guest room. I can't stand to look at your face a second longer. Take the kids to school in the morning, then go stay somewhere else. I don't care where; anywhere but here."

"What do I tell the kids?" he asked.

"I don't know, Ethan," I snapped. "Figure it out. You got yourself into this mess, you can find your way out of it too. Get off my bed. I'm going to sleep."

He stood and opened his mouth to speak, then shook his head. I walked past him, avoiding brushing against him. I couldn't risk his touch creating a fluttering in my belly like it still did, even after so many years. I crawled into bed and pulled the covers over my head. The sound of his footsteps dragging him to the door was followed by it opening, then clicking shut.

I used a pillow to muffle my final choked scream before falling asleep.

SIX

ETHAN

THE BED in our guest room was uncomfortable. With everything going on, that shouldn't have been a concern, yet as I laid there on top of the flower-patterned comforter, staring at the ceiling, I couldn't help being annoyed by the sleepless night ahead.

What was she thinking sending that shit?

I dug my phone from my pocket and typed out a text before deleting it. It was the tenth attempt. I loved Cass. No words in the English language were adequate to describe how deeply. I was filling a void with Emma. Did Cass scoop out that missing piece, or was it my doing? It didn't matter. I was caught; there was no talking myself out of this one.

I typed *What the hell was that about?* and sent it to Emma.

I rubbed my face and took inventory of my situation. Work: I lost my two biggest clients, with no new ones to fill the gap. When your job is sales, and you aren't selling anything, that tends to upset your boss. Every day I opened my email and readied myself for the calendar invite: the one from HR, where they'd finally fire me. Family: cheated on my wife, may lose Cass, may lose the kids.

And her.

I fell in love—not with a person but with a feeling. She found me when I was lost, and had been lost for a long while. It's not her fault, it's not Cass's fault, at least not entirely. However, Cass isn't as innocent as she believes herself to be. I tried to reach out and explain how desperately I needed her. She didn't listen. She didn't slow down or hear my cry for help. I guess I wasn't screaming loud enough.

There's no excuse for what I did, but it wasn't without reason. Whether or not that made a difference, I had no idea at that point. Probably not. I was fully aware I had a life most men would be envious of. A beautiful, smart, successful wife, two amazing children, financial comfort—even if I managed to get myself fired—so why was I so unfulfilled?

I'm not doing this over text. If you want to talk to me then we can talk in person. Emma replied.

I stared at the text. My temper took hold. It always came on so fast, making me do things I instantly regretted. It had been a point of contention between Cass and me our entire marriage. A bowl would have been nice, but my bag of weed sat on the top shelf of our closet. Getting to it would require disturbing Cass. I considered it but feared what I'd face. I'd been yelled at enough for one night and had no intentions of putting myself through more torture. My head throbbed, and I felt terrible for what I'd done, but I was over women and their drama.

There was a light knock on the door.

"Dad?" Ben said from the other side, his voice tentative. The kids must have heard the entire fight, and knew I'd been banished to the guest room. 'My room,' she had called our bedroom, as if it wasn't just as much mine.

"Come in, Bud," I replied.

"Is Mom okay? I thought I heard her yelling or something. She didn't look so good earlier, she said she was sick."

"Yeah kiddo, Mom's fine. She had a bad day at work."

He looked like he wanted to say more but tipped his head down and shut the door.

I rubbed my chin and tried to think about how I'd get myself out of the disaster I'd created. No light bulbs were flickering on above my head, so I reached for my phone and called Tyler.

"Ethan, everything okay? It's late."

"Yeah, sorry for that. I've gotten myself in a bit of trouble."

"Ah hell, that doesn't sound good. Should I get dressed and come post bail?"

"Not that kind of trouble."

I explained everything. Tyler had been my best friend since we were kids. We grew up in the same neighborhood, our families vacationed together, and we were the closest thing to brothers friends can be. With that much history, we'd both seen the best and the worst of each other over the years, including Tyler's dark years in college. His life took a horribly wrong turn when drugs and alcohol replaced everything good about him. He reached his rock bottom when I found him in his room at three in the morning, a girl lying on his bed half-conscious and him crawling clumsily on top of her.

I've spent many nights replaying that night in my head. If I'd walked in even one minute later two lives would have ended that evening. I can only assume he would have done something terrible, the addiction demons finally getting their wish and killing off the last good piece of Tyler left. He would have ended up in jail and deserved every second spent there. And a sweet girl would have been left emotionally damaged, possibly scarred for life.

The hate I felt for him was instantaneous the second I opened the door. It was one of the few times my temper was used for good. I ripped him off the bed and beat the shit out of him. He was too drunk to feel the blows. With Tyler unconscious, it was safe enough to leave the girl for a few minutes to get her friends. After wandering around the frat house and only finding remnants of a typical college rager, I returned to the room and managed to wake her up long enough for her to slur her building name and room number. I picked her up and carried her back to her dorm. Julie, her roommate, and I stayed up with her all night, forcing her to vomit, checking her pulse and her breathing. Ready to call for help if things took a turn for the worse. When I was sure she was okay, despite a massive hangover, I walked back to the house and found Tyler in the same spot I left him, bloody and bruised, snoring on the floor of his room. I slapped his face until he woke up, then explained what he almost did while he cried with shame. Then I drove him to the campus clinic and helped him check himself into a long-term rehab program.

The next day I went to the girls' dorm room to check on the girl. The incident left Cass shaken up, but she seemed to be doing much better. I offered to take her to lunch, with Julie insisting on escorting, which was fine. I appreciated her protectiveness, because despite only knowing her for less than twenty-four hours, I felt the same.

Tyler came out of rehab six months later a different man. He hasn't touched alcohol or drugs since. He has also accepted responsibility for his actions, repented, and changed. It's amazing how our lives comprise millions of moments where decisions are made—some tiny and insignificant, some monumental—but regardless of size, the actions we take during these microcosms determine our fate.

On the night I saved Cass, the decision to go to Tyler's room when I did, altered the course of all three of our lives for the better.

The night I slipped into bed with Emma? Not so much.

If Cass would have just listened, given me a chance to explain, we could have worked it out. Another decision and that one out of my control. We didn't, though. It was no longer Cass and Ethan against the world, and that world exploded around us.

SEVEN

ALICE

"ALICE, what are you doing here so early?" Julie asked.

I straightened and dropped the pile of papers I'd been organizing on Cass's desk.

"I could ask you the same thing." Julie's spine visibly stiffened. I chuckled. "I'm used to having the building to myself this early. I like to have Cass's workspace prepared for the busy day ahead. Fresh coffee in the break room for everyone and all that. You know Cass, and how she likes everything tidy and in its proper spot."

"Yes...I know Cass. Right, well, okay." She looked like she wanted to say more but turned and left.

I rolled my eyes and sat in Cass's chair. My gaze swept across the room, checking for anything out of place. The day prior, after she'd quite unexpectedly left right after the presentation, I couldn't help but notice the broken frame and smell of vomit in her trash can. Normally the two of us would download after such an important meeting. After cleaning up, I'd waited in her office twenty minutes before realizing there would be no follow-up meeting. That's when I found the trash can. Trouble in paradise it seemed. I couldn't help the giddiness I felt fluttering in my chest. One less distraction for Cass, and another opportunity for me to prove how useful I could be. I went home and wrote down all the ways I could help Cass through these awful times. Divorce can be a messy affair. Emotions so heightened. It didn't have to be hard for Cass, she had me. What more did she need?

I stayed in her chair for a while longer going through my list. Of course I memorized it. I needed to be ready for action at any moment. The sound of my phone made me shoot up from my chair. Cass's special ringtone. I scurried back to my desk and checked the message. *Oh dear, this is worse than I thought.*

I swallowed my pride and crossed the building to knock on Julie's door.

"Yes, Alice?" she said without looking away from her monitor.

"So sorry to interrupt, I'm sure you've heard. I'm very concerned with Cass's wellbeing. I think it's best I stop by her house and check—"

She whipped her head toward me. "Absolutely not. That would be highly inappropriate." Her face didn't give her emotions away, but her eyes bored into me. Anyone else would have cowered under that gaze, but she didn't faze me. I'd been dealing with women and girls like her my entire life.

I nodded curtly and walked back to my cube, regretting that I had given her the courtesy of asking. She wasn't Cass's ruler. She hadn't a clue how close Cass and I were. How much Cass relied on me, especially during a crisis. I opened my drawer and took a half of Xanax from the stash I kept for Cass emergencies. She'd suffered from panic attacks since childhood. Therapy and dealing with her past trauma had lessened them greatly in her adult life, but often during times of high stress those sneaky little buggers would come back. Because those times were few and far between—Cass was so strong—she often forgot to refill her prescription. I'd gone to a doctor and listed out the symptoms to get my own prescription to keep on hand when she ran out. That's just one example of how many steps ahead of Cass I am. I am always fully prepared for any situation. I know for a fact Julie couldn't say the same.

I wondered again what the agency, and Cass, would be like without Julie in the picture. Julie held her back. She's too much. Too domineering. She overshadowed Cass in a way that made me sick.

Best friend, I think not.

This was certainly something I needed to ponder further. I took out my notebook and scribbled *J? Needed? How?* A reminder to myself to put more thought into that much stickier situation once I'd rescued Cass from her current predicament.

I tapped my lower lip with my pen, then wrote an additional note. *With no E, no family. C and A family?*

EIGHT

CASS

ETHAN CREPT into our bedroom the next morning while I pretended to sleep. My plans didn't include speaking to Ethan that day. Those plans did include staying in bed, wallowing, and crying. I allowed myself one day to fall apart —just one day. Then I'd pick up the pieces of my broken heart and put myself back together. I'd be fine; I'd survived worse.

When first confronted with the affair, my immediate instinct was to gorge myself on information. I was starved for every detail. Who was she? When did they meet up? What was their sex like? But like someone famished for too long who found themselves standing at a buffet, if I devoured it all too fast, I'd be sick from it.

After sending Julie then Alice a text letting them know I'd be staying home, I squeezed my eyes shut. When I opened them again, I was at our wedding. The scene was bright and sun-kissed, with hazy edges. My sleeping brain became aware

I was moving through a dream. I walked down the aisle toward a smiling Ethan. Our love and the possibilities of our future hummed in the air. When I reached him, we intertwined our hands. I looked from his eyes to my left hand while he slipped the wedding band on my finger.

My joy morphed into horror as the gold band turned rusty and black, contracting around my finger, cutting off the circulation and turning it an angry red, then blue. I looked up to meet Ethan's eyes, but a head of smooth flesh sliced open by a wide, menacing grin with sharp teeth hovered above me. As a forked tongue shot from the mouth, I jerked awake.

Drenched in sweat but not ready to get up, I willed myself back to sleep. This time I was in a bar with a vodka and soda—tall, single shot, with two limes—sitting in front of me. I lifted the glass and enjoyed a long refreshing sip from the straw. The bar wrapped around in a half square, framing the area that held the taps and liquor bottles. The only other customers were a couple seated on the other side. An odorless smoke rolled and curled, creating a living haze, concealing the couple's identity. A grinning bartender dressed in a tuxedo walked past, idly swinging his arm in a wide arch. The smoke dissipated, revealing the couple's identity.

Ethan brushed a raven-colored strand from the woman's face, and the black hair hovered around her head like she was floating in water. I strained to see who she was, but the way she sat, angled toward Ethan, made it impossible. Ethan lifted his head, switching his focus from the woman to me, then smiled. He then leaned into the woman, and they exchanged a deep, passionate kiss. An unseen force paralyzed my body. My mind screamed at me to run over and rip them apart but couldn't move. I tried to scream, but no sound came from my outstretched mouth.

With heavy breaths, I bolt upright into a sitting position. I looked around the room, my bedroom, and clutched at my heart, sure it would explode through my chest. When my breathing calmed, I stretched my neck to rid the crick that had formed from sleeping too long. A groan escaped my lips.

After pushing myself out of bed—a simple action that took significantly more effort than usual—I walked to the bathroom. My legs felt heavy, like I was trudging through quicksand.

With the shower turned on, I undressed and spread a towel on the floor. Standing took too much effort, so I sat on the towel to wait for the water to warm. Filled with shame, my throat ached from wailing. I was a successful, strong business owner. People looked up to me, they wanted to *be* me. It took one moment, one single second in a sea of millions of seconds, one single email in a sea of a billion emails to destroy that image I'd worked so hard to achieve.

What would those people who looked up to me think if they saw me like this? A pitiful shriveling mess, naked on the bathroom floor, broken by a man.

Steam seeped from the top of the shower. I heaved myself off the floor and stepped in.

Still too tired to hold myself up fully, I leaned a cheek against the cool tile while the water burned my skin. Images of women flashed through my mind: friends, colleagues, business partners. The potential of betrayal from each one made me sob harder. I gave my whole heart to someone and look what he did with it. People had been letting me down my entire life, starting with my worthless mother; I should have known Ethan would be no different.

Ethan didn't have any female friends, other than wives of his college buddies or those of the guys he'd grown up with. Would he sleep with a friend's wife? He was in sales at a large IT firm. Plenty of women worked there, leaving so many opportunities to hide an affair behind work excuses like late nights at the office, dinners, or trips. The same charisma that made him so good at his job and that sucked me in and won my heart, could have easily charmed the panties off a colleague. I thought back to the last holiday party and strained to recall the evening. Did any of the women pay particular attention to him? Flirtations beyond acceptable friendly banter? No one I could think of—none with long black hair. The flip-flopping emotions returned, and images of other women turned my anguish into anger once again.

I should leave him. I imagined my life without him. Moving on, finding someone new. That thought brought more tears, and I finished my shower, choking on them.

Determined not to crawl back in bed, I got dressed and walked downstairs. I was proud of myself for taking such a big step. What a mess I'd become, where getting dressed and leaving my bedroom were accomplishments.

In the kitchen, I went to make myself a cup of coffee. I opened every drawer and searched through the pantry, but there were no coffee pods to be found. A simple thing. It should have been easy to shrug off, but I picked up the coffee maker and smashed it on the tile floor. I was staring down at the remains, regretting my decision, when the doorbell rang.

I answered it to find Julie. She held a Starbucks cup in one hand and a brown paper bag in the other.

"I'm not going to bother you, or drag you into a lengthy discussion, but here are supplies. Coffee and vodka. Drink them alone or pour some of that vodka in there and drink them together. No one would judge."

I hung off the side of the door, smiling. "You're my hero." I took the coffee and vodka from her. "Want to come in for a bit?"

"I have to get back to the office," Julie answered, turning to leave. She stopped. "Unless you need me here. I'll cancel my meetings, get drunk and cry with you."

Yes, I need you. Hold me, rock me, tell me it's going to be okay. That it won't feel like this forever.

"Can't let the inmates run the asylum while we sit here getting tipsy," I replied, forcing a laugh. "I'll be fine. I desperately needed this, though." I held up the coffee, not telling her the reason was that my smashed coffee maker lay in pieces on my kitchen floor. "You're a lifesaver. Seriously."

"You let me know when you're ready to sit down and have a long talk about it, 'kay?" Julie replied.

"I will, I promise. Love you."

"Love you more." Julie blew a kiss and jogged down the front stairs to her Jaguar. I closed the door and then moved to stand at the window, clutching the coffee and vodka so tight it's a wonder the cup didn't collapse under my grip. A few tears slid down my cheeks, and I had to remind myself she wasn't leaving forever. Julie would always be there. I may not be able to count on anyone else, but she was my person, the closest thing I had to family. My walls had to remain down for her.

I angrily wiped the tears away with my sleeve and admonished myself for being so melodramatic. Before turning, I glanced out the window one more time. A woman with a baseball cap and sunglasses stood across the street staring at my house. I placed the drinks on an end table and ran to the front door. By the time I flung it open the woman was gone.

The neighbor's lawn crew was working on their front yard, not wanting to draw attention to myself I walked casually down my driveway and pretended to check the mailbox. I turned my head straining to see down the street to find the woman, she'd disappeared. I considered getting in my car and driving to look for her but shook my head. *A neighbor out for a walk is all, no need to start stalking the neighbors now.*

I returned to my house, grabbed the coffee and vodka, and sauntered into the kitchen, stepping over the ruined coffee maker. I placed the vodka and Starbucks next to each other on the counter. *Just a bit, enough to take the edge off.* I peeled the lid off the coffee and poured in a shot of vodka before taking a long gulp. I winced. *Not the best combination. ...Not the worst, either.*

The rest of the day was a blur. The spiked coffee may have been partially to blame, but the roiling emotions were the main culprit. The juxtaposition of the reality I'd been living in for the last nineteen years and the reality I was floating in now was impossible to digest. Like eating nails. Another swig of vodka straight from the bottle down the hatch.

Ethan accused me of being too focused on work. As if I was some heartless robot who never made time for its family. A completely unfair assessment. I began mentally cataloging all the ways I was, in fact, full of heart.

Unfortunately, the best examples I came up with were work or kids-related. Maybe he was right; I'd given too much of my attention to the agency and didn't allow enough space for him. Ethan was the person who was supposed to understand me better than anyone. He should have seen through my sharp tongue and understood why I had such a hard time trusting people. As if the circumstances we met under weren't bad enough, he was the only person outside of Julie who knew my past. He knew why touching and affection didn't come easily or naturally for me. At least he had always said he understood. Another lie to add to the growing list.

I huffed air through my nose and chugged more vodka. Screw Ethan for making me doubt myself. Cheating on me was bad enough, but he had to tear me down and hold a mirror up to all my flaws, too?

AUBREY AND BEN came home bickering and complaining about riding the bus to find me on the couch, staring at a blank TV. Ben stomped past, grabbed a bag of chips and a Coke from the kitchen and ran upstairs. Aubrey stood in the doorway with her hands on her hips and eyes squinted.

"Do you plan on telling me what's going on?" she demanded.

I chewed on my lower lip. The vodka had worn off and was replaced by a slight hangover thumping behind my right eye. Day drinking was always fun while doing it, but not so much once the day ended. I considered finishing off the bottle and passing out.

"Your dad and I had a fight. It's nothing to worry about. Adult stuff."

"You and dad never fight," Aubrey said, crossing her arms. I was looking at the mirror image of myself during last night's fight with Ethan. I started laughing hysterically. She dropped her arms and stared at me like I'd grown a second head.

I composed myself with a slight shake of my head. "I can't talk about it." I sighed. "Another time, okay?"

I willed her to drop it and go upstairs.

"Is Dad coming home tonight? He brought a suitcase with him this morning," she said.

"Probably not," I said, leaning my head back on the couch and shutting my eyes. "Do you think you can manage dinner on your own tonight? I'm going to bed early."

"Fine. Then we'll go back to our rooms so we can listen to you and Dad scream at each other. Perfect. Or will we be listening to you cry all night with no idea what's going on? And will we have to listen to you make up more lies? So sorry for giving a shit about you, Mom." Aubrey ran out before I could answer. I mourned the loss of my family and worried we'd never be the same again.

I dragged myself upstairs and grabbed a sleeping pill from the medicine cabinet. A dreamless sleep. No creepy bars or weddings with monsters. In bed, I reached over to the empty side and ran my hand over the cool sheets. The time for wallowing was over. Tomorrow, I'd find out who she was and make them both beg for mercy. I'd make my plan.

I'd have my revenge.

NINE

CASS

I DROVE to work the next day, singing along with Alanis Morissette's *You Oughta Know.* The song had taken on a whole new meaning now that I was a woman scorned, and I performed a solo concert in my car for not only the woman Alanis wrote the lyrics for, but myself.

Head held high, and shoulders rolled back, I pushed through the glass doors and strode through the front lobby with purpose. My heels, while not designer, confidently carried me through the office. I still looked like a powerful executive, someone to be feared, but with feet that didn't throb with each step.

I called out my joyful greetings to each staff member. There were a few tentative waves, and eyes slid down to avoid contact. *Do they know?* My smile faltered. *No, how could they?*

"Mrs. Mitchell, good news!" Alice shot up from her chair. "Tara's assistant called. She requested a meeting with you as soon as possible. I told her you were all booked up yesterday but that you'd be available today at ten. Does that time work?" She smiled and gave me a thumbs up.

"Great, yes. Ten works for me," I said. The week was getting better already.

In my office, I pulled out my laptop and scooted my chair forward, determined to get some actual work done before the call. My phone buzzed, jolting me from the moodboard I was reviewing.

A text from an unknown number: *Had a great time with your man last night xoxo.*

It was fifteen minutes before my call, so I turned my phone over and ignored it.

I'd had a few bad days where I was someone else, but no more. I would not let this text, which should be vomit-inducing, deviate me from my mission. I closed my eyes and took a few seconds before returning to the collage of California-inspired images including carefree surfers and models posing with longboards.

Thankfully, my Blaxten presentation fumble didn't screw up the entire deal and we got the account. A multi-year agreement where we would be their agency of record for all channels of media buying including creative development and kicking off with a rebrand. Normally, I would have been ecstatic but all I could muster was a half-smile when I hung up the phone. It vanished before it could fully form.

I picked up my phone.

"Where were you last night?" I demanded when Ethan answered.

"Huh? What do you mean?" Ethan asked.

"Hang on, I'm texting you a screenshot. Another love

note from your side piece. She's been so helpful in keeping me informed of your whereabouts."

"I stayed at Tyler and Sandra's. There's no way she could have sent that," he said.

"Look at the screenshot, Ethan? Are you calling me a liar?" My grip tightened on the phone, I considered throwing it—an aggravating habit I'd formed lately. I promised myself no more hurling inanimate objects.

"What? No!" Ethan's voice rose in an annoying way. I shuddered. It was as bad as silverware scraping on a plate. I may be throwing things like a child, but at least I wasn't whining like one.

"I'm calling Sandra. If you're lying about where you were last night, you better get it over with and fess up now."

"I'm telling the truth. Call her." He sounded so sure of himself, but he *was* a liar. Tyler would certainly cover for him. Even with the guilt for The Night. The one we all pretend never happened but sits with us when we all get together like a fifth person. Regardless, Tyler remained fiercely loyal to Ethan, much more so than to me. But Sandra would never pass up an opportunity to show she had information I didn't.

"Maybe I will," I said, giving him one more opportunity to falter.

Ethan exhaled heavily into the phone. I held it away from my ear, and glared at it as if it was the phone's fault he had suddenly become the most obnoxious person in all humanity. He started yapping again, so I put the phone back to my ear.

"What did you say?" I asked, venom sharpening the question.

"I said, can we please meet tonight and talk?"

"I'll meet with you on one condition. You *will* tell me her name."

The silence dragged on much longer than acceptable. My finger hovered over the end call button.

"Fine. I'll tell you who she is. If that's what it takes for us to have a chance," he said.

"You will answer every single question I have. And if I think you're hiding anything the conversation will be over. And don't think I won't be calling Sandra the second I hang up." I said this knowing full well I'd have no way of discerning fact from fiction. It was quite the predicament, having to rely on someone who couldn't be trusted. I told him to come at seven and ended the call. Before I had a chance to tear apart our brief conversation, I pulled up Sandra's contact and hit call.

"Cass, hun. I'm so sorry." Sandra's nasally voice assaulted my ear. She drew out the 'o' for so long I worried the suffering would never end. Her overly honeyed tone produced a sound as counterfeit as her personality.

"Sandra, hi. I'm fine. Did Ethan sleep at your house last night?" I asked.

"He did. He told us—"

"Okay, thanks. I really must jump off, work stuff. Sorry," I sang, hanging up before she could respond. There would be at least one benefit to divorcing Ethan: never having to sit through another dinner with one-up Sandra again. No Ethan also meant no Tyler. I'd forgiven him many years ago. When he came out of rehab, Ethan and I had been dating officially for a few months. Ethan sat me down and said, 'If you tell me it's you or Tyler, I pick you.' This made me feel wanted, but also uncomfortable. How could I ask him to give up over twenty years of friendship for a girl he'd only known three months? I agreed to sit down, the three of us, see what Tyler had to say, then make my decision. I forgave Tyler. I always forgive too easily. It's my Achilles' heel.

But I never forget.

"You look much better today." Julie walked in and sat on the couch tucked into the corner of my office, she ignored my glare at her crossed feet propped on the glass coffee table.

"Getting there," I said. "We got the Blaxten account. The contract should be finished today."

"Of course we did. Ready to get your online profiles up on dating apps?" Her maroon lips turned up in a mischievous grin. With her dark hair in a tight bun, and brown eyes lit up, she looked witchy and conniving. It was the look she always gave me before we made bad decisions. Only our mischief would usually have much fewer permanent after-effects. Like a terrible hangover, not a date with a stranger.

I choked on the latte she'd bought me. "I wouldn't go that far. Oh my god, I can't even imagine dating again. What do you even talk about on first dates?"

"A lot of things have changed over the last two decades, but I can assure you first dates have not. They are as awkward and terrible as always. Remember that one psycho chick I dated before Victoria, who slept over one night and wouldn't leave, for like days?" Julie laughed.

I rolled my eyes. "You're doing an excellent job convincing me."

"Has the jerk told you who she is yet?" Julie asked.

"Nope. But he's coming over again tonight. I told him that was part of the deal." The anticipation of finding out who the woman was hummed beneath my skin. It was close to excitement. But once I had a name, it would only be a temporary high, like a shot of heroin. An addiction, shooting myself up with the disgusting details until I'm left sick and strung out.

"Some crushed laxatives in his food wouldn't be a bad idea." Julie chuckled.

"Hilarious," I said.

A loud bang made us both look toward my door. Alice stood hands stretched over her head and waved when she made eye contact with us through the window. I returned the wave and smiled, Julie did not.

"She's so weird."

"Stop it, she is not," I chastised.

Julie chortled. "Right, doing her hourly *stretches* I see. Funny how they always seem to occur when we're in here talking, and right outside your office."

"She takes her back health very seriously." I laughed. "Besides, Alice is harmless. She's just a bit—"

"Obsessed, over the top, *present.*"

I waved my hand dismissively. "She's a hard worker. It's hard to find people with that type of work ethic these days."

"I hate that I agree with that."

"Anyways, moving on. *She* texted me. Said she was with Ethan last night. I called Sandra and she verified he was at her house the entire night. She's baiting me."

"Ouch, you had to call Sandra. Bet she loved that."

"Oh, for sure; this is like Christmas morning for her. So close to all the action." I snorted.

"The whole thing is super weird. Something isn't right." Julie visibly shivered.

"That's exactly how I feel. At least *you* see it. Ethan's making excuses for her. 'She's hurt, just lashing out.'" I rolled my eyes again.

"Ethan lost his right to an opinion when he jumped in bed with a psycho. We'll find her, and she'll pay. No one screws with my Cass and gets away with it."

"That is why I love you the most." I kissed the air in her direction.

She stood and crossed the office, then opened the door to find Alice with one hand raised ready to knock.

"Done with your stretches I see? She's all yours." Julie stepped around her. Alice stood in the doorway watching Julie walk down the hall. I brushed aside the weird feeling the expressionless look on her face gave me.

The moment ended and the life returned to her eyes. She walked in beaming.

"How'd the call go?" Alice asked before taking a seat in a chair facing my desk.

I filled her in on the good news and leaned back, already crafting campaigns, once again using work as a distraction from my problems.

"That's wonderful! And of course, not a surprise. You deserved a win after the week you've had."

"Oh, it was a small stomach bug, nothing serious." I shrugged.

Her eyebrows rose slightly. "No, I meant the other thing."

"What other thing, Alice?"

She wrung her hands but continued. "You know, with Ethan and Emma. It's so—terrible. But I understand if you aren't ready to talk about it. My apologies. That's wonderful about the Bla—"

"What did you just say? Ethan and who?"

Alice's face collapsed, her eyes slid to the door, and she shifted in her seat. "The reason you stayed home yesterday."

I said nothing. Silence is a powerful tool. If you use it to your advantage, people will always fill it to save themselves from their discomfort. You can find out so many things by asking nothing and simply being patient.

"I assumed the reason you weren't here was because of the email Emma sent you."

My entire body vibrated. "How do you know about the email?"

She started to stand.

"Sit, Alice. Tell me how you know about the email. And what name did you just say? Emma?"

She slowly lowered herself back into the chair. "Emma. She works here." Her face turned the color of blood and her eyes expanded in her head. "Oh my god. You ... did you not know?"

An eerie calm washed over me. Alice became the keeper of the information I needed, and if I maintained my composure, I'd finally have the answers I'd been seeking.

"You're telling me Emma, the account manager who works for us, is the girl who sent me that email?" I threw my head back and laughed.

Alice nodded meekly. Concern warped her features.

"Okay," I said. My head bobbed up and down slowly. "That's something I'll have to deal with."

Alice gulped and pushed her glasses up her nose. "Yes, what can I do? How can I help?"

"First, I'd like you to tell me how you know all this."

She cleared her throat and her eyes fell to her lap. "It took some prodding, but something seemed to be amiss with the account managers. While you were out, I decided to do some investigative work. I got a confession from Delaney. Emma called out sick two days ago. Delaney called to check on her. I guess they had plans for the weekend, you know how close they are. Emma told her about the affair. Though if I were to guess, that wasn't the first Delaney had heard of it. Emma told Delaney that she and Ethan were going public with their relationship and she was waiting for him to tell you. He was taking too long for her liking, so she took the matter into her own hands. Once everyone knew, Emma said she wouldn't need the job here anyway. I'm sorry, Cass."

If Delaney knew, then the entire office did based on how fast gossip moved through those halls. Which would explain the odd looks I'd received on my way in this morning.

Ants crawled across my skin, tap, tap, tapping away over every bit of flesh covering my body. Their little legs created pricks of anxiety growing more unbearable as the seconds ticked by.

"I need you to go find Julie and Carla. Quick, Julie may still be close. I don't care if they are in a meeting, the bathroom, or where they are, tell them to come to my office. Now."

"Yes, of course. I'll go get them right away." She was already opening the door and sliding out.

I massaged my temples.

He had an affair with one of my employees. Is he insane? I ripped a page out of the notebook on my desk and stuffed it in my mouth, hoping to stifle my scream. It didn't matter if anyone heard; the entire office currently had front row tickets to my humiliation. My hands shook with a desire to destroy my office. Smash everything made of glass and throw everything else at the wall. *No more fits, no more tantrums.* I had the information I was after. I should have been happy, finally satisfied. Once I knew who she was, I thought there'd be no more questions, but that turned out not to be the case at all. I chose a spot on the wall to stare at, to center myself.

Emma's face materialized behind my eyes, along with her long waves of black hair. I slammed my fists into my head. How stupid of me for missing it. She was so close, right here in the same building as me the entire time. I hated myself as much as I hated her. *You couldn't fathom he'd be so foolish to sleep with your employee. That's how you missed it.* The words of comfort did little to make me hate myself less.

I typed a text to Ethan: *Emma?!?!?!* Then hit delete as the door opened and Alice, Carla, and Julie walked in. I'd deal with him later.

"What's wrong, dear?" Carla asked, her wrinkles creased further with worry.

"What has he done now?" Julie demanded, making a much more dramatic entrance.

"Alice, if you could give us a minute, please?"

Shock overcame her face. "But I can help."

Julie pointed to the door, "Not now, Alice."

Her eyes narrowed, and with a huff she walked to the door and shut it behind her.

Ethan's office was a short drive. If I had to experience this humiliation at work, he should too. I contemplated how to make that happen while Julie and Carla sat.

My fingers rubbed my temples and my hands slid down my face before steepling against my lips, I blew a slow breath between them.

I opened my eyes and looked at Carla and Julie. "We have a problem."

"Haven't we had enough of those lately?" Julie asked.

"Emma," I said.

"Wait. Is this the homewrecker? Who is she? Where'd

they meet?"

I sighed. "Julie. I need you not to be you for two seconds. I'm a disaster right now. I can barely function. Please, think." I was crumbling and needed Julie to take over. Or at the very least, remember the names of our employees for once in her life.

"I need a minute to catch up here. Emma? Homewrecker?" Carla asked.

She didn't know. That was one person at least. Tiny victories. Not that she wasn't about to find out, but still. If Carla didn't know, maybe there were others? *Not for long.* That asshole Self-Doubt wasn't about to let Optimism ruin his fun.

"Holy shit, Cass! The Emma who works for us?" Julie shot from her seat.

"Yes. That's the one." I pinched the bridge of my nose. The distant throbbing of a migraine grew behind my eyes.

"I will kill her. And her career." Julie snarled.

"Okay, pause," Carla jumped in with an uncharacteristic rise in her voice. "I need you both to fill me in."

So, I did, leaving nothing out. Carla managed employment laws and compliance. We needed her to help us navigate how to fire Emma without getting sued.

"Here's what we're going to do," Carla soothed. "I'll get the paperwork ready. Call her and tell her to come in tomorrow morning. Julie and I will let her go. We'll offer her four weeks of severance to keep the entire thing less messy. It will be professional, quick, then over with."

"Severance?" My fists clenched. "Why would we pay her a dime?"

Carla frowned sympathetically. "Severance will incentivize her to sign her exit papers. It's the only way we can guarantee she won't turn around and sue us, not that she would win, but it's better this way. No lawyers. No bad publicity. I know it's not what you want to hear, but this is how to make it go away as fast and painless as possible."

"All I'm hearing here is I cannot strangle her during said meeting?" Julie asked.

Carla looked down her nose at Julie with pursed lips. Julie slumped in her chair and crossed her arms, pouting. I grinned, watching the scene unfold. A few people could put Julie in her place: Victoria, me (occasionally), and Carla. Alice had a feistiness in her I would leverage as well, but only when absolutely necessary.

"She can't see me when she's here. I'm afraid I'll cry. I can't give her the satisfaction," I said. My voice shook at the thought and tears pricked at my eyes.

"It's okay to cry, you know? You feel whatever way you need to. And if you need to, just stay home that day," Carla said. Tears shined her eyes, too. If she cried that would be it. I'd be sobbing behind my desk again.

"I know. I just. God. The thought of our entire staff knowing is embarrassing. They'll lose respect for me. I can't hide at home, though. I won't let Ethan and Emma win."

"No. The staff, clients, everyone loves you, Cass. If anything, we'll have to keep the mob from hunting her and Ethan down with pitchforks and torches," Julie said.

I snorted at the image of our team marching down the road, screaming for their heads.

"You're right. I know I can't be in the room, but this is my company, I will be in this building." My confidence grew. I almost tasted revenge on the tip of my tongue, and it was delicious.

"That's the spirit," Julie said.

"I wonder if she has any idea I've figured out who she is?" I asked.

"Who knows? But who cares? She'll find out tomorrow, and she'll learn you are *not* the woman to mess with," Julie said.

"I'm sorry he did this. I can't believe—"

"Knock it off." Julie cut me off. "No apologies. You did nothing wrong here. You can tell that loser of a husband he owes me an apology, though. One of our employees. What the hell was he thinking?"

"Exactly what I'd like to know," I said. "I think I'm still in shock. It's weird. Like I'm sad, and mad, and everything. But it still doesn't feel real. It's hard to explain."

"We're all shocked. Victoria was reduced to tears when I told her; you'd have thought *I* cheated on *her*." Victoria was the exact opposite of Julie in so many ways. This reaction wasn't a surprise. "She loved Ethan. We all did. But we love you more. You didn't deserve this. You were a good wife to that man. You know that, right?"

"I thought I was. But this sort of thing really makes you question yourself." A tear dripped down the side of my face. How many tears does a body hold?

"Well, don't. You did everything right. He had it all. And he pissed it all away. Or banged it all away, I should say."

My fingers curled into fists. "Okay, Carla, you'll get everything ready for the morning, and we'll meet at eight so we can be waiting for her, if she shows up."

Both women nodded in agreement before leaving.

I stared at my computer with intentions of getting work done. A debate raged within my mind. Once again, impetuousness won, and I packed up my things and left early.

TEN

ALICE

CASS BREEZED BY, briefcase and purse in tow. Clearly leaving early...again.

She really needs to get it together. If she would come to me, trust me, I could help. She knows this. We've been through plenty before, there is nothing we can't handle. But there's not much I can do if she won't let me help.

I took a stroll around the eerily quiet office. At least the employees knew better than to feast themselves on this latest turn of events. Their gossiping mouths were sealed shut. Cass was in no position to pay mind to who may have a knife poised, ready to stab her between her shoulder blades. I wouldn't be letting any indiscretions or further damage to Cass's reputation slip past me, though. Oh no.

Once satisfied that I could trust the office to run without me, I also packed up my things and left.

Now where would she be running off to this time?

Her house being the most obvious choice, I started

there. On the ride over I thought about what I should do upon my arrival. Knock on the door, ask what, if anything, I could do for her. Or I could park a few blocks away and take a peek inside unannounced and unnoticed.

I pulled into the driveway. She would appreciate my persistence, understanding how well intentioned I was.

My knocks on the door went unanswered. I leaned against the window to scan for movement from within. A quick walk around the house's exterior indicated no one was home. I found myself back at her front door once again. A quick shrug and I entered the code to unlock the front door.

"Cass," I called. "Hello? Anyone home? It's Alice."

I took a tentative step into their home and listened. There were no sounds from upstairs, music blaring, or other signs the kids may be home and ignoring the visitor ringing their doorbell. I stood in the entryway listening to my breathing for a few minutes. One more call of her name and I made my way upstairs to her bedroom.

After spritzing myself with her perfume, I walked into her closet. Rows of organized outfits fit for any occasion greeted me, along with a wall of shoes to match. I ran my hands across the luxurious fabrics and smiled. So beautiful.

The section of evening gowns called to me. I had a few dresses hanging in my own closet, but none like these. I quickly undressed and slipped one over my head. Twisting and turning in front of the floor-length mirror I admired how the beading caught the light.

Cass is very particular about her things, so I carefully placed the dress back on the hanger where I'd found it before selecting another one to try on.

The dress felt right, so different, so Cass. With my eyes closed I imagined, not for the first time, what it must be like to be her. To walk into a room and have every head turn, rather than eyes avert. To say words, any words, meaningless words and have people lean in, begging for more. To not be told you're worthless, annoying, a very bad girl, who deserves very bad things.

The darkness of my closed eyes became unappealing. There was no need to think about things that happen in the dark, no need at all. That was then and this was now. A different girl in a different life.

My stomach dropped. I'd lost track of time. That happened occasionally. I over-fixated, got lost in a task and, poof, the seconds, minutes, hours had departed. I checked my watch. The kids could be home any minute. Or Cass. While I quickly changed back into my boring clothes and gathered my belongings, I tried to think of a good reason for me being in their home. My hands fumbled for my phone, I quickly logged into their camera app and deleted the footage of me entering their home. Neither Ethan nor Cass ever have their notifications on, so I knew they wouldn't have been alerted.

Down the stairs and out the door, I heard my name called from the driveway just as the door shuts.

Forcing myself to gather my wits, I turned and smiled. "Aubrey, how wonderful running into you. My gosh, you've grown since the last time I saw you. How long has it been ..."

I pretended to think, knowing full well I could name the exact date and time.

Her face changed from surprise to confusion.

"Silly me, you must be wondering why I'm here. I was coming by to see your mom. Do you know if she's home?"

She stepped around me to unlock the door. I held my breath hoping there'd been enough time between my closing the door and seeing Aubrey for it to lock. The keypad beeped, indicating the door unlocked, and I forced myself not to breathe a sigh of relief.

"She's at work, wouldn't you've seen her there?" she said to the door with her back facing me.

I chuckled. "Normally, but I had business to attend to at the location of our upcoming event. I thought she mentioned she'd be leaving early and wanted to brief her on the meeting."

Aubrey twisted to face me and looked displeased by what I'd said. I smiled sweetly and waited for her to move on.

She shrugged, turned back to the house and opened the door.

"Well, it looks like our meeting will have to wait until tomorrow. No emergency, nothing to fret. Wonderful to see you, Aubs."

Her eyes widened followed by pursed lips. "I'll let her know you stopped by."

Without so much as a chance to bid my farewells, I found myself staring at a closed door.

If I hadn't been so nervous about the close call, I'd have been quite perturbed by her rudeness. Nevertheless, I'd gotten away with my fun. It was time to leave before she changed her mind and decided to question me further about my appearance on their front step.

ELEVEN

CASS

I PULLED into Ethan's office's parking garage and looked for his car as I wound my way through the rows of expensive vehicles crammed into the dark, cramped cement structure. My tires squealed around each corner. I didn't see his car, but that didn't mean anything. His office was one of many in a fifteen-floor building. Besides, I could have easily missed it in my haste. After parking, I sat in my car for a few minutes, breath ragged, staring through the windshield.

I didn't know what I planned to do or even say when I saw him, but I knew it wouldn't be pretty. I didn't care what his co-workers thought of me. I didn't care what anyone thought of me. Rational thinking had gone the second Alice said her name.

Finally ready, I opened the door and flinched when it slammed into the car next to me. I looked up and scanned for cameras. Old Cass would have left a note, *so sorry, please call me, I will pay for the giant ding I just left on the side of your over-priced luxury sedan.* That Cass wasn't in control today.

I ran to the elevator and punched the up button repeatedly. It wouldn't make the elevator cab move any faster, but I had to feel like I was doing *something.* The doors slid open, I jammed my finger on the button for the fourteenth floor and tapped my foot watching the numbers above the doors taking me up. Ten, eleven, twelve, thirteen.

I stomped across the hall before throwing open the glass doors and marching up to the reception desk where Rosalie —the office manager and receptionist—sat.

"Mrs. Mitchell," Rosalie called, surprise circling her eyes and mouth.

"Is Ethan here?" I asked, harsher than I intended.

"I'm sorry, but Mr. Mitchell left about thirty minutes ago." She checked her wristwatch then confirmed. "Yes, almost exactly thirty minutes. Is there an emergency? Something I can help with?" I considered telling her, but she wasn't the type to gossip so it would do me no good.

"Buzz me in, Rosalie, I need something from his office."

"Mrs. Mitchell, you know I can't do that. Authorized perso—"

"Since when am I not authorized?" I demanded.

We stared at each other like two enemies waiting to see who would break first.

I put my hands on the desk and leaned forward. "Rosalie. Buzz me in."

She thought a minute and hit the buzzer without taking her eyes off me. I watched her pick up the phone and cover her mouth as I marched past her through the second set of glass doors. When I got to Ethan's office, I shut the door and looked around before my focus landed on his neatly organized desk. A small cry escaped my lips. The last time I stood there we both, by some miracle, had meeting-free afternoons.

"Let's do lunch?"

The welcoming had been much friendlier that day.

I leaned against his desk. "How about a quickie before we head out?" he had said, arching an eyebrow and running his hand up my leg under my skirt.

"Simmer down there, I'm starving."

"Same," he replied, grinning like a schoolboy and moving his hand up farther.

We'd laughed and chatted up a few of his co-workers before grabbing a bite on the water at one of the nearby restaurants. How long ago had that been? I no longer measured time in weeks or months, it was now pre-Emma or post-Emma. I blinked and returned my focus to the desk.

The drawers were as good a place as any to start. I pulled out each one, scooping the contents out onto the desk and the floor, looking for what I didn't know. Next, I moved on to the desk, then the shelves, I was running out of places to search. I sat on the floor, papers and folders spread around me, frantically flipping through them all.

The sound of the door opening sent me scrambling up. Kevin, Ethan's boss, walked in and shut the door behind him.

"Cass? Is there something I can help you with?" he asked with the soothing tone you'd use while approaching a rabid animal.

I smoothed my wild hair. My pulse raced, and I wildly grasped for a good explanation for why I was there tearing apart my husband's office. "No, Kevin. Just looking for something Ethan lost. You know how he is, always losing things." I released an odd screechy laugh.

"Mmhmm. Why don't you come with me? I think whatever it is that's lost, Ethan will probably have better luck helping us find it. Don't you think?"

I glanced around, noticing the aftermath of my 'search' for the first time. Pens, paper, notebooks, folders, and other various supplies were thrown everywhere. It looked like the place had been ransacked.

I cleared my throat and my face filled with heat. My hand shot to my cheek trying to cool away my shame. "Yes, yes of course. I was just, you know, so into my search, silly me. Didn't realize what a mess I was creating. I'll just get out of here."

He nodded once and stepped over a pile of manilla folders bleeding papers. He placed a hand on my lower back and led me out of Ethan's office.

I halted before we reached the entrance doors. "Maybe I could wait in your office until he got back? Or the break room. Do you happen to know when that might be? Or where he is?"

The pressure on my back strengthened, my feet started moving again. I swatted at his hand and said through gritted teeth, "This isn't necessary. Have some respect. I know my way out."

He leaned down. "You've caused enough of a scene today, Cass. Keep moving."

I pinched my lips between my teeth and bit, hard. On my way out I managed to flash Rosalie a smile and waved goodbye to Kevin. This was a perfectly normal visit to my husband's office. An office I hadn't just destroyed. All was fine.

Back in my car with my fingers curled around the steering wheel, I stared at my lap.

What's your plan, Cass?

Get home without killing yourself or someone else. Must drive safe.

Get the kids fed and upstairs. Need privacy.

Wait for Ethan. Don't destroy the house while doing so. No more throwing things.

Stay in control, remain calm, calm, calm.

Deal with Emma later.

Twelve

ETHAN

I SAT across from Emma with my knee bouncing beneath the table. My gaze shifted around the dark restaurant. As more of my secrets leaked out, these meetings were riskier, harder to explain away.

"An email *and* text? I thought we had an understanding."

"Well, she had to find out somehow." She sipped her martini and shrugged. I ran a hand through my hair. After putting the glass down, she lifted the cocktail pick and wrapped her lips around the olive impaled through it before biting down. She was trying to be sexy, but she looked like a teenager desperate to be grown.

"It wasn't your place," I said.

"What exactly gave you the impression you have any say in what my place is? You don't control me, or have any right to tell me what I can and can't do. You can have an opinion, but I can also not care about that opinion."

My hands gripped the edge of the table. *Christ, it's like having an argument with Aubrey.* Regret was firing through my chest like bullets ricocheting around my ribcage. What did I ever see in this girl? What a fool. I threw my life away for a petulant child. I looked around the room again. *They probably think I'm here with my daughter, a fun daddy daughter date.* A woman at the table to the right of ours met my gaze. Her lips pressed into a thin line. She looked from Emma and back to me before turning to the man seated with her. She leaned across the table and said something to him. He looked our way, not even trying to hide it.

Whatever. He's probably cheating on his nosy wife, too.

I turned my attention back to Emma. "You have created such a mess here, and for no reason."

She laughed and sat forward, pulling her hair over her shoulder. "Oh, Ethan, darling, you still don't get it do you? You're still looking in all the wrong places for the source of your woes. Here let me show you." She reached into her purse and pulled out a compact, cracking it open and holding the mirror to my face. "This is the person who created this mess."

I flew back in my seat. This was a side of Emma I'd never seen before. She was always so sweet and kind. She never spoke to me this way. Even if I'd had a shit day at work and took my mood out on her, she would never snap back, not like Cass. Usually, she'd stay quiet and dote on me, try to fix whatever was bothering me.

"You can't contact her anymore."

"I'm sorry, did you not hear me earlier? I will do what I want."

"Excuse me, bathroom." I stood and grabbed my phone.

"Okay, babe, I'll be here waiting." She smiled as if the entire insane exchange hadn't just happened.

I walked away and noticed five missed calls from Kevin. *Shit, am I about to be fired too? Wouldn't that be perfectly fucking fitting.*

"Kevin, hi, Ethan here. Sorry, just seeing your calls. Something the matter?"

"Ethan, not sure what's going on, but Cass was here. She appeared—unwell."

My stomach plummeted. "In what way?"

"She came here looking for you. Rosalie explained you weren't here, but she wouldn't take no for an answer. I found her in your office tearing the place apart. She said she was looking for something."

I looked back at Emma happily sipping her martini. I couldn't remember what I'd found attractive in her.

"Where is she now?"

"No idea. I escorted her out. Not sure what's happening in your personal life, Ethan, but this is the last time it's brought to my business, understood?"

"Understood," I said, holding the phone to my ear long after he hung up.

My hand gripping the phone slowly lowered to my side. I walked back to the table and grabbed my wallet from my back pocket. I threw four twenty-dollar bills on the table.

"There's an emergency at work, gotta go. Can you take care of closing us out?"

"I don't think so, Ethan. Sit. I'm not done. My salad hasn't arrived, and I don't plan on eating alone."

"Did you not hear what I said? I have to go."

Something flashed in her green eyes. "And I said I don't plan on eating alone. Now sit down or I'll scream and tell this entire restaurant that you've kidnapped me and I'm afraid for my life."

My jaw flexed. We stared at each other, unmoving. She opened her mouth and I held up my hands in defense, then dropped to the seat.

"Knock it off. Enough of this. What's gotten into you?"

She lifted a strand of hair and inspected the ends before looking at me and smiling. "Who called?"

My mind blanked. "I just told you," I said slowly. "Work, there is an emergency. Some of us still care about our jobs."

When Emma rolled her eyes, she looked just like Cass but with dark hair and green eyes. "Emergency at work? Or Cass called and you're being summoned home? And why should I care about my job when I have you?"

The waiter came and placed our food on the table. As if sensing the tension, he quickly asked if there was anything else he could get us. His friendly banter from when we first arrived was gone.

"Thanks, we're good," I said, trying to sound casual.

Emma placed her napkin across her lap and ate her lunch while happily humming to herself. I'd lost my appetite.

"You don't like it?" She gestured to my burger with her fork.

"Not hungry."

"Oof, someone's grumpy." She giggled.

This entire scene couldn't be real. I was ready to wake up from this nightmare.

"What is going on here?"

She paused, fork halfway to her mouth, and cocked her head to the side. "What do you mean Ethan? I'm enjoying a lovely meal with my boyfriend, one I'm so grateful for. I've missed you so much. I really appreciate you taking me out today."

She reached her hand across the table to take mine. I jerked back and put my hand on my jiggling knees. The nosy couple from the table to the right had left. I loosened my collar and wiped the sweat on my forehead with my napkin.

"Are you done?"

"We can't just leave. We need to pay for our meal, duh. But yes, I'm done. Again, thank you for the lovely meal."

I glared at her and caught the waiter's attention. I handed him the cash and told him to keep the change.

"Yeah man, you two have a good one," he said.

"Oh, we will," Emma said with a saccharine smile.

We stood and she looped her arm around mine. I would have pushed her off but didn't trust her to not follow through on her threats. The last thing I needed was the police being called and an accusation of abuse. We walked out of the restaurant, and I pulled my arm free.

"I don't know what is going on with you, but this is over. We are over. Don't call me, my wife, or anyone in my life. We're done, Emma."

A few people walking by glanced at us.

She stood on her toes and wrapped her arms around my neck. Just a day ago this would have had me carrying her to bed and ripping her clothes off, but instead I wanted to throw her on the pavement.

Her lips grazed my ear and she whispered, "We're done when I say we're done."

THIRTEEN

CASS

I WASN'T MYSELF. I was the twigs scattered across the floor of a forest. I snap, snap, snapped with even the slightest weight. My poor kids. They couldn't even breathe without me lashing out at them. I rushed through dinner and ushered them upstairs. Then I sat in the kitchen waiting for Ethan. I wanted to wash my face and change into pajamas but going into battle without my armor wasn't an option. Sitting on my hands so I wouldn't chew through my fingernails or scratch the skin off my face, I waited. Still as a statue, scarcely drawing a breath, but beneath the surface the threads that kept me sewn to sanity were fraying.

The doorbell echoed through downstairs. My forehead wrinkled. After looking at the clock, it dawned on me, it was Ethan. It had come to that. My husband now rang our home's doorbell rather than let himself in. How strange. I sent him a text telling him to come in and meet me in the kitchen, not sure my legs could support the walk there and back.

A disheveled Ethan entered. He must have gone to Sandra and Tyler's before coming over, because he was in a T-shirt and jeans. His five o'clock shadow looked more like a midnight one, and the skin beneath his eyes looked bruised. Despite that, he looked absolutely delicious, almost rugged. I was the absolute worst.

My eyes slid from his face to his hands and back to his face. I pictured his hands, big masculine hands, and how they felt against my body when picking me up and throwing me into bed. I studied the scar beneath his eye and imagined all the nights lying in bed, tracing it lightly with my finger. I'd ask him how he got it and each time he'd make up a new story, more outlandish than the last time. Hundreds of nights in bed, hundreds of stories, and he still made me laugh with each new one. Then I imagined those same hands on Emma, and her tracing the scar with her delicate finger. It made me furious, and yet, there was something else churning in my stomach along with the fury. Some animalistic instinct. The competition for him was turning me on. I was a disgusting beast. What was wrong with me?

His jaw wasn't clenched, and his face wasn't doing that exasperated judgmental thing it did when he was about to lay into me. News of my office visit hadn't reached him yet. So, I figured I'd pretend it didn't happen.

"Emma?" I asked through clenched teeth, remembering my purpose, remembering the reason for my rage. "What were you thinking? Not only have you jeopardized our family, but you're going to take my business down too. It all makes sense now why you wouldn't tell me who she was."

Ethan's face paled. "How did you find out? I planned on

telling you, but—" he stammered. He was reduced to a weak, pathetic man unable to ignore his desires, and too scared to face me.

"Alice told me. She found out from another employee. It was humiliating." I hated the shake in my voice. "Not even a senior employee, not someone who'd at least keep their mouth shut. An account manager told her. How can I face my employees after this? If I don't murder you, Julie may."

"Shit." Ethan collapsed into a chair across from me, then leaned back and looked at the ceiling.

"Shit is an understatement, Ethan. It would be hard enough to figure out all this," I waved my hand between us, "privately. But now I'll be the laughingstock of my office. Which makes working it out nearly impossible."

"Okay. Let me explain. That's what you want, right? An explanation." Ethan met my eyes.

"Yes. I want to know exactly how this happened and how long it's been going on. And so much more. But I'm so furious I can barely speak." I clenched my hands in fists on top of the table and resisted the urge to jump across it and pummel his face with them.

Ethan let a long breath leak from his lips before continuing. "It's Emma, she works for you. So, I'm sure you know how old she is. Both facts make me a dick. Together, I don't even know. We met at one of your client's launch parties. I couldn't tell you which one; you know how they all blend together. I'm not complaining." He rushed out the last part. He was walking through land mines, carefully choosing his words to avoid triggering one. Maybe this time I wouldn't have to sit through a lecture on how awful I was in never making time for him. I bit back my words, letting him fill in the blanks and answer the questions I didn't even know to ask.

"At first it was harmless flirting," he continued. "She was so over the top with her attention, and it was nice. We started texting, then we met up. Before I knew it, I got myself wrapped up in something I couldn't get out of. Months had passed, and I was in this *thing*. This relationship, stuck with no way out."

As I watched tears trace lines down Ethan's face, I strained to remember everything I loved about him, besides his good looks. How he made me laugh. He was kind. A good father. All the things that would stop me from standing, grabbing a kitchen knife, and stabbing him through his heart. I squeezed my eyes shut and dug deep. All those good things were so far out of reach. It was becoming harder and harder to connect the man I loved with the intruder who sat across from me. While I thought his explanation would be the information that bridged the gulf, it only widened the canyon between us.

I sighed. "I'm trying not to hate you but you're making it impossible. And now I have this crazy child, because that's what she is, a child, coming after me. First the email, then the text. Who knows what's next? Especially after I fire her tomorrow."

Ethan's shoulders fell and his eyes dropped to his lap.

"I could talk to her," he said.

"Are you serious? In what universe would you think I'd be okay with you talking to her?"

"Yeah, that was a stupid suggestion. I'm sorry, Cass. I'm totally lost here."

There was no easy answer. Nothing Ethan said would fix it. Our marriage was like a shattered vase. One that Ethan himself had held over her head and thrown to the ground. I could painstakingly find every piece and glue it back together, but it would never be the same. If anyone looked closely enough, they would see the lines from the old fractures; they'd always be there.

"I'm not sure if I want to be with you, Ethan. That's the problem. My trust is gone. I'll constantly be wondering and worrying. That's no way to live."

"Can I come back home at least? I'll stay in the guest room. It will be easier to figure things out if we're still living together. Plus, I can't take living with Sandra much longer. I wish I had a hearing aid to turn off every time she opens her mouth. Like Grandpa would do when Grandma would nag." We both chuckled, and in that microsecond things were normal. We were Cass and Ethan again. With a history and shared jokes. If only I had been able to grab onto that moment and make it last forever. It passed as quickly as it had come.

"That's not a good idea."

"Cass, please. I'm begging. I know I don't deserve it, but I think being here with you and with the kids is the only way I can earn back your trust. I'll stay out of your way and give you your space, I promise. What about counseling? It was Sandra's idea, which kills me to admit. But it's not a bad one. She gave me the name of a doctor she got from someone. I can't remember who she said exactly. I'm not going to give up on us, Cass. Never. I'll try anything. Would you be willing? To try, for the kids at least?"

"Oh, don't use the kids for your own sick advantage. Not after what you've done."

My options multiplied. I could scream and yell and throw things, which is absolutely what I preferred to be doing, but that wouldn't get me what I wanted. The idea of counseling was horrifying—another person to know how easily replaceable I was. But what other options did I have? I still had to raise kids with this man. Additionally, him being here, under my watch, did have its benefits. I could always kick him out again later. Ethan's weathered face looked at me, his blue eyes begging. His knee bounced nervously.

"You can move into the guest room. I'll let you know when, and I'll agree to one counseling session, but that's all I'm committing to," I said.

"That's fair." His face relaxed into a smile. I should have reached out and tugged his lips down. If he thought we would be moving forward, pretending none of this had happened, he was wrong. "I'll call and see what times are available. Thank you, Cass. I know I've screwed things up here. I love you. I hope I can win back your love, eventually. I can't imagine my life without you. Just the thought—"

"That thought should have crossed your mind before you crawled into bed with Emma. I have photos showing how hard it was for you to imagine being with someone else. You didn't seem too in love with me when your head was between her legs. Spare me your bullshit, Ethan. I will go to counseling, but this is for the kids, not for you. Whatever happens between us, we're stuck with each other in some capacity. We still have to raise these children together, and I would prefer your life choices didn't ruin theirs. You deserve nothing from me."

"Okay. Understood." His smug smile collapsed.

The anger began churning in my stomach again. He needed to leave before I did something I'd regret like punch him, stab him, or rip his clothes off and sleep with him. Too many emotions were colliding. That confusing line between passion and hate began to blur my decision-making skills again. I told him to leave and come back the next day.

After he left, I sat staring into my glass mulling over my options. When I was satisfied with the plan I'd formulated, I crossed the kitchen to the sink and poured what was left of the ice into it. A flash from the backyard caught my attention. Cupping my hands to the window above the sink, I peered into the darkness. Shades of black bathed the backyard. My eyes adjusted, but the only thing moving was the water in the pool. The privacy bushes lining the lanai blocked the view beyond our back porch. I leaned back from the window, my brows furrowed.

It must have been an animal, or my mind playing tricks on me. I walked upstairs, got changed, and climbed into bed. Staring at the ceiling, trying to sleep, I wondered if firing Emma would be enough. It would feel good, and I would be in control, but she ruined my life. The punishment wasn't fitting the crime; her sentence was still too lenient.

I needed more.

FOURTEEN

CASS

I TRIED to convince myself I was a lioness waiting for my prey but, in truth, I was a scared child sitting in a dirty trailer wishing her mother would tell her why she loved drugs more than she did her daughter. I chose a fitted, black dress for the occasion and painted my lips red. I had lined my eyes with the sharpest wing, which I was feeling pretty great about earlier that morning until I sneezed while my mascara was still wet. Rather than shooting off a funny tweet about the mess beneath my eyes, I sat on the bathroom floor and cried. I eventually washed my face and walked into the boardroom with the same red lips and mascara only.

"Okay, loves. I think we're all set. Ready for me to grab her?" Carla asked. I shifted my gaze from the door to her and smiled, grateful for her presence. She reminded me of my grandmother. I wanted to wrap my face in her wrinkled hands. I imagined they'd feel like crinkled silk, just as my grandmother's did. They looked nothing alike, other than being older women. My grandmother was long dead, but her loss gutted me like I'd just received the phone call telling me she'd passed. A lioness doesn't need help though. She is fierce, she is independent. I looked at Julie to dismiss the longing for comfort that Carla was dredging up.

Julie hissed yes, and I nodded, afraid if I opened my mouth I'd betray my strange thoughts. What if I said something weird like call Carla Grandma? That would have them both questioning my sanity.

With an abrupt nod, Carla hauled herself up and went to get Emma.

I stood to leave, and Julie grabbed my hand and squeezed.

"You just sit tight. If you happen to see her on her way out, make eye contact but keep your big mouth shut. We don't need that temper of yours getting you in trouble. We need controlled Cass. There will be time for psycho Cass later. You do look properly scary, though, nice work."

I nodded and walked out of the boardroom. She was right; I'm not good at behaving when angry. I lose control of my actions. I might do something I'd later regret, like fly into the room, jump across the table, and stab her in the eye with my pen. Or say something that gets us sued. Or burst into tears and humiliate myself. There was no telling, and I preferred to come through this unscathed, not in jail, and with our business still intact.

Carla appeared at the end of the hall with Emma dragging her feet behind her. I stepped back and used the wall's corner to position myself where I could see her, but she couldn't see me. I suppressed the urge to laugh. Her eyes didn't leave the floor. I wanted so badly to jump out and yell *boo*. Without her phone and keyboard to hide behind she'd been reduced to nothing but a scared child.

I leaned further into the hall and they walked silently into the room.

"Let's go listen."

I jumped and whipped around. Alice grabbed my hand and pulled me away from the boardroom. I'd never seen her so excited.

"Go listen? What do you mean?"

"Hurry, we might miss something. The meeting room next door shares a vent with the boardroom; we'll be able to hear the entire thing from there."

I didn't have time to consider how Alice knew this or more importantly, how she'd used it in the past. I obeyed and let her pull me into the smaller meeting room. She turned to face me, a crazed smile split her face and made her eyes light up in an uncomfortable way. Were everyone's secrets slipping out this week?

She slowly lifted her finger to her lips to shush me.

"Now, Emma." Julie's muffled voice came through the ceiling. My eyes widened in shock, and Alice's head nodded excitedly. "Surely you do. We're all professional women here; let's not play dumb. It's so unbecoming." Julie sounded like a teacher lecturing a naughty student.

I tried to picture Emma's reaction. It was clear what Ethan saw in her physically. She was a beautiful girl with her perfectly symmetrical face, striking green eyes, long dark lashes, and heart-shaped lips. I wasn't so blinded by jealousy I couldn't admit that. But besides that, what more did she offer?

"No, Julie, if you wouldn't mind filling me in, that would be great. I've been sick, you know. I could be contagious, spreading my germs around. Wouldn't that be a shame?"

Alice and I looked at each other with our mouths in matching O shapes. Was she actually denying it?

My memory flashed back to our last monthly all-hands. Emma sitting in one of the seats in the very room she sat in now. Julie and I were at the head of the room giving an update on the last quarterly performance and most critical priorities. I remembered being annoyed that she seemed more concerned with checking for split ends than what Julie and I had to say. *The hair, how did you miss it?* First the affair, then Emma. Things were slipping past me, big things. It was so unlike me. Was my comfortable life getting *too* comfortable? Making me soft?

A bang from the ceiling made Alice and I jump and look up.

Julie's icy voice came through clear as if she was standing in there with us. "You're fired. Hand over your keycard. Carla will explain the severance agreement and the time you have to sign it. She will also pack up your belongings and mail them to you. Carla, please escort Emma out."

Emma laughed. Alice looked at me, and I avoided eye contact. The heat on my chest crept up my neck.

"Have any of you taken one second to consider the other person involved here? Since you seem so uncomfortable coming out and saying it, I will. Ethan. What about him? He took advantage of someone half his age, one of *your* employees. Are we not going to talk about that? Just pretend that's not why we're really here."

My throat constricted making it hard to swallow.

"We should go," I whispered.

Alice shushed me again.

"I've no clue what you're talking about, Emma. I recommend signing the agreement and moving on with your life." I hoped Emma understood the layers of meaning in Julie's statement.

Emma continued, "Tell Cass she should start looking inside her own home, or in the mirror, before all you come at me pointing your judgmental fingers. You let her know she can stop lying to herself and get her house in order."

A flurry of activity sounded, and I started to run out of the room. Alice grabbed the top of my arm with a firm grip. "Cass, no!"

I turned and glared at her. "Don't ever touch me like that, Alice."

She dropped her hand and jerked back. "I'm so sorry, Mrs. Mitchell. Forgive me. I don't think going out there is a good idea."

I was already ripping the door open.

Emma came out of the room first with Carla rushing behind her. She stopped so abruptly Carla almost ran into her. Her neck twisted, and we locked eyes.

We held each other's gaze. Then she winked, smiled, tossed her hair over her shoulder, and practically skipped to the exit.

I hadn't noticed Alice until she steadied me. I didn't mind the uninvited contact that time.

"I'm sorry," I murmured. "Thank you."

"Don't be silly, Mrs. Mitchell. You know I'd do anything for you."

"I'm going to my office. Can you tell Julie to give me like thirty and come see me? I need a few minutes alone."

"Of course, do you need help?"

"No, no. I can make it there on my own. Thank you

again."

TIME SLOWED, or maybe it sped up. I stood in my office staring at nothing with unfocused eyes. I replayed Emma's and my encounter in my mind. This wasn't over. It was clear we were just getting started.

"That went as well as can be expected," Julie said, walking in and knocking me from my thoughts.

"What the hell?" I shivered. "Something's not right with her. Do you think she's going to sue us?"

Julie plopped in the seat across from my desk.

"No way. And for what? It's Florida, an at-will state, we don't need a reason to fire an employee. How does Aubrey react when she's done something wrong and gets punished? She blames you. Emma is a child. You're seeing a spoiled little child who didn't get the toy she wanted," Julie spat.

My chest tightened. "Aubrey is nothing like Emma."

"Whoa, slow down, killer. I didn't mean it like that. Oh, never mind, you're right, bad analogy." Julie stood, walked over, and bent to give me a quick hug. She leaned on the desk and looked down at me. "Are you okay? Like, really okay?"

I laughed and swiped at a tear away before it betrayed me. "Let's see, my marriage is a sham, my kids are barely speaking to me, my entire staff is aware my husband fucked their co-worker, oh, and I may or may not have a psychotic stalker. Life couldn't be better."

"You and Ethan will either work it out or you'll move on; you're a catch. Kids are resilient; they'll get over it. Someone will make an ass of themselves at a happy hour, or someone will start sleeping with someone else, and the gossip mongers will move on. And as for Emma ... if she doesn't go away, I've got that covered."

"You make it sound so easy," I said. "I can't become my mother." Panic tightened my throat. "I need the kids to know I'm there for them no matter what. Every time another man of the month would figure out my mom was a leech they'd disappear, and my mother would sleep for days and sometimes weeks. Those were always the worst times. I can't let a man turn me into her. But I feel like all I'm doing is drinking and sleeping. Acting exactly like my mother."

"You are *not* your mother. You're an amazing mom, and those kids adore you. Aubrey would kill to be you. She looks up to you and worships you like a superhero. That's why they're so mad at their dad right now. They can't stand to see you hurting. When they find out the full story they're going to be crushed. You're allowed to have a few bad days; that doesn't turn you into your mother. I could shake you for even thinking you're anything like that woman. You're overwhelmed by your feelings right now. You need time. 'This too shall pass,' as they say."

I groaned. "We've been reduced to clichés." I didn't want my kids to hurt, but I also wanted them to know what their dad did to me. More people on my side. More people to hate Emma and Ethan. Was I willing to use my children to get back at Ethan? If so, I was a fraud and not a good mom. I'd be exactly the kind of mother I'd been terrified of turning into: selfish and mean. The kids deserved so much better. There was always the option to follow in my mother's footsteps. To go to sleep and never wake up.

"You should order takeout for the kids tonight and come over to my place. I'll have Victoria make dinner. Keep yourself busy, keep moving. And get out of that house with Ethan reminders everywhere you look. It will be good for you," Julie said.

I looked up and smiled. "How about tomorrow? I'll be on my couch decompressing tonight."

"Perfect. Victoria will be ecstatic. She'll go overboard with preparations and cook more courses than necessary."

I laughed and told her to make sure she told Victoria not to go to too much trouble.

"I'm not telling her that," Julie said. "I like my bed and prefer not to be kicked out of it tonight. Victoria will make exactly as much food as Victoria wants to make." On her way out she called over her shoulder, "You know where to find me."

Once again alone with my thoughts, I imagined what the last twenty minutes would have looked like if there were no rules, no repercussions. I would have walked into the room, grabbed a handful of that damned shiny black hair, and snapped Emma's neck back before smacking her face into the table. That perfect button nose of hers would have been crushed beyond repair. Like my marriage. I slammed the heel of my hand against my forehead and begged my mind to evict her.

My phone vibrated, sending a chill down my spine. Conditioned like Pavlov's dog, the vibrating of my phone made me instantly think of Emma and Ethan, and when I thought of them, I imagined them in some dingy hotel room, sweaty and riding each other. I considered turning the vibration alert off, but then I'd constantly be checking my phone, worried I'd missed a text from the kids. A chime wouldn't work either, as the ringing or dinging would make me lose my mind more than I already had. I cautiously picked up the phone to read the text from Ethan. He'd sent a list of times the marriage counselor was available. I didn't think he'd actually call her when I had agreed to go to counseling. He never followed through on things like that, especially if it required him to take the initiative. I shot back a reply with my selection, annoyed the one time I was counting on his laziness he let me down. It was a common theme with him lately. I went to put my phone away, then paused. I added a warning if Emma contacted him, I expected him to ignore it.

I thought of Emma's exit once again and my frown deepened. Everyone in the office would have witnessed her death march. Which she treated more like a walk on the red carpet than one of shame. Their whispers about me were like a distant swarm of hornets. It grew louder until the inside of my head was a nest. I slapped my hands to my ears and squeezed my eyes shut to make the buzzing stop.

It was the same drone that invaded my thoughts as a child. Every day I'd come to school in ratty, ill-fitting, second-hand clothes. Everyone knew I was the daughter of a whore. Some kids had the grace to look away and ignore me, but most weren't so kind. 'Trailer Trash Cass, your mom's a slut and you smell like ass' was a song the nasty little girls would greet me with. Then they'd giggle amongst themselves, always buzz, buzz, buzzing behind my back, coming up with new names, new ways to break me down and make me hate myself more than I already did. Thing is, I didn't hate the girls, as every insult, every whisper, and every name was all true. Who I hated was my mother. And myself. I decided in those years that the truth wouldn't work for me. Lies were much more effective. I began snipping away my true self, my authentic self, bit by bit, bone by bone.

FIFTEEN

ALICE

A DISAPPOINTING EXIT; I hoped for more excitement and dramatics. A crying Emma running through the halls with her pretty little face in her hands, perhaps. She walked past with her chin lifted, marching like she was far superior to us peasants. Girls like her always think more of themselves than they should.

I walked over to Delaney's cube. "Delaney."

She twisted tentatively in my direction. "Hi, Alice."

"I can't tell you who to be friends with, obviously, but I highly suggest you keep your relationship with Emma strictly personal. There will be no talk of Cass or the agency. Are we clear?"

"Of course, I would never—"

I held my hand up to stop her. "Good, we have an understanding. I don't think I need to stand here and lecture you or anyone else on the importance of loyalty. This agency, including its highly respected owners, are loyal to those who show the same in return. I expect you and anyone else who is friends with that—girl—to remember who signs your paychecks and whose hands your careers are in. Advertising, as you all know, is a highly competitive and tightknit space. I have many contacts, and I'm not afraid to use them." Without giving her a chance to answer, I walked away. I had more important things to tend to, like Cass's heart.

At my cubicle, I considered what she would need and how to make her day better and easier. I took out my Cass notebook and flipped through my pages of notes. Most were memorized, but I'm never one to leave a stone unturned. I read the lists of her favorite items, dislikes, and other things I'd considered noteworthy over the years. I chewed on my pen and decided I must put more thought into the broader picture. Cass would survive this, but we needed to ensure she came out the other end stronger and better than ever. Squeaky clean. *She's not alone though, as she has me.* I smiled to myself. *We've got this, Cass, don't you worry one bit.*

After ordering her favorite launch, I canceled her afternoon meetings and laid out everything for the Blaxten campaigns on the table in her office. I stood waiting for her, ready to distract her with work.

"Alice, you scared me," she said, hand flying to her chest after walking in.

"Your lunch has been ordered. I'll go pick it up in a few minutes. I've organized the campaigns you were working on here for you so that you could dive right back in. I also canceled your meetings for the remainder of the afternoon. Would you like to begin going over the brand launch event? I've started a list; I just need to run it all by you."

She looked at me. My stomach tightened slightly. Had I missed something?

"Is that to your liking? Is there something else I can do for you?"

Her brow furrowed slightly. A Botox appointment may be needed; I'd have to figure out the most delicate way to suggest it and schedule that in. We couldn't have her perfect face lined with imperfections. Especially not now.

"It's just—you know what, never mind. This is a great idea. I'll throw myself into work and forget about this morning."

Her shoulders visibly relaxed, and her smile reached her eyes. Were those tears shining in them? A fluttering erupted in my chest, like a bird flapping his wings. I always know what she needs.

"What would I do without you, Alice?"

"Oh, Mrs. Mitchell, you flatter me. You would be just fine without little old me."

I smiled tersely and left to leave her to her work, grabbed my purse from my desk, and headed toward the exit.

A gaggle of account managers huddled together in the lobby. Their heads turned in my direction. One of the bolder ones spoke first.

"How's Cass doing?" The informality of her approach made my spine stiffen. I hitched my purse on my shoulder and glared at them.

"None of your business. All of you. Loose lips sink ships; you'd all best remember that." I pointed a finger and wagged it at each of them.

"Yes, ma'am," a few of their high-pitched voices said in unison.

They thought I was out of earshot when they burst into giggles. Or they simply didn't care. I stood outside in the muggy air and stopped on the sidewalk with my eyes closed repeating my affirmations in my head.

No what ifs.

You are living the life you are meant to live.

You have a purpose. Your life has meaning.

You are exactly who you are meant to be.

"Alice?"

I opened my eyes and Julie towered over me, looking confused.

"What are you doing? You look...unwell."

"Oh! Everything is wonderful, Ms. Parker. Couldn't be more fantastic in fact."

"Alright. You looked lost there for a second."

I huffed a laugh. "No, no. Not lost. Just taking a minute to enjoy this beautiful day. The sun is shining, and our little problem has been taken care of. Yes. I do believe things will be taking a turn for the better."

Julie still looked unsure. "Yeah, I mean, it's a bit humid, but sure ... nice day. Anyway, gotta run. Have a good one."

"I will," I said to her retreating back. "And don't worry, Ms. Parker. Cass is in very capable hands."

She stopped and turned. "You are an excellent employee; I know Cass appreciates your work. But why don't you leave her personal life for me and her to handle. Sound good?"

My smile tightened. There were many things I'd have liked to say, but unlike Emma and her pals I knew when and how to keep my opinions to myself. There's a time and place for everything, and I filed my response away for another day.

"My number one goal is this agency and making it the most efficient, successful advertising agency. I serve Cass, but also Parker & Mitchell. Cass's current, how should I put it, *situation*, is none of my business, and I don't plan on making it my business. I will continue to serve her here and leave the best friend role to you."

Julie's head tilted, and her eyes narrowed. I returned her inquisitive gaze with a pinched smile. Finally, she nodded and walked away.

Bitch.

I straightened my purse strap on my shoulder, pushed my glasses up my nose, and enjoyed the pleasant noise the tapping of my shoes made on my walk to the café to get Cass's lunch.

Sixteen

Ethan

"I got fired, you know," Emma snapped into the phone.

I sighed. I didn't have time for her today. "And this is a surprise?"

"Would it kill you to show some sympathy? They gave me four weeks' severance. How am I supposed to pay my bills? It was my first job, and now I have no references. Who the hell will hire me? I'm totally screwed."

She sniffled, I couldn't tell whether it was fake or if she was actually upset. After our weird lunch I had no idea who this girl I'd gotten myself mixed up with was. I also had too much going on at work, and this conversation was making me impatient and mean. I wasn't sure how any of this was my problem. She was a big girl. She knew the risks before getting involved with me. She pursued me, not the other way around.

"Put my name down. Give me some fake title. My last

name is in the company's name, no one will know the difference."

"Are you dumb? The agency world is as small as a flea. Everyone knows perfect, wonderful Cass. And they all think they are best friends with her. She'll be the first person they call."

My teeth clenched. I couldn't stand when she trashed Cass or talked about her like she knew her.

"Get a job at Starbucks," I snapped.

Kevin knocked on my door and I took my feet off my desk and covered the mouthpiece of the phone.

Kevin stood in my doorway, hands in pockets, face hard and impassive.

"Hey there, Kev, how's it going?"

He slipped one hand out and motioned me with a finger. "Can we talk a minute?"

"Sure, no prob. Let me finish up this call, new potential client, it's looking good," I said, giving him my broadest 'I got this' smile.

He made a noise, something between annoyance and agreement, and told me to meet him in his office when I was done.

"Who was that?" Emma asked when I uncovered the phone.

"My boss. I can't talk. He wants to meet about something."

"Oh, babe. Is it that promotion you've been hoping for? I bet that's it. I'm so excited for you."

How she went from crying, to angry, to excited within the time it took to unscrew a beer cap was beyond me. Another thing different about her. She used to be so ... predictable. What else was she hiding?

"Yeah promotion, maybe."

"Are you listening to me?"

I wasn't. It hadn't even registered she had been talking.

"No, I told you I'm at work. I'm working."

She huffed into the phone, another personality coming out to play. "I need money, and you are going to give me some until I can figure out work. That's what boyfriends do."

"I'm not your—you know what, I don't have time to get into this now."

She laughed into the phone. I used to love the sound, but this new noise she made was not like wind chimes. It didn't make my pulse speed up. It made my body break out in sweat.

"Put ten thousand dollars in my account by the end of today." Her voice changed from sinister to sweet. "Because you love me, remember?"

"That's an insane amount of money," I yelled.

I calculated my current funds in my head. Commission checks had been pennies lately, and I was barely scraping by after the monthly transfers into the joint account we paid our bills from. Cass was already watching my every move, so if I started transferring less, the questions would come. Questions I wasn't ready to answer.

"I can get it to you in a week."

"Babe, that's not going to work. Rent and my car payment are due, and food. Surely you don't want me homeless and starving. I need that money today."

"You *just* lost your job. How are you broke?"

"This isn't about the money, baby. It's about us. You want to take care of me, don't you?"

No, I didn't. I wanted her gone. "Fine. I'll get you the

money by the end of today, tomorrow at the latest." He's such a dipshit.

"Don't forget," she said before hanging up.

I grabbed my notebook and pen from my desk. Do you take notes when getting fired? Probably not. I put it back down and walked to Kevin's office while trying to convince myself it was something else. He wanted to talk about Cass's scene again or a new client he'd be charitable enough to pass my way. I was good at lying to my wife; maybe it would work on myself, too.

"Come in Ethan, grab a seat," Kevin said, gesturing to a chair. Belinda, the head of HR was sitting in the other.

"I'm afraid we're going to have to let you go Ethan. We've had several talks over the last year about your performance. I'm not seeing the improvements I'd been hoping for. Belinda will go over the severance and paperwork. I'm sorry, Ethan, wish I had better news for you."

"Is this about Cass? I told her she can never do that again. I assure you, it's the first and only time. She was having a bad day. Not herself. You know Cass. Both of you do. She owns a company, she's a great mom. It was a bad—" I looked at each of them, my eyes wide, desperate for them to believe me.

"Your personal life is none of my business. But as a friend, Ethan, we all know what's been going on the last year. You haven't hidden it well. My advice is to get out while you can, save your marriage, get your career back on track, and knock off this schoolboy shit. We've known each other a long time and you're good at what you do. It's time to get your priorities in order and your head on straight. Just not on my dime. Feel free to use me as a reference though."

Belinda took over. "Ethan, please follow me down to my office. We can review the severance paperwork and schedule a time to come in after hours to pack up your office." She gave me a sympathetic smile.

I nodded curtly and stood, extending my hand toward Kevin. "Sorry, Kevin, nothing but respect for you. I let you down. Wish things ended differently."

Kevin shook my hand with his firm grip and turned back to his computer. "Best of luck to you, Ethan."

Back in my car, the one I could no longer afford, I punched the dashboard. My rage wanted to blame everyone including Kevin, Belinda, my accounts that dropped me, Emma, Cass, and even Julie who I'm sure had something to do with Cass's visit to my office. The ten grand Emma demanded seemed even more impossible.

If I hadn't told her about the other women, she'd have nothing to hold over my head. Unfortunately, it wasn't just Emma. There were countless Emmas. The only difference was this time I got caught. Telling her was such a mistake. Without that information, I'd block her and move on with my life. Convince Cass to take me back and get my shit together. No more affairs. Get my career back on track. Life had gotten in the way of *us*, and we'd somehow turned into roommates. This woman who meant everything to me. No one could make me laugh like Cass, no one could look as beautiful as she did, whether in a fancy dress or sitting on the couch in sweats. She wasn't my wife, she was home. Without her, I'd be lost. I leaned my forehead on the steering wheel. I couldn't keep paying her off forever. I had to figure something out.

The only positive thing I had going for me was Cass agreed to let me move back in. I wasn't homeless—yet. I could stretch my twelve-week severance for about two months, after Emma's payout. I would have to find a job between now and then. Explain to Cass an opportunity arose that I couldn't turn down. She wouldn't have to know I lost my job at all. What she didn't know couldn't hurt her. Just like the affair.

If only Emma had kept her damn mouth shut.

I started driving home but halfway there I changed my mind and drove to an apartment complex I'd been to many times before. An older maroon Toyota was parked in the lot.

I stared at it, trying to place where I knew it from, but plenty of people drive the same car. I shook my head and got out of the car.

If I was going to pay Emma ten grand, she'd earn it.

SEVENTEEN

ALICE

IN MY TINY HOME, at my tiny table, eating my tiny bowl of soup, I imagined what it would be like if Cass were there with me. I'd listen to her, nod at the right moments, frown at the precise time, and make her laugh exactly when she needed it.

Instead, she was probably headed to Julie and Victoria's house, where she'd be breaking bread with them instead.

"Don't ever touch me like that again."

My hand clenched the spoon a bit tighter.

I am a chameleon. A professional impressionist. I am a mirror. At one point I may have had my own personality, but I've been other people for so long, I haven't a clue who Alice is at this point. The real Alice ran far, far away when it all became too much. So, I learned another way. I found people whose lives were easier, who had the things I wanted. And I would take a piece of them for myself. A patchwork quilt of personalities—that's what I became.

Becoming other people requires watching, researching. It's easy to watch when you blend into the background. And I've always blended into the background.

After finishing my dinner and tidying the kitchen I walked to my bedroom where the bags from my earlier shopping trip sat neatly on my bed. My meager salary didn't afford many luxuries; however, my prudent lifestyle didn't require lavish funding. Treating myself on occasion came without worry.

The fitted blazer and pencil skirt made me feel smart, confident, Cass-like. Even the department store employee felt the same, she nodded and smiled and told me so. I'd stopped at the beauty counter and had one of the ladies do my makeup. She didn't seem pleased when all I'd purchased was a lip gloss for her trouble, but that wasn't my problem. I removed my clothes, careful to not mess up my newly painted face, and changed into the new outfit. One bag remained to complete the look.

In my bathroom, I retrieved the blonde wig and pulled it tight over my head.

"Alice, would you mind running to Ponte and grabbing me a salad? I'm so busy," I asked my reflection. My heart fluttered like a butterfly. The resemblance, oh it was perfection. The pride swelled within my chest.

My face sobered. "Ethan, what you did was despicable, unforgivable even. My attorneys will be drawing up divorce papers immediately. And Julie, we've been through a lot, but all good things must come to an end. I do believe it's time we go our separate ways. I hope you understand."

My lips curved upwards; the not-Cass-Cass grinned along with me.

I nodded, satisfied. And walked back to the kitchen to make myself a cup of tea.

EIGHTEEN

CASS

IT HAD BEEN years since I'd lived anywhere with a true winter, but I remembered the feeling of cold mornings. Standing in our barely heated trailer, preparing myself for the long walk to school where I'd trudge through snow with an inadequate spring jacket three sizes too small. I'd grip the door handle, preparing to leave, my muscles tense, and my jaw clenched, knowing when I opened the door and stepped outside the air would smack me and steal my breath.

That's how I was feeling every second of every day. Like I was back in the trailer bracing myself for what lay on the other side of that door. Muscles perpetually tense, I was in a constant state of waiting for the next thing to smack me and steal my breath. Not knowing what I was bracing for was the worst part.

When I approached Julie and Victoria's front step, my shoulders relaxed. I didn't need to brace myself for what laid on the other side of the door in front of me. Victoria welcomed me into her home with a giant hug, enveloping me in the smell of lavender. With an arm wrapped around my lower back, she nudged the door shut with her foot and ushered me into the house.

"Sit, sit," Victoria said, pointing to the living room. "What can I get you to drink? I have a fresh bottle of Tito's. Soda with two limes?"

I almost cried. I was so sensitive, like pregnancy hormones without the pregnancy.

There are only a few people I have ever truly trusted in my life. None of them had ever met the *real* me, but they knew enough. Those people include my grandmother, Julie, Ethan, and Victoria, in that order. Before I met Julie in college, my grandmother had passed and I was untethered. Alone. I focused on my studies while pretending I didn't need anyone. Another lie I told myself to maintain my sanity.

My worthless mother, who earned her title by giving birth, not by doing any actual mothering, was good at two things: drinking and drugging. Well, three if you counted manipulating and using men to fund those other two things. By the time she died from an overdose, I was so used to being alone I had no clue how lonely being alone could be.

The state shipped me to Florida to live with a grandmother I'd never met, but I learned what it was like to be loved and cared for. If my mother had miraculously risen from the dead, I would have killed her again. How dare she starve me of love when it was right there, a phone call away?

She could have given me up earlier, sent me to live with my grandma and removed herself from my life, then I wouldn't have had to work so hard to pretend. I wouldn't have ended up like the apple I was, glossy and red on the outside, but rotten in the core. I would have been good, rather than pretending I was.

When my grandmother died, I covered my depression by putting my head down and distracting myself with schoolwork. Then I met Julie. We clicked immediately, became instant best friends, and have been inseparable ever since. She pulled me out of my cave of loneliness and gave me hope that love wasn't something for other people. She showed me I wasn't doomed to wander this earth, having only had a nibble of affection, but never getting the chance to enjoy much more than that.

When Ethan bounded into my life, saving me from even more trauma, I experienced an entire meal of love. A year after we started the agency, Julie met and married Victoria. Everything was good. Everything was perfect.

"I'll be down in a minute," Julie yelled from upstairs. "Just changing into something more comfortable."

As I relaxed into the couch, the familiarity of Julie and Victoria's home filled me with warmth. The feeling of sitting in that comfortable space jarred me. My home had become cold and uninviting.

With Ethan and me barely speaking, I'm ashamed to admit I didn't know who I was without him. The perfect loving wife was a role I'd slipped so easily into. It was a costume of mine that fit comfortably. So comfortably, I'd almost forgotten it was a role I was playing. A kiss hello, dinner on the table every night, ask him about his day, compliment and feed his ego, sex at least three times a week, check, check, check, check, check. I'd mentally check off the boxes throughout my day. Always completing my tasks. Without him there, I had no tasks to complete.

I know these wifely things should have felt natural, not

like a daily to do list, but they didn't come naturally to me. I'd never give him the satisfaction of admitting any of that.

Regardless of my emotionally stunted heart, Ethan was always with me, and had been every day since I'd met him. That wasn't forced. He was always there, floating in the back of my mind, often without me realizing it. Insignificant things connected us, such as wondering what he was doing, what he was thinking. Had it always been that way? Or had that omnipresence grown along with our relationship? Now that my thoughts of him weren't insignificant, it opened my eyes. Without him physically there and part of my everyday life it was like I'd lost an appendage. I read a news article once about Phantom Limb Syndrome. Where someone who loses a limb still feels pain or sensation in the now empty space where it used to exist. When I read the article, I couldn't fathom what it must be like. With Ethan gone, I understood, because I was living with it.

At home I was pacing the rooms each night with my skin crawling or sitting and staring at nothing losing hours of time. It was too much time for my mind to be left to wander. Too much time to obsess over Emma and for my bitter heart to concoct ideas on how to make her experience the same agony as me.

Being here, with Victoria and Julie, I felt closer to whole than I had in a while. I considered driving home, packing bags for me and the kids and moving us in. I closed my eyes and let my muscles unclench. Just a few miles away, Ethan was moving back into our house. We wouldn't be sharing a room, but we'd be sharing a roof.

"Nap time?"

I hadn't heard Julie enter. My eyes snapped open, and I smiled. Julie had her dark hair pulled into a messy bun. She sat and crossed her outstretched legs on the ottoman. The furry slippers on her feet made them look comically large.

"Those slippers are ridiculous," I said.

"What? These are the best. They're so comfy," Julie replied, lifting one leg up for me to admire her footwear.

"It looks like you have dead animals on your feet. You've got some nerve forcing me into four-inch heels every day," I teased.

Victoria walked in balancing three glasses on a tray. Her curvy form maneuvered this world like she was constantly swimming through water. I glanced down at my stick-like figure society constantly forced on women and felt a twinge of jealousy for Victoria and her curves and softer frame.

"That's at work. At home, it's perfectly acceptable to look like a slob. Encouraged, in fact. Isn't that right?" Julie asked, grinning at Victoria.

"Mhm." Victoria handed me my bubbling glass of vodka and soda, and Julie a glass of white wine. "You shouldn't listen to her anyway, Cass. She's all bark and no bite. You wear what you want. It's your company, too." She winked at me.

"She knows that," Julie said, laughing before taking a sip of her wine. "Any more out of you-know-who?"

"Which one, Ethan or Emma?" I asked. I'd hoped for a night where we talked about anything other than my cheating husband. It was impossible; I probably would have brought it up myself. The affair, Ethan, and Emma were always there, tumbling around in my head, refusing to adhere to their eviction notice.

"Either one," Julie said.

"Ethan's at the house tonight, moving back in, and I have that counseling appointment in three days. Marni the marriage counselor. Funny right? Like a nursery rhyme. Not a peep out of Emma," I replied, taking a long sip of my drink.

"I knew you'd cave too soon. Can't believe you didn't make him suffer through Sandra for at least a month. Emma might be smarter than we thought, and she'll, poof, disappear. Carla told me the account managers are glad she's gone. Apparently, Emma had been blabbing about the affair for a while now, and they were shitting their pants not knowing whether to say anything."

"Seriously? The entire company knew about the affair before I did? And I've just been walking around like a grinning idiot. Not one of them thought to tell me?" My worst nightmare coming true. The humiliation made my temperature rise.

"I mean, you're their bosses, bosses, boss. The owner of the company, and they are a bunch of babies."

"Look at you, all involved and in the know. Seeing things from other people's perspectives. I'd love to be excited if, you know, it hadn't taken an employee screwing my husband to get you there," I said. Trying to hide my discomfort.

"No, no. I've not changed a bit. You are both stuck with me just the way I am, forever. Carla mentioned it when she brought me Emma's box of things to sort through before mailing it. Before you ask, there was nothing in there you'd care about. Not much at all, actually. I'm sure she packed up most of her stuff when she fired off that email. She likely figured the firing was coming soon enough."

"It's terrible what you're going through. I'm so sorry," Victoria said.

I squirmed in my seat under her caring frown.

"Thanks. It's pretty insane, isn't it? Like a bad *Lifetime* movie."

Victoria nodded, eyebrows scrunched together.

"I could always kill him." My delivery must have been off, because Julie and Victoria stared at me with curious expressions. I clutched my glass and took a drink of the cold liquid, hoping it would cool the embarrassment rushing heat from my chest to my face. "Just kidding." I chuckled awkwardly, then took another long swig of my drink.

Julie started cracking up. "Just tell me when it's time to hide a body."

"Alligator Alley, for sure. Dump his body in the Everglades, he'd never be found," Victoria added. We both looked at her, shocked. Victoria usually chastised us for our dark sense of humor. She shrugged and smiled while bringing her wine glass to her lips.

"We're terrible influences, Cass. Now we're taking sweet, innocent Victoria down with us. Cheers to karma and bad behavior," Julie said, and we all held up our glasses and collapsed into a fit of giggles. It felt so good to authentically laugh. I longed to wrap my arms around both of their necks and hug them. The gesture would have been more unexpected than me planning my husband's murder, I'm sure.

"Dinner is probably almost ready. You two have a seat at the table, be good girls, and try not to plan any other murders. I'll bring the food out," Victoria said, once we'd regained control of ourselves.

"Need any help?" I asked, grasping for anything to keep my hands and mind busy.

"No, love. It's your night, I don't want you lifting a finger," she called over her shoulder.

We walked into the dining room, drinks in hand, mine reduced to ice. Vodka was going down much faster and easier since I'd found out my husband was a lying cheater. As expected, Victoria served four courses of delicious food, bringing my depleted appetite roaring back to life. Her cooking may very well have been the thing that saved me from death by starvation.

"It's a nice night out. Want to light a fire and sit outside for a bit? Or do you need to get home to the kids?" Julie asked. After we'd finished dessert, a mouth-watering tiramisu. Unlike my dinner parties, this was definitely not purchased from Publix and placed on a fancy plate; it was homemade.

"That sounds wonderful. The kids should be fine, hiding in their rooms from their dad. I'll shoot them a text." I tried to keep the slur from my words. My dead mother's spirit had snuck back into the land of the living. It was a fine line I walked. *Tomorrow I'll cut down on the drinking; I'm not her.*

I dug my phone out of my purse, looked at the screen, then threw it onto the table as if it had burned my hands.

"Something wrong?" Julie asked, concern washing over her face. "You're bright red."

She snatched the phone and read the text from a private number out loud.

"This isn't over. I'm not done playing with you or your husband."

The silence hardened around us.

"Bitch," Julie spat. She swiped the text to delete it.

"Guess she's stalking me now." I studied their faces to see if they agreed.

"She can't do anything she hasn't already done. She's

hurt and now she's trying to hurt you." Victoria squeezed my hand.

"She's hurt?" I threw my hands up in exasperation. "He wasn't hers to take. He was mine. She may have rented him for a few months, but that's it!"

Victoria stood and pulled me from my seat into a hug. I leaned my head on her shoulder. The time for sadness was over. I was shaking with rage. I'm sure Victoria confused it for sobs, as she rubbed my back and whispered soothing reassurances in my ear.

"I know. She's just hiding behind her phone. I'm sure she'll get bored and move on soon." Julie suggested.

"I guess." I peeled myself from Victoria's embrace. "It's freaking me out. I wish she'd just—disappear."

Julie and Victoria exchanged a glance.

"We were having such a fun night. We can't let her spoil the mood. No reason to worry until she gives us a reason to," Victoria chimed in with her natural cheeriness. I wished I could be so happy all the time. It seemed to come so effortlessly. "I'll fix us all drinks. Julie, you two go outside and start the fire." She stood and began collecting glasses.

"I'm just going to run to the bathroom for a second. I'll meet you out there," I said.

I stepped up to the mirror and wiped the mascara that had smudged beneath my eyes, pinched my cheeks, and straightened my back. I watched my reflection smile back. As if text messages were even remotely scary. My eyes rolled upwards. Please, after what I've seen it would take a lot more than a few text messages to ruffle these feathers. But I needed their sympathy, their mutual disgust; it was my oxygen. I unfocused my vision and returned to that dirty hotel room, pictured Emma's head flung back and that damn hair cascading down her back, eyes closed and mouth open in ecstasy as she rode my husband. Anything I did from then on was absolutely justifiable. I practiced my scared and whimpering face in the mirror for a few seconds, slumped my shoulders, and walked slowly to meet Julie in the backyard. A distraught and hurt wife. How sad. How pitiful.

I drank the rest of my feelings away, and the night blurred. Around midnight, I called for an Uber. I'd need to come back for my car, so Victoria and I decided we'd meet for yoga in the morning and I'd come back to their house and grab my car after. It was one of those drunk decisions that always end up being much better in theory than in practice. Julie was very anti-yoga. She would not be joining us.

I MUST HAVE FALLEN asleep in the Uber because when we pulled into my driveway, I couldn't remember the ride home. I'm sure my driver, Paul, found it amusing, taking a shit-faced, middle-aged mom home from being over-served at her suburban dinner party. My hand fumbled with the door handle and the door opened with a groan. Paul twisted in his seat to say goodbye. He was hot, too young for me, maybe twenty-something, but not too young for someone like Emma. I paused and considered giving him her number. She could release her talons from my husband and run off with Mr. Uber. It's too bad I was too drunk for schemes. It was an interesting idea I'd come up with but was much too tipsy to execute. Next time. I hoped my sober brain would remember my drunk brilliance.

"Odd time to go for a run," Paul said before I shut the door.

I froze, my head tilted to the side. "What? I'm not going for a run."

The woman running by must have sensed us talking about her, because she turned just as we looked and sped up her steps.

I shrugged. "It's cooler at night."

"It's also dangerous at night."

I shut the door. I was too tired for safety lectures from Paul.

Every window in the house was lit up. I expected to walk in and find Aubrey and Ben, and potentially Ethan, sprawled on the couch watching TV. I concentrated very hard on walking straight and not slurring my words. *I am not my mother.* After struggling with the code and several incorrect attempts, I unlocked the door before the alarm alerted the cops. I walked—stumbled—into an empty first floor.

I stood at the bottom of the stairs with my hand on the railing. Aubrey's muffled voice floated down the stairs, merging with sharp retorts from video game guns and Ben's rambling over his headset. I walked around the first floor, turning off the lights and locking up for the night. After flipping the last switch down, the room turned monochrome, and the shadows seemed to morph into fingers, growing longer as they crawled toward me. A strange energy lifted the hairs on my arms, and I twisted around, trying to find the source of the fear clawing at my spine. I grabbed a vase then put it down, feeling silly. I was drunk and overreacting.

Still, I ran up the stairs. When I reached the top, my grip

tightened on the rail and I steadied my breathing to slow my racing heart. Was I afraid of the dark now? Or did some part of me understand, an unconscious instinct that recognizes danger, that Emma was just as scary as I was? Did I know that underestimating her would be as foolish as underestimating myself? I wiped my clammy hands on my pants and walked to my room. The light from the guest room created a triangle in the darkened hall. I glared at the closed door and hoped Ethan didn't attempt to come speak with me tonight.

"I'm home. Goodnight, you two. Love you," I called to Aubrey and Ben. I shut the door and crawled into bed without changing. A sober me would have stared into the darkness, terrified by every creak and groan of the house. Or, I would have re-hashed every Ethan conversation from the past six months, continuing the desperate search for the signs I'd missed. All the lies he'd slid past me. I licked my lips and tasted a hint of lime juice. Not quite as delicious as revenge. But almost.

NINETEEN

CASS

MIRACULOUSLY, I woke up the next morning before my alarm. With my eyes still closed, I assessed the damage. Only a slight pain pulsed on the right side of my temple. I considered the lack of a hangover a depressing sign that I may be overdoing the vodka too much. I threw on a pair of leggings and T-shirt and gulped down the cup of coffee Ethan handed me. He offered a ride to get my car, but I declined. I put in a request for an Uber to take me to meet Victoria at yoga, while wishing I hadn't agreed to it all and could simply fetch my car and lay on the couch all day. When the little car on the Uber app turned into my neighborhood, I grabbed my yoga mat, and walked outside to meet my driver. Unfortunately, it wasn't Paul. Too bad—I was in a much clearer state of mind and could have orchestrated that setup.

"CASS, HELLO!" Victoria was waiting for me outside the studio. I gave her a hug with my free arm. "How are you doing? Any more crazy texts?" she asked.

"No, thank God." I held open the door, then followed her in.

"She'll get tired of it all and move on. If she hasn't already. Just hang in there. This will be behind you soon."

"I hope you're right." I found a spot and unrolled my mat. Victoria did the same next to me and sat with crossed legs.

She wrangled her red curls into a bun. "I just hate that this is happening to you," she soothed while patting my leg.

"Yeah, it's pretty terrible," I said, tucking my knees to my chest and wrapping my arms around them. I rocked back and forth and blew out a slow breath to show just how terrible it was. "One second, I'm so sad I can't imagine how I can go on. The next, I'm so angry I can't think."

"Have you thought about having Ethan tell her to knock it off? So you have one less thing to stress over?" Victoria asked.

"Why would I encourage Ethan to have any contact with her?" I snapped.

Victoria smiled sympathetically. "I'm sorry, I didn't mean to upset you. It's all so unfair."

The teacher came in and interrupted our conversation. I was getting myself worked up, so I focused on the instructor's voice to tune out the noise for a blissful hour. When class was over and we were rolling up our mats, my smile reached my eyes. An entire hour free from the weight of revenge and hurt. I told Victoria how glad I was she suggested it and surprised myself when I meant it. I was so used to pretending. The lies were so easy; white lies covered by bigger lies. My whole life was a lie.

"Yoga cures all," Victoria said, returning my smile. "Want to grab a coffee at Starbucks across the street before we head to the house for your car?"

"A vanilla latte sounds amazing," I replied.

We stepped out onto the sidewalk when I halted and grabbed her arm. With my words glued in my throat, I dug my nails into the flesh of her bicep.

"Ouch, what—" Victoria said, but someone else had my attention. The noise of the street fell silent, and the corners of my vision darkened.

I'd finally regained my footing, felt in control but seeing Emma's face released something inside of me. She sat with a friend on the patio chatting and laughing as if she hadn't destroyed a family and my life. I released Victoria's arm, dropped my mat, and barreled across the street.

A horn blared, mixed with rubber tires screeching on pavement. The sounds barely registered.

"Cass, watch out!" Victoria's scream pierced through the silence. She later told me the car came within inches of hitting me, but I was too focused on reaching the other side of the street I didn't notice. Without even so much as pausing, I continued running toward Emma.

The commotion had captured Emma and her friend's attention, and they were staring at me. Her friend's eyebrows wrinkled in confusion and her jaw hung open. Emma's eyes grew wide, then narrowed into slits. A smile played at the edge of her lips.

"You bitch," I screeched while jabbing my finger in Emma's face. It confused me for a half-second, as I'd never heard that sound come from my mouth. Emma and I made eye contact. "Stay away from my husband and stop texting me with your crazy shit."

Victoria caught up to me and stopped at my side. My breath was coming out in raspy huffs, I was sweating, and my eyes bulged from their sockets.

"Cass, what—?" Victoria's head whipped from me to Emma and back again. "Is this her?"

"Yes." My voice and body pulsated with hatred.

"What are you on about, Cass?" Emma asked. My face whipped toward her, and she had the gall to laugh.

It was all too much, her nonchalant attitude toward me and the situation. "You fucked my husband."

"Calm down. You're causing a scene. I slept with Ethan, so what? He told me you two were practically divorced. You should take that up with your husband and not me." She shrugged, then took a sip of her iced latte. "I'm not texting you anything. You're the one who needs to stay away from me." She turned back to her friend and resumed their conversation as if I wasn't there. She destroyed my life, and it was so inconsequential to her she couldn't even apologize. I stood there staring at them, shaking, with my mouth hanging open.

Other people sitting at the nearby tables stared at me whispering to each other. The buzzing came, grew louder.

As I was about to turn and run away from my mortification, Emma threw her head back and started laughing. I stumbled backward. Thankfully, Victoria took over.

She took me by my elbow and whispered in my ear, "Come on, sweetie, let's get you out of here." With her arm around my shoulders, we walked across the street. Emma's cackling blended and faded into the background. The world unfroze, and people continued on with their lives. If only they knew how fortunate they were. I was one of them, not too long before that day. But now, I was an outsider. Staring through a window into an organized and predictable land, a world I used to fit so neatly into, a world where I was no longer welcomed. Instead, I stood outside, banished, looking in on what I used to have, while a storm of chaos raged around me.

Victoria eased a stunned version of myself into the passenger seat of her car. I leaned my head on the cool window and closed my eyes.

"I'm so embarrassed," I whispered. The rage poured out with the tears trickling down my face.

"Don't even think about it." Victoria reached over and squeezed my white-knuckled hands clasped tightly in my lap.

"I don't know what came over me. I saw her sitting there and—" I placed a hand on my forehead. "I just...lost it."

"Who could blame you? I'd have done the same. I'm just glad that car didn't hit you. You ran right in front of it. Scared the shit out of me."

"Ha. That would have made Emma's day," I said dryly.

"What a nasty little cow she was. Laughing like that." Victoria filled her cheeks with air and released it. "Now that I've seen her in action, the insane texts make sense. What a psychopath. No guilt at all."

"I just need a minute."

"Sure, of course. Whatever you need."

Victoria was too kind to admit I'd made a fool of myself. I didn't need her confirmation, though. I'd lost control. I'd let Emma take my power—again. It was all fun and games when it was a few texts. I'd been shamed enough by the entire situation. That day was my breaking point. I sensed the shift.

Things would go my way soon.

WE WALKED into the house to find Julie in the living room, sitting on the couch reading a book.

"Hey, how was—"

It was as if I'd just walked away from a terrible accident. I was numb, shocked. Like I could vomit at any minute.

"Let's get you comfortable." Victoria pointed to the couch. I must have looked a mess from how they were both staring at me. Victoria spoke to me as if my skin was as fragile as an egg and loud noises could crack it.

"I'm going to wash my face," I replied.

"We had an incident," Victoria explained to Julie on my way out.

"What kind of incident?" Julie asked.

I must have been gone long enough for Victoria to fill Julie in because when I returned, she was pacing the room.

"This has gone too far," she said to me. "I'm calling Ethan right now. It's time for him to clean up his mess." She may as well have been frothing at the mouth.

I should have felt something, perhaps anger, definitely shame, but I felt nothing. Every cell in my body had been anesthetized. Just when I had downward dogged the tension from my body, the encounter with Emma left my muscles stretched like a rubber band about to break. But if it took me embarrassing myself for everyone to see Emma for who she truly was, perhaps it was worth it.

My phone vibrated in my purse. I dug it out and looked

at the text, a private number with no words, just five laughing emojis. It came as no surprise. I turned the phone for Julie to see.

"It's a game to her," I said.

Julie ripped the phone from my clammy hand and deleted it. "Not today. We're not giving her one more second of our headspace."

My stomach was on a roller coaster. Suddenly finding my voice and energy, I jumped up. "I'm done with this shit." Snatching my phone back from Julie, I pulled up Ethan's contact and smashed the call icon.

"Ethan? No, stop talking. Are you at the house? Something happened." Julie and I switched places, and I now paced the room. "I'm not talking about it on the phone. Just don't go anywhere. I'll be home in a few. Bye."

Julie cocked an eyebrow. "What's the plan?"

"I haven't figured it out yet, but I'm done playing the victim. She will *not* humiliate me ever again. I'm heading home. I'll see you at the office." Technically, the person responsible for my humiliation was me, but I didn't have time for technicalities. I turned around and almost ran into Victoria.

"Are you sure you're okay to drive?" she asked, still talking to me like a child. Now that I had regained feelings, it was grating on my nerves. I had to get out of there before I said something I would regret.

"Yes, I'll be fine. Promise. I love you both and owe you. But right now, I need to get home and figure out how to rid my life of this girl."

"She's worse than herpes." Julie chortled.

"Julie, hush." Victoria pulled me into a hug, and I focused intently on not tensing. My skin was itchy and uncomfortable. I didn't want anyone touching me. "Text us when you get home, so we know you made it. Driving angry can be just as dangerous as driving drunk."

I pulled away and forced my lips into a pinched smile, then grabbed my yoga mat before running out of the house. In the driveway, I fumbled through my purse for my keys, dropped them, picked them back up, ripped open the car door, threw the mat in, and slammed the door closed. My face dropped into my hands, and I screamed before slamming my body into the seat repeatedly.

With that out of my system, I inspected my reflection in the rearview mirror and straightened my hair. I'd been the person I promised myself I'd never be. Seeing her made me lose control, even worse, I lost control in public. But some sacrifices are worth it. She had baited me with the email, and I swam up and ate it like the tarpon swimming around our dock. Who knows what bystander-shot videos would be making their rounds across the internet? No one who witnessed the encounter knew why I was screaming at her. All they saw was me acting like a maniac. Victoria and Julie's eyes were open though, and now it was time for Ethan's eyes to open as well, even if I had to pry apart his eyelids with my nails.

TWENTY

CASS

EMMA'S LAUGH played on repeat in my head, the soundtrack for my drive home. Thoughts and plans and schemes flew through my head as my car sped from Tampa to St. Pete. I stepped out of my car and into my driveway. Our neighborhood had a lumbering stillness to it, the calm before the storm. Moisture bloated the air and left a metallic taste in my mouth, weather that perfectly complemented my current disposition. I'd had a minor slipup, one in which I'd allowed my mask to slide down a bit too far, but I was beyond that now. I stood in my driveway and listened to the distant rumbling from the bay. The first drops of rain plopped onto my upstretched face, and I smiled. A thunderstorm would be the perfect ally for the upcoming battle with my husband.

I walked into my house and told Aubrey and Ben to go upstairs. Ben groaned and stomped away. Aubrey lowered her chin and narrowed her eyes.

"Why do we have to go upstairs?" she asked with that typical teenage attitude that sliced my nerves.

"Where's your dad? We have things to talk about and need privacy. When I'm done, I'll take you and Ben out to dinner. We can do something fun." It was as if I was bargaining with an enemy, using bribes to get my way. My mind had returned to its precise and methodical state, and I could maintain the high standard of composure I held myself accountable to. It was back to acting the way I'd trained it to act. But my daughter had spent her entire life observing and learning from me. She was a worthy competitor.

"He's out back on the dock. Fishing, I think. Why can't dad come to dinner with us? And why isn't he sleeping in your room?"

I appreciated her persistence. I found datasets with holes just as annoying.

"I'll explain everything tonight at dinner." My eyes slid to the back door. I pictured him standing on the dock, beer in hand, happy as can be. *Asshole.*

Aubrey's eyes narrowed further. How far was she willing to dig? If it were me, I'd keep going until I'd reached the earth's crust, then dig further.

I could visualize the synapses within her brain firing, connecting the dots, putting the pieces of the puzzle together. After a pause, her eyes widened.

"Did dad cheat on you?"

I dipped my head in a slight nod. "Don't worry about your dad and me. Everything will work out the way it's supposed to," I said, my voice clipped yet falsely cheery.

"What a dick." She uncrossed her arms and placed them on her hips with her face twisted in anger.

"Language, Aubrey." I sighed and dropped onto the couch. Gravity's pull, strengthened by the blanket of my growing public shame, was too strong for my muscles to fight against. She'd have found out eventually, so I wasn't inflicting any unnecessary damage. I was just speeding up the process. She'd already guessed. It wasn't my fault. There would be nothing to tell if Ethan hadn't had the affair.

I clasped my hands and leaned forward with my elbows on my knees. "Aubrey. I'm asking you to please go upstairs. I know this is confusing for you and Ben. I hate that it's affecting you, but I need this from you right now. We need privacy. Please."

"Fine." Aubrey snatched her phone and ran up the stairs. I knew it was coming, but still winced at her slamming door.

"Cass?" Ethan walked in through the back door. I leaned over the back of the couch and called out so he could follow my voice to me.

He walked in with his face twisted. He looked old and worn. I hoped he felt as bad as he looked.

"Is everything okay?" he asked.

"I'm fine, but something happened." I explained the humiliating scene I'd caused outside Starbucks. Playing down my bad behavior and playing up Emma's, of course. Most people would do the same.

"She sat there laughing like a deranged witch," I finished. "I'm scared of her. She's going to do something. I'm afraid for myself and for the kids." There I went, using my kids as pawns in my games again. It was fine; the ends justified the means. His feelings were straddling the line, and it was time for him to pick a side. The right side. Mine.

I let Ethan retreat into his thoughts, and the room grew silent. I chose my next words carefully, a test.

"I didn't have a ton of interactions with her at work. As hard as it is to say, she was a normal, sweet girl. Okay at her job. She got along well with everyone in the office. I *never* imagined she'd turn into this—whatever this even is." This was a lie. My feelings for Emma were most definitely on one very clear side, not even a millimeter in any other direction.

But were his?

"Me either. It seems out of character." *Idiot.* As suspected, I still had work to do. She was still providing me with plenty of material to mold the narrative the way I needed. We'd get there.

"What did you promise her, Ethan?"

He flinched and ran a hand through his hair. A curious response. He *had* promised her something and it was clear he was trying to hide whatever it was. More secrets. My familiar friend Curiosity sauntered into the room and pulled up a chair.

Let's dig a little deeper, shall we? she whispered in my ear.

"Well?" I pushed.

"You did nothing, Cass. Neither did Emma. This was all me." *Avoiding the question.*

"Tell me what you promised her."

He spun his wedding band around his finger. Was he thinking back on our marriage? Every special moment we'd shared. Memories now tarnished and rusted. Or was he remembering his time with Emma and contemplating how to answer the question without sending me flying across the room and scratching his eyes out? "I probably wasn't firm enough with her."

"Stop muttering," I snapped.

"Do you want to hear or not?" The force behind his words surprised me. *That's the spirit.* Finally, the Ethan I could love was here with me. It brought a tickle to my stomach. My mouth chose before I had time to debate the options.

"Fuck you, spit it out." *Calm, calm, calm, calm.* I repeated the word and focused on soothing the rage brewing in my chest while I hung onto my control by the tips of my fingers. Emma was the crazy one, not me. That was the goal. Stick to the goal. Once he was fully on my side, I'd decide if I still wanted him there.

He swallowed, steadied his voice, and continued, "Looking back, she would talk about our future. I just kind of laughed it off to spare her feelings. I should have been more forceful. More direct."

Every muscle contracted. *Liar.* He wasn't telling the full story. I sensed it in his shifting eyes and in the way his voice had lost its charisma. Should I push farther? Ethan had a temper. He was like a wild animal, especially when we fought. There was only so far I could back him into a corner before he'd lash out and start yelling. The second his voice would raise I'd retreat into my head and review the next day's to do list. I'd grown up listening to emotionally stunted men scream when they got angry. They'd use it as a defense mechanism to cover their lack of emotional intelligence and ability to use words to communicate effectively. It was a boring act, and so below him, below both of us. When he was like that, he wasn't worth even a smidge of my attention. That wasn't the path I planned on walking down that evening, but sometimes it was fun, a little drama to spice things up. *Just a bit more prodding.* I couldn't help myself, I never could.

"Women don't just assume they have a future with a man unless that man has given them some sort of signal or sign. Try again. She didn't spin a future up in her head. I'm not an idiot; stop treating me like one."

"What do you want from me, Cass? For some reason, she's convinced herself I was leaving you for her. She found out she was wrong when I dumped her, and now she thinks it's your fault."

The more he spoke about her, the more possessive I grew. Ethan was the prize in some sick game, and I wasn't winning. I'm not sure why I felt that way. He was there with me. She was alone and now jobless. My emotions were probably because she got to laugh while I stood in the street like a fool. Losing made me desperate. I needed something more, something to regain my sense of superiority over her. I pictured leading him upstairs, ripping off my clothes, and claiming my prize. Sending her a few photos of my own.

"I did nothing," I said coolly. "Yet you're getting to live your life, not a care in the world. And I'm being harassed by your crazy ex-mistress. How is that fair?"

Ethan held both hands up in mock surrender. "It's not, Cass. I want her to stop, too. Believe me, I care, a lot. The guilt is eating me alive. My life is pretty shitty right now. You're all I think about. Seeing you like this, so destroyed, so broken, it's killing me."

"Then you shouldn't have fucked her," I muttered under my breath.

"I'll call her tonight. It's the only way."

"No!" I screamed. "Absolutely not. There is to be no more contact between you two, ever. Are we clear?"

"I'm just trying to help—" Footsteps pounded up the

stairs, and both our heads whipped in the direction of the sound.

"Shit," he said. "Which one do you think that was?"

"Aubrey already knows about the affair. She figured it out, and I'm sick of covering for you."

"Doesn't look like you'll have to cover for me anymore. I guess they've figured out what a terrible person I am. If Aubrey knows, Ben will know soon enough." His shoulders slumped. *Poor, poor Ethan. He's always making everything about him.*

"Forgive me if I can't find it in my heart to sympathize with you," I said dryly.

Ethan gave a slow nod and stood. "Do you want me to go talk to them?"

"Up to you." I shrugged. "They can hear it from you, and you have a chance to earn back their trust. Or they can hear the full story from me tonight. I'm taking them out to dinner."

He shuffled his feet and walked upstairs to face his children. I slammed my fisted hands on my thighs. I couldn't stand Ethan moping around like he had been victimized, like his life was in shambles. I regretted letting him move back in and regretted marrying him at all. He'd spent our whole marriage talking incessantly about his needs, but I had needs too. At the very top of that list of needs was—in big, bold capital letters—for him to not fuck other women.

I'd be left to clean up another one of his messes. Emma, the kids, my heart. Only these messes were much more distressing than picking up discarded beer bottles, clothing, and other forgotten items he'd leave sitting around the house. I checked the time and got up to make myself a drink. If I drank it quick enough, it would wear off in time to drive the kids to dinner. Probably not the most responsible parenting decision I'd ever made, but none of us are perfect.

Ethan came back down an hour later with red eyes and his hair a mess. I assumed the conversation hadn't been an easy one.

"I told them everything. And they hate me, too."

I swallowed my anger and slipped on my sad, hurt wife mask. "Don't you hate Emma too? For what she's done to the kids?" Wrapping my arms around my stomach I hid the hand I was using to pinch my side until the tears fell from my eyes.

He looked at me with his head tilted. His gaze penetrated too deep. I felt naked, but not sexy naked. I panicked and wondered if I'd gone too far too fast.

"I have no idea how to answer you anymore. Everything I say just makes you angrier and angrier."

I sighed. This wasn't going to be resolved tonight. He wasn't ready to give me the reactions I needed.

"They don't hate you," I said, the mention of the kids softening my heart and words. "I don't hate you either. Most of the time." Our eyes met, and we exchanged a half-smile. "They only get one dad. And they're kids. They get over things a lot easier than adults. Me, on the other hand, I'm excellent at holding a grudge." Both our smiles curved higher. It was these flashes of *us* that made it easy for me to lie to myself, pretend an *us* still existed.

"Ha. That's true. You are the most stubborn person I know."

"Besides you." I laughed.

We both retreated into our thoughts.

"Aubrey told me you guys are headed to dinner, and I wasn't invited. I asked if they wanted to go out with me another night to spend some time together. Ben ignored the question and Aubrey said, and I quote, 'hell no.'" His hand ran through his hair as he stared at the wall.

"She'll change her mind," I said. "But I can understand her anger, and it would probably be best if you gave her a few days. Then try again. We can ask the therapist for some suggestions."

"I hope so. I'm going to run up and grab a shower. Have fun at dinner if I don't see you before you leave," he said, standing and walking upstairs.

After he left, I looked at the bottle of vodka and longed for a glass. The kids didn't need another parent letting them down. I walked to the kitchen, put the bottle away and poured the ice from my glass into the sink. Something crashed against the window. I ducked and threw my arms over my head. The glass I was holding hit the floor and shattered.

What the fuck?

I stood slowly, sure I'd find the window shattered too. Unlike the drinking glass, the window was intact. *What the —?* I ran a hand down the cool and surprisingly sturdy window, then leaned my head closer. My eyes strained against the darkness but couldn't make out the source of the noise. *Surely this wasn't like the last time. What I heard was real.*

I ran to the back door and flung it open, then looked under the window. A bird lay dead on the ground beneath it, its head twisted at an odd angle. The lanai door banged repeatedly against the frame filling my ears with the clattering of metal against metal. The entire scene was strange.

The blood flowing through my veins turned to ice, and I

hugged myself, freezing despite the hot evening. A guttural crash of thunder made me jump, and I almost peed myself. The sky opened with the storm I'd been waiting for.

"You're late," I called to the clouds. I stood shivering and staring at the dead bird as the rain soaked through my clothing.

"What the hell happened?" Ethan shouted over the storm. "I heard a glass shatter. Why are you standing out here in the rain?"

His eyes followed my gaze, and he saw the dead bird lying beneath the window. Ethan walked over and locked the lanai door before running back into the house. A puddle formed at my feet while I stood shaking and waiting for him.

"You must have forgotten to shut the door. The bird hit the window while I was standing right by it. Scared me so bad I threw my glass."

"No, I didn't. I remember shutting the door. It didn't shut at first, so I had to jam it closed, I remember for sure, because I made a note to check it out tomorrow. It may need replacing," Ethan said, shaking his head.

I glared into the back, the palm trees started bending from the wind, the fingers of their fronds whipped sideways with each gust.

I turned back toward him. "Maybe Emma has decided she wasn't getting what she wanted with phone and email stalking. I'm going to shower. You use the kids' bathroom." I stepped around him. Flashes of lightning and crashes of thunder followed me into my room. I got ready, hoping to put the whole disaster of an afternoon behind me and take my children out for a meal. I'd ensure they enjoyed themselves. They deserved a relaxing evening, where they didn't have to worry about their dad or me.

TWENTY-ONE

ETHAN

I DECIDED to wait until I couldn't hear the water rushing through the pipes anymore before getting in the shower. Cass was always nagging me for how long I took, using up all the hot water, she'd complain. Already in enough trouble, I didn't need to give her anymore ammunition. In the guest room, I sat on the bed propped up against the headboard, scrolling through my phone.

Using my fake accounts, I checked Emma's social media. My stomach dropped when I saw a video she shared. It shocked me how fast she'd been able to find it. I watched the entire scene my wife described play out on my phone. Furious for Cass, I wanted to find every person who shared, commented, and liked the video and murder them—including Emma.

Where's my money? That was the last text I'd received from her. I hadn't replied.

When Cass was done, I showered then clomped

downstairs. Cass and the kids had left. I'd grabbed a beer and bag of chips and had just settled on the couch to watch TV. After an hour my phone vibrated with a text alert.

I'm out back, come see me or I'll walk up to the front door and wave for the camera.

I ran outside; the lanai door was jammed.

"Open you stupid—"

"Ethan." A giggle came from the dark. "Calm down babe, it's just a door."

I wiped the sweat from my forehead and looked through the screen. She stepped out the shadows and wiggled her fingers in a wave.

"What are you doing here?"

She sauntered up to the door and opened it for me. "Why don't you come out here and we can have a chat"

I followed behind her, convincing my hands not to reach up and wrap around her neck. "This is *my house*. Are you insane?" My entire body shook with fury. "My kids live here!"

"You mean the kids and Cass."

My hand unconsciously ran through my hair. "Yes. The kids *and* Cass."

"I saw them leave. I knew they weren't around. I'm not that dumb."

No, but you are that insane.

"Is this about the money? I'm still working on it. I'll get it for you tomorrow."

She sighed and looked toward the water. "It must be nice."

"What are you on about?"

She gestured to our house with her arms. "All of this. This life. Big house on the water. Family. It must be nice.

Cass is so lucky. She's always had your whole heart, while you were throwing me scraps like a dog begging at the dinner table."

"Emma that's—"

"No, stop. It's true. You know it's true. I loved you, Ethan. Still do. I thought you loved me too. I thought this life was mine or at least would be mine."

She stopped talking and moonlight reflected off her cheeks wet from tears. The anger melted from my muscles, replaced by guilt. I wrapped my arms around her and pulled her into me.

She pulled back and wiped her face with her sleeves. "I'm so stupid." She laughed. "I believed you. I thought we had something special. Was it ever special for you? Was I special?"

Her eyes pleaded with me. I should be honest with her, and myself, for once.

But I lied.

"It was real. It still is. And you *are* special. It's me. I'm totally screwed up. What I did was wrong. I shouldn't have dragged you into all of this before I had my life in order. I have kids, and a marriage, it complicates things. I don't know—"

"Do you want to be with me or Cass?"

I didn't know how to answer that question. I couldn't leave Cass now. I was jobless with no viable prospects on the horizon. I needed her, and I still loved her. I didn't want to be with Emma, but the information she had on me would ruin my life even worse than I already had.

"I need more time to answer that."

Her face hardened. "Your time is running out." She turned and called over her shoulder, "Money better be in my account tomorrow, or you'll have a lot more problems than deciding who you want to be with." She stopped and faced me. "Even though we both know who that really is." She blew me a kiss and disappeared back into the shadows.

I walked back into the house and heard the garage opening. *They're back already?*

"Hey Ben, hey Aubs," I said.

Aubrey glared at me and ran upstairs. Ben looked at me a second longer than normal. My stomach flipped. I tried to keep the panic from my face. He shook his head and followed in his sister's wake.

"How was dinner?" I asked Cass.

"It was fine."

I relaxed. If they'd seen Emma, she would have been yelling.

"Want to watch a show?"

"Not tonight, I'm going to read in bed for a bit."

"Sure."

She went upstairs, and I sat in the living room staring at the TV. After a few minutes I received another text from Emma. *Close call, next time I won't be hiding in the shadows. I'll keep your secrets for now. But I'm getting bored.*

TWENTY-TWO

ALICE

"I LOVE MY JOB. It is an important job. I am valuable and imperative to the success of Cass and this wonderful advertising agency. We do not look back; we only look forward," I repeated to myself sitting in my car in the parking lot at work. A morning mantra. All true, all I believed, however the drama exhausted me. Some extra morning motivation had become more necessary. On top of keeping Cass mentally sound, there was an event to plan, and she needed to stay on task. Who unravels when they've landed their biggest client of the year? Certainly not Cass Mitchell. I would not allow her to destroy her reputation over some man and his silly indiscretions. I sat in the whirlpool's center of her distracted mind, swirling with Ethan and Emma thoughts, trying to stop its spinning with a feather.

I checked my face in my rearview mirror and watched Cass's much newer, much more expensive SUV pull into the parking lot. I had come into work early hoping for a few uninterrupted hours, but no such luck.

"Morning, Alice." She waved. I rearranged my face into a smile as I left my car, and we walked in together.

"How's the new branding coming along?" I asked.

"Oh, you know, it's coming."

"Should I schedule a meeting with the team for a first concept review?"

From the pinching of her smile, I knew immediately it was in fact not coming along. Julie said to stay out of Cass's personal life, but she was obviously not doing what needed to be done to get our Cass back. Which of course was no surprise. When you want a job done right, you must do that job yourself. I learned that bit of wisdom very early on. I had big plans for Cass, and this little breakdown of hers was not aligning with those plans. Although, it certainly could be used to my advantage. Everything good and bad is a door opening.

"Yes, reach out, see what times they are available next week. Plenty of time to put the finishing touches on everything." Her steps quickened.

"Did you enjoy your time at Julie and Victoria's?"

She halted. "How...?"

I laughed. "You told me you were having dinner there." I reached out and laid my hand on her arm. "You have so much going on, it must be hard to keep everything straight." I frowned and shook my head.

She looked at my hand, I could practically see her mind trying to remember the exact moment she told me about their get together.

"Yes. Now I remember. Such a silly question. I don't even know why I asked." She shook her head and laughed.

"Where would I be without you Alice? Your memory is like a bank vault, nothing slips by you!"

"Simply doing my job." I lowered my voice. "I know you have a lot going on outside work, but if I may suggest, perhaps, at least for the short time, fewer late nights out may be in order. Frankly, if you want my opinion, it may be time to consider leaving Eth—"

She stepped back, her face morphed from surprise to anger. "No. I don't want your opinion. I think it's best to keep your suggestions focused on Blaxten and the upcoming event. Which, you are right, is exactly where my focus needs to be as well."

I smiled sweetly. "Of course. My very top priority."

I stood at my cube and watched her walk toward her office. She glanced back one more time.

"Have a great morning, Cass. Please let me know if you need anything." The door shut with no response from her.

My face dropped as fast as I dropped into my chair. After settling in and getting my desk in proper working order for the day, I caught up on email, put a few calls in to vendors, then decided to check in with the graphics department. Just to be sure they had everything they needed for the rebrand. Normally I wouldn't babysit Cass's work so closely, she was brilliant enough I didn't need to, but it was clear on this project she would need the extra help. She could use the extra help with her life as well yet refused to accept it. Perhaps she wasn't as brilliant as I or everyone else had always believed.

I used the trip to walk by the account managers' area. Cass needed to be paying very close attention to that crew of Emma's friends, and since she didn't realize this, I would have to do it for her.

I stopped before turning the corner, using my notebook to appear busy and inconspicuous. They always thought they were so discrete, but all of them were loud mouths. I got close enough to hear but remained out of sight.

"Did you hear what she did?"

My entire body stiffened, as expected they delivered what I needed.

"Oh my god, yes. Apparently, she went like totally crazy, screaming with all these people around too. I can't picture it *at all.*"

Who was this 'she?'

"Wait, what'd I miss? Someone spill the tea immediately."

I could hug the body connected to that anonymous voice.

I waited long enough to learn about Cass's public scene and the video making the rounds on the internet before marching around the corner and giving the team a passing lecture on gossiping.

A few red faces and round eyes stared back at me, but not as many as usual. Several were covering their mouths with their hands to stifle laughs.

"Do you think this is funny?"

Delaney, who had the good graces not to laugh, shook her head and held out her phone.

"Don't show her," one of the girls said in a panicked voice.

Delaney shot her a look, then handed the phone to me. "I think you should see this."

I watched the appalling video, keeping my face impassive. Cass's embarrassment would not be these girls' entertainment.

"Delete that vile thing off your phones. And if I catch any of you with it, you'll all be fired."

One of the girls stood. "You know you can't fire us. You aren't our boss. It's all over the internet. What good will deleting it off our phones do? It's out there. You should be worried about our clients seeing it, not us."

My hand shot to my chest. They'd never spoken to me this way before. Behind my back, sure, but never had they been so bold as to do so to my face. I smoothed the front of my shirt and shook my head. "Well then. We have nothing more to discuss."

We were losing control. I was losing control. Something more had to be done. I quickly walked away. My feet froze when I reached an empty hallway.

You aren't my only friend Alice. Don't ever touch me like that. You stupid, stupid girl, this is why your mother abandoned you. I don't want your opinion. Get in the closet, no dinner for you. We told you, you aren't our friend anymore, leave us alone...

My fists slammed against my head. I gasped, forgetting where I was for a moment. I twisted and turned, ensuring no one had borne witness. A stretch of my neck, ear to shoulder, ear to shoulder and a slight shake of my head, I continued to my desk.

TWENTY-THREE

CASS

MARNI THE MARRIAGE COUNSELOR, whose name I sang in my head now anytime I thought of her, had an office inside a converted bungalow in downtown St. Petersburg. The house creaked and groaned like a living creature. How many secrets and sins did those walls hold from listening to the couples who'd passed through its halls?

I perched on the edge of the sofa next to Ethan, though I'd have rather been in the office working on the project that was very much not coming along. On the one hand, I was excited to have another person tell Ethan how terrible he was. Because surely Marni would be on my side. How could she not be? Anyone, especially a woman, would be repulsed by him. However, the idea of airing our dirty laundry to a stranger was nauseating. She was someone else now aware of how unworthy I was of my husband's affection. So unworthy he had been forced to seek comfort in Emma's arms.

I was trying to hide my nerves but couldn't stop fidgeting. The room was stuffed with so much junk, my gaze flitted around it. Taking a deep breath, I inhaled the woodsy smell of the pine floors mixed with jasmine. The smell should have put me at ease, but it only tied my stomach into more complicated knots.

Marni sat across from us with a leather folio sprawled open on her lap. She was saying something about communication and how the sessions would work, but I was only half-listening. A framed photo among the clutter on the walls caught my eye, a silhouette of a raven with the words *Nevermore* scrolled across the bottom. What an odd choice of wall décor for a therapist's office. As a huge Poe fan myself, anywhere else I would have loved it. Here it felt out of place and made my mind wander to raven black hair and dead birds. I imagined the hair wrapping itself around my neck and suffocating me. Emma's name echoed through my skull. I squeezed my hands between my legs so I wouldn't cover my ears with them and forced myself to focus on the present, the room I was in, Marni, Ethan, and marriage counseling. Marni was still droning on. I had anticipated minimalistic, modern leather furniture, but Poe and ravens surrounded me. My confidence in her abilities was plummeting along with my stomach.

I forced myself to concentrate on us and not Emma. To help my cause, I shifted so I could face him and pictured life without him. The kids would be off to college soon. Then what? I'd float around an empty house, eating meals alone, sleep, work, rinse, and repeat. Every day until I died. Or worse, I'd have to date again. I imagined painful, awful, and awkward first dates, hoping to find some other woman's leftovers who wasn't more damaged than I was. Because let's face it, at forty, the dating pool has evaporated to more of a puddle.

Everything about us—Ethan and me—fit together perfectly, including our bodies. I pictured us naked in our bedroom, rolling around laughing and him kissing every part of me. So many people search their entire lives for their soulmate. I found mine. And Emma stole him while my back was turned. The flash of euphoria I'd found remembering the good times was gone before I could enjoy it.

"Can't imagine my life without her. She's my everything." Ethan's voice snapped me from my thoughts. *Did he read my mind?*

"Mmhmm." Marni nodded her head full of silver curls and looked over the rim of her glasses at me. "And Cass, how do you feel?" Marni had kind eyes. They warmed me to her instantly. Looking into them, the cluttered room seemed less oppressive and more cheerful and welcoming.

"I feel a lot of things right now. Mostly angry. Hurt. Terrified."

"All of those are perfectly natural. What each of you needs to decide, and not today, but eventually, is what the goal of our sessions will be. Whether we will work on saving the marriage, or work to establish a mutually agreeable way to dissolve the marriage and co-parent the children."

"I don't want a divorce," Ethan said, looking quickly between us.

"And Cass? What do you want?" Marni asked, focusing her attention on me.

I puffed air through my cheeks and looked at the ceiling.

Their gazes crawled over me. What I wanted was for Ethan and Emma to experience the soul-crushing pain they caused me. I wanted them to wear it around their necks like an iron ring. Then, along with their pain, they'd be overcome with humiliation. I wished their lives would crumble at their feet and turn into burning coals they'd be forced to walk over, barefoot.

"I want her to leave me alone. I feel scared all the time. Like someone is always watching me. Terrified what she'll do next. As far as Ethan, I'm not sure I'll ever be able to forgive him. Or trust him. And how can I stay married to someone I don't trust?" Tears filled my eyes, and not ones I had to manufacture. It had become so easy to hide my hurt behind my hate for Emma. But it was always Ethan if I thought hard enough. I loved him so deeply, which is why the betrayal hurt so deeply. It was death by a million paper cuts—slow and more painful with each slice.

"Those are important and very good questions. I have counseled couples through infidelity, and it *is* possible to move past it. But it's a personal decision. If you can't forgive Ethan, your marriage won't work. You must commit to not bringing up the affair in every disagreement and not using it as a weapon. And Ethan, you must commit to earning Cass's trust, of course. It's not easy, but it is possible. As for Emma and the harassment, you may want to consult the police and obtain a restraining order."

"I don't think the restraining order will be necessary, but I'm committed. Fully," Ethan rushed out. "I'll do whatever it takes."

I cocked my head and searched his face for a lie, also wondering why he was so quick to shut down the restraining order suggestion.

"Look." I leaned back on the sofa, crossing my arms across my chest like a shield protecting my heart. "I'm not saying that it's not a possibility. I'm just not ready to give him—" I turned back toward Ethan. The pain on his face almost made me reconsider my next words. It looked so real, so believable. I turned away to remain strong. "No. I can't answer that. Not yet. I need more time."

"No one is rushing you, Cass. That's perfectly understandable," Marni said. "I want to show you both a communication exercise. As Cass explores her feelings and ways to come to terms with what happened, and decides what she wants to do, this will help you two navigate the tough conversations you'll have to face."

I was hoping to spend the hour ganging up on him; I looked forward to having someone else tell him how terrible he was and how wonderful I was. I should have done some asking around before the session. I would have learned that it's not how these things worked at all. I pushed that minor inconvenience to the side and remembered we did still have kids to raise. For them, I committed to Marni's lessons, uncomfortable as they may be. She walked us through various communication methods, and we went back and forth practicing. The entire thing was forced and unnatural. It did allow me to expel some of the poison that had been burning my insides. When the hour was up, we scheduled our next appointment for the following week. *Maybe Marni will be less of a disappointment the next session.*

We walked out. I was so awkward around Ethan when I wasn't yelling at him. Yelling was easy. But when we weren't fighting, I wasn't sure how to act or what to say. He stopped on the sidewalk and looked at me. My face twitched, and I cursed this new inability to control it.

He looked calm and confident; the old Ethan was shining through. I guess the session gave him hope. Or he was happy he'd deceived me. He was thrilled his ploys were working, and his smile would have me melting into him at any moment.

"Are you hungry? Want to grab dinner?" he asked.

I pretended to consider his offer, knowing I wouldn't agree to go, but teasing him with hope. I hadn't figured out what I needed from him or how he could prove himself to be worthy of my trust and love, but I was painfully aware he hadn't succeeded yet.

"Not tonight. I'm emotionally drained. Can we just go home and order in?"

Ethan nodded, then held out his hand like he wanted me to hold it and walk to the car with him. I recoiled and moved my purse to my chest. He towered over me with his broad shoulders and thick arms. I imagined how good those arms would feel wrapped around my body. The loneliness was playing tricks on me. I had to stay sharp, not give in to my heart and desire just yet. I took two steps backward, just in case.

"Yes, right. Sorry. I—um—okay." His smile fell and likely took his confidence with it. I stepped around him to walk to the car, and he stuffed his hands in his pocket and followed behind me.

Once in the passenger seat, I threw my sunglasses on, not trusting my emotions and needing to hide any tears that might make their escape. I spent the ride home stewing on my frustration and trying to figure out what to do about it.

We got home and after checking in with the kids, I announced I was going to take a bath. Ethan agreed to order food, then asked Aubrey and Ben if they wanted to watch some TV. Neither took him up on his offer.

In my bathroom, I shed my clothes and perched on the lip of the bathtub as I waited for it to fill. A rush of adrenaline shot through me. Something was off. I walked to the sink and looked across the countertop. A crystal vanity tray in the center of our two sinks held my perfume, moisturizer, toothbrush holder, and other toiletries and makeup. The one there now was a replacement since the prior version had been smashed during our fight. I organized it the same way every morning after getting ready. Every item had its place. Aubrey knows this and had caught enough hell for trying to sneak in and use my makeup and the other items. It couldn't be her. But who else could it be? I'd ask her to be sure.

Nothing was missing or broken, but things had been moved. My perfume had been taken off the tray and placed by Ethan's sink, and my moisturizer was sitting on the counter in front of the tray. My makeup brushes were on the tray's right side, but they belonged on the left. I walked around our bedroom searching for anything else amiss. It was exactly how I'd left it that morning. I quickly organized the items back to their proper places and took a step back. No longer in the mood for a bath, I turned off the water and pulled the drain to empty the tub.

Wrapping myself in a towel, I turned the shower on, walked back into the bedroom and sat on the edge of my bed. *Am I being paranoid?* I tapped my bottom lip with a finger. It was just like the lanai. Not alarming enough to cause panic, but still—not right. After concocting a million different imaginary explanations, I returned to the bathroom and screamed.

Ethan barged into the bathroom. "What's wrong?"

I stared at the mirror, horror twisting my features. A giant smiley face had been traced in earlier condensation in the center of the mirror, the fresh steam fogged the mirror everywhere except the crude finger drawing. Someone *had* been in there.

Someone is fucking with me.

Twenty-Four

ETHAN

I STOOD in the bathroom staring at the mirror, watching the smiley face slowly disappear along with the shower steam.

"I think you're overreacting, Cass," I said looking at the mirror. "It's probably one of the kids being funny. They trace doodles on the shower's glass wall all the time." I leaned in and studied the remnants of the face. I was trying to convince Cass as much as I was trying to convince myself.

"And I think you're *still* defending Emma. I'd like to know why."

I grabbed the sides of my head and looked down. "Not everything is about Emma. I'm not constantly thinking about her. No one is except you."

"Who else would it be?" Her hands were on her hips and her face told me all I needed to know. She'd formed her conclusion. Her mind wrapped around it and wouldn't be letting go anytime soon.

"Exactly who I said, the *kids*. Or you and you don't remember. Hell, if I know. You think she broke into our house, moved some of your stuff around, then drew a smiley face in our bathroom mirror? That's weird. What could she possibly gain? A few texts and emails are one thing but actually breaking into someone's house is illegal."

"The kids have their bathroom. Why would they use ours? I would remember doing it, and I'm not losing my mind. It's insane you can't see she's way past texts and emails. She's unhinged. I've seen things, a woman following me, *the bird*. It's more. I know these are all connected. There is no other explanation for this." She jabbed her finger at the mirror then jerked back when she caught sight of her reflection. She held her head in her hands and her face changed. She was trying to control herself. It drove her mad to not be in charge of everything, big or small.

"Wait, people are following you? Why are you just mentioning this? I think you're taking every random thing and forming connections that just aren't there. What you're suggesting is unbelievable. If you're not losing your mind, stop acting like it," I said. I knew if I could distract her with anger, I would have time to figure out how to deal with Emma. I was starting to worry Cass may be right.

Her eyes squinted before she stomped from the bathroom.

"What now?" Aubrey said outside the room. She must have cornered her mom in the hallway.

"Nothing, everything's fine," Cass replied.

"You're a shitty liar." The sound of more heavy feet was followed by a slamming door.

I scrubbed the area of the mirror with a towel so it wouldn't return every time someone showered. I turned and leaned on the sink with the mirror at my back. It didn't make any sense why Emma would come into our house and move stuff around. The kids either. Or Cass.

The effects of my actions pulsed through me. Hurting Cass has been devastating. But the guilt surging through my body was paralyzing.

What kind of man destroys two women he loves?

I pulled my phone from my back pocket and dialed Emma's number. I didn't bother with pleasantries. "Were you in our house?"

"Ethan, I can't answer your weird questions. I'm out with friends. And thanks for the money."

My grip tightened on my phone. I heard the commotion of a bar in the background and knew exactly what my money was funding. "Yes or no. Just tell me if you came into my house."

"You sound funny. Is everything okay?" It seemed sweet Emma was back. Money must be the key to her heart.

"Yes, well, no. Someone's been in our house. Just be honest. If it was you, I just need to know, I won't tell anyone."

"I have much better things to do with my time than break into your house." The sweetness had evaporated from her voice. "Is that all you called for? I'm busy."

I crushed the end call button, undressed, and stepped into the shower. I didn't fully believe Emma, but I was worried about Cass. She had been drinking a lot lately. With her family history, it was always something she was super careful with. Could my infidelity be enough to burst the dam she'd been holding up her whole life? Were her genetics rushing in and taking over?

Our house felt too small, like a prison. But if I took off

anywhere, Cass would use that to validate whatever story she'd spun in her head.

I jogged down the stairs. Cass sat in the living room watching a true crime show.

"The husband did it," I said, testing the waters.

"If the husband did it, it's not interesting enough to be a show."

"There wouldn't be enough content. What would they show then?"

We both laughed, and I knew I had my chance.

"Need me to do anything around here? I was thinking of heading out and fishing some dock lights. The tides are perfect right now. I mean—if the whole thing upstairs has you too freaked out, I can stay in no problem."

"No, I'm fine. You can go."

She was already engrossed in her show again. I ran to get my things before she changed her mind. After tugging on pants and a long sleeve shirt I went into our closet and pulled out the stepstool. I went back into the hallway to listen one more time to ensure she wasn't coming up the stairs, then went back in the closet and grabbed the box hidden on the top shelf on my side of the closet.

I tucked it in a duffle bag and called goodbye on my way out. I undocked my skiff and motored quietly through the intercoastal. When I got to John's Pass I veered away from the homes, hotels, and restaurants. The lights from shore faded and became fireflies blinking in the distance. I turned off the motor and grabbed the box. The boat floated and I turned my face into the salty breeze blowing off the rolling waves. I pulled each item out, smelling them, caressing them against my face. Then, one by one, I threw them into the ocean. My souvenirs from prior affairs sunk into the murky water. I'd miss them, but I needed to be more cautious moving forward. At least until this was all in the past.

Twenty-Five

Cass

I STOOD and smiled when I spotted my friend Lara making her way through the tables at the café. She looked stunning. At 5' 9" and all legs, she always looked like she'd stepped straight off the runway no matter what she wore. Today, in her wide-legged linen pants and fitted white T-shirt, it was no different. I looked down at my leggings and loose T-shirt and felt very self-conscious. When she got close enough, I stretched out my arms and we hugged before exchanging cheek kisses. The familiar scent of Chanel No. 5 filled my nose.

"I hope you don't mind sitting outside," I said. "It's so nice out today."

"Not at all. I'm so glad you called and suggested lunch. It's been way too long," Lara said, wrapping her thick brown hair into a perfect knot, an impressive move. Not a single strand was left out of place. My hand unconsciously patted my hair. "How have you been?" she asked.

I sighed. I knew this question was coming. It's the standard way all conversations start. But it wasn't a filler question anymore. Not since my life had become in every way not okay. I couldn't simply reply 'great' and move on to other topics.

"Not great, actually." I sulked.

Lara looked up from her menu and frowned. "Oh, no. What happened?"

Gossip travels so fast. She was most likely playing dumb and preferring to hear me say it. Enjoying my torture. Regardless, I explained the Ethan situation.

"Yikes," Lara said when I finished. She took a sip of her water, then continued. "Well, honey, I'm sorry. That doesn't help, though, does it?"

"I have to ask you a question. I don't mean to be forward or bring up the past." I paused. I planned on sliding the true reason I'd asked her to lunch after more pleasantries and small talk, but I saw my opening and snatched it.

"You want my perspective on the whole thing, being a cheater myself," Lara cut in.

I fiddled with my napkin and stared into my lap. "I'm sorry. I don't mean to be rude." My hand raised to my forehead as if I had a headache and I met her gaze. "Everything is a mess. I shouldn't have brought it up. It was so long ago, your affair, I mean."

"Don't be silly." Lara patted my arm. "Look. My secret was the worst kept secret in the history of secrets. Hell, I married my secret. I will tell you this, though. My situation is nothing like yours. Mike and I had been over long before I started sleeping with Lucas. You all saw how much we fought publicly. It was shameful, such a spectacle we made of ourselves."

"Yeah. It got pretty bad," I admitted. No one had wanted to invite her and Mike out anymore, not at the end. I'm sure they noticed—especially Lara. She's too intelligent to not have figured it out. She was extremely concerned with public appearances, though, we all were. The public spats always perplexed me; they were so unlike her. I was learning the hard way, however, that people will do strange things when emotions take control.

"Anyway, regardless of Mike and my issues, what I did was horrible. Even with my disaster of a marriage, the guilt from the affair was awful. It ate me up inside. Plus, I was always bracing myself. I woke up every day wondering 'will today be the day?' Mike and everyone else would finally find out, and you'd all know what an awful person I was." Lara looked away at nothing, I let her wander off with her thoughts. She blinked her eyes a few times and smiled, making eye contact again. "What a mess. It was a terrible thing I did. I love Lucas, and I'm happy with him. But Mike didn't deserve that. I should have gotten a divorce before moving on. Done the right thing in the right order. And I have to live with that for the rest of my life."

"Yes," I said. "You should have. What made you do it?" I asked. Prior to Ethan's affair, I had no opinion of Lara's infidelity. We all knew about the affair as soon as Mike found out, and had all suspected it before then, too. He walked in on them—in their bed of all places. It was the scandal of the year, fun to talk about as more and more of the story leaked out—a distraction from our own boring, drama-free lives. Once things settled and she married Lucas, they were just another boring married couple like the rest of us.

Being cheated on changed that; I hated all cheaters now.

Lara was a friend, but I found myself mad at her, as if someone flipped a switch and every inconsequential annoying thing about her shone as bright as the Vegas strip. Still, I was curious to hear her response. The concept of cheating was so alien to me. If you didn't want to be someone, you left them. It was so simple. I couldn't make sense of the motivation: hers, Ethan's, every other cheater. Being with one person was enough work. Managing two seemed so draining.

"I was miserable. But I can guarantee my motivations aren't the same as Ethan's. I've seen you two together—"

"Cass? What a surprise, I was walking to the farmers' market and I thought that was you, I hope I'm not interrupting but I couldn't walk by without coming by to say my hellos."

I looked up and squinted, Alice stood over our table, the sun blazing behind her making her face hard to make out.

"Alice. Don't you live in Tampa? You came all this way for the market?" I asked.

"Have you never been? They have the best fresh veggies, absolutely worth the drive."

No one said anything, I hoped Alice would get the hint and leave us to our lunch, but I didn't want to be rude.

"Well, I didn't want to interrupt, you ladies enjoy your lunch. See you at the office." She pushed her glasses up her nose and walked away.

"Who was that woman?" Lara asked when she was out of earshot.

"Oh, just my assistant."

Lara's perfectly shaped eyebrow arched. "No offense, but she seems a bit...strange."

I laughed. "She's harmless."

Lara didn't look convinced.

The waitress approached the table, interrupting our conversation. Lara ordered a salad, and I ordered a burger and fries. I felt zero guilt about the side of ranch I added before she walked away.

"Anyways, I'm obsessing over it all the time. I'm trying to find things to stay busy. But my mind always wanders back to Ethan and Emma. It's like I'll never be normal again." It was the most honest thing I'd said in days.

"He fucked up. That's all there is to it. You'll drive yourself insane trying to find a reason. It's unreasonable. There's no reason *to* find."

I contemplated her words. They brought no comfort. People don't do things without reason; life doesn't work that way.

"What's your plan? Are you two going to try to work it out?" Lara asked, taking a bite of her salad.

I shrugged. "He wants to. I haven't decided yet. He's still staying at the house, not in the same room though. And we've done one counseling session. Not sure it made much difference."

"Well, if it makes you feel better, Mike has told me he's forgiven me. Not that we would ever consider getting back together, of course. He's like a kid in a candy shop with online dating, and Lucas is stuck with me until we grow old. Mike told me it took a long time, but the anger finally passed, and he forgave me. I didn't deserve it, but it helped me heal and let go of my guilt. No matter what you two decide, you will heal, and you will move on."

"Maybe I should call Mike and ask him how he finally

got rid of the rage." I laughed. "Because right now it feels like it's permanently tattooed on my bones. A scar I'll be stuck with forever."

Lara sucked in a breath. "I have to admit, this is dredging up some bad memories. Watching someone else I love being ripped to shreds by something I myself have done to someone else."

"I'm so sorry. I didn't mean to make you feel bad." I wasn't sorry—not really, but it felt like the right thing to say. Deep down I knew Lara was my friend and I was simply projecting my anger at Ethan onto the wrong person.

She held up her hand, "No, stop right there. You don't need to apologize to me, Ethan, or anyone else. It's so easy to get wrapped up in our needs, to forget the impact our actions and selfishness can have on people. I need to remember to be grateful for what I have. And to tell and show people how much they mean to me. Every day." She paused. "Calling Mike is a good idea, actually. Ask him what helped him get through it. I'm the idiot in our situation. He may have some better insight for you. And if nothing else, he can fill you in on his online dating sagas. He has some doozies."

"Oh, my gosh. I can't imagine dating again. All those apps to learn, starting over, weeding through all the junk. Julie was ready to launch my profiles the second she heard."

"Then she wanted to hunt down Ethan and kill him, I imagine." Lara laughed.

I snorted. "Yes. She probably has a spreadsheet of possible methods. Or at the very least has her assistant preparing one."

We busied ourselves with eating. I considered what Lara

had suggested and decided I'd send Mike a message when I got home later that night. It would be nice talking to someone who truly *got* it.

My phone buzzed. We had moved on to catching up on work, kids, and life, so I ignored it. The vibrating became more frequent, making us both stop talking and look down at it.

"Let me make sure this isn't one of the kids," I said, picking up my phone. I gasped. "Look at this!" I turned my phone to show Lara the endless scroll of texts I'd received from a private number. Every text, there were too many count, just said one word repeated over and over: *Bitch.*

Lara's eyes bulged. "I don't understand. What is this? Some sort of spam?"

"No, not spam. There's something else I didn't tell you." I threw the phone in my purse and puffed my cheeks. "Emma, the girl he cheated with, told me about the affair over email. Ever since that email she's been kind of harassing me."

"Kind of?" Lara asked. Concern dripped off the question.

"There have been texts, emails. I'm pretty sure she was in our house. My bathroom was rearranged and—this sounds so odd saying it out loud—someone drew a smiley face in the steam on the mirror. I went to take a shower and it showed up. I just about shit myself when I saw it." I chuckled uncomfortably.

Lara's head bobbed between me and my purse. "This is insane. I've never heard of anything like it. A smiley face." Her eyes were bulging, and her hand was clasped at her neck. "Why would she be harassing you? And breaking into your house ... did you call the police?"

"No, Ethan doesn't believe it's her. He thinks it's me or one of the kids."

"Why would you mess up your own bathroom? That's nonsense."

Ethan's words from that evening floated around me. *You.* It couldn't be me. He had me questioning my sanity. It's probably what he wanted. A diversion. Or had I been in a rush, consumed by thoughts of them, and just didn't remember leaving the bathroom a mess?

"I don't know. I assume she's doing it all because she got dumped by her boyfriend and lost her job within the same week. I was actually feeling bad for her after that, while still hating her, of course. I'm sorry, I just need to go to the bathroom for a minute. Collect myself."

I grabbed my purse and ran to the bathroom. The single stall offered the privacy I needed. I took screenshots of the texts and sent them to Ethan with a *WTF??!!* text. After turning on the faucet, I splashed water on my face and leaned on the counter, staring at my reflection. The reply came fast. I straightened and picked up the phone: *I'm sorry. I'll fix it, I promise.* I reapplied my lipstick and tucked a stray hair behind my ear. With my chin lifted, I returned to the table with my lips curved into a smile.

"It's fine, really," I assured Lara after I sat. "I've dealt with worse. This will blow over too."

"Okay," Lara replied, which came out almost as a question rather than a statement.

"It will all be fine. Don't you worry about me. I think I'll take your advice and shoot Mike a message tonight, though. See if he has any advice."

"That's a good idea. And you'll call me if anything else crazy happens. Promise?"

"I promise," I said.

We finished our meals, paid, and hugged our goodbyes. I sat in my car for a few moments before turning it on. I was starting to lose my grip on who I was and what I wanted.

Was Ethan even worth it?

TWENTY-SIX

CASS

SIX HUNDRED AND forty-two pages sat fanned out across my kitchen table. I knew the exact number because I'd counted each one as the printer at work spit them out. Julie had stood over me, arms crossed and shaking her head, watching the hot pages slide into the collection tray. Over six hundred emails and texts sent in one day. They kept coming, from the time I arrived at work until I left early for home. Julie happily agreed to pick up the kids and take them to her house to stay for the night.

"Those kids don't need to be around that pig," she had said. "You tell him this, word for word, from me. If she doesn't leave you the fuck alone, I'm getting involved." She stood scowling while the papers continued to print. "You'll come pay my bail, right?"

We smirked at each other.

"Always," I said.

It took thirty minutes to talk her out of driving over to

Emma's to 'put a stop to this shit myself.' I had enough going on that night. Bailing her out of jail didn't need to be one of them.

I made myself a Tito's and stepped out into the backyard. It was a beautiful evening, the kind of evening Floridians suffer through stifling summers for. There was a breeze blowing off the canal, tickling my face, and the sunset was painting the water, boats, and houses pink.

After dragging one of the lounge chairs from the lanai to our dock, I watched the water for dolphins and manatees. I'd lived in Florida for more than half my life and our wildlife still left me awestruck. Ethan and I used to do this often, sit together and enjoy the sunsets from our dock. I glanced at the empty space next to me and an uncontrollable loneliness rushed through me. Alone time was something I'd always cherished. In fact, it was something I yearned for almost daily before the demise of my marriage. There was always someone needing me. Kids needing a ride, money, or their questions answered, Ethan needing affection, conversation, and attention. Employees needing decisions or their questions answered as well. That constant need was debilitating. It left me depleted, drained, never feeling like I had time to care for myself, and my needs.

"You've finally got your alone time, Cass," I said to myself. "It's not so great, is it?" I was always wanting the wrong things and never realizing they were the wrong things until it was too late.

Our driveway camera picked up motion, and my phone alerted me to Ethan's arrival. I walked back into the house to meet him.

"This isn't right, Ethan," I whispered after he sat at the

table next to me. My voice cracked and tears streamed down my cheeks. "I did nothing. Why is this happening to me?"

Ethan took one of my clammy hands in his warm one and rubbed the skin between my thumb and pointer finger. The familiarity of the motion slowed my beating heart and sent butterflies fluttering in my stomach. He squeezed my hand then let go to read through the papers. He shook his head. Her words were ugly, revolting. The names she called me in her relentless texts and emails. Vile hate filled page after page.

"This is insane," he finally said. My muscles relaxed.

"See, this is what I've been trying to tell you. I'm scared, Ethan. Look at all of this." I motioned to the table. It was all right there for him to see. He couldn't deny it or brush it off as if it would go away. Or as if it was all in my head.

He shook his head again and ran his hand through his hair. "I need a drink. Do you want one?"

"Yes, please." I sniffled and blew my nose. I began organizing the pages back into a stack.

With the two drinks made, Ethan motioned with his head for me to follow him into the living room. "Come on babe, let's go sit in there and get you comfortable. We can talk about what to do." The term of endearment both startled and warmed me. I smiled inwardly and followed him before tucking myself into the armchair.

"I think we should call the cops. File a report or something," Ethan said.

A flash of panic clutched my stomach. I didn't want the police involved. But if I said as much, he may start to question the seriousness of the situation again. He may go back to feeling sorry for Emma, or worse, loving her, and even worse, not loving me. I took a sip of my drink to buy myself time to think.

"Do you think that's necessary? What if it gets out? If my clients find out? It could destroy my reputation and the agency."

His body visibly tensed. "The agency? That's what you're worried about. What do you want me to do here? I'll talk to her and tell her—"

"No!" I forced my voice to calm. "No, that's not what I want at all. I guess we'll have to call the police." The thought of Ethan talking to her was enough to curdle my blood. "Can you call them?" I asked. "I don't think I could handle it. I'm just—"

"I'll call them right now. I don't know how this all works, but I'll see what they say."

Ethan found the number for the non-emergency line and spoke with someone at the local precinct. I focused on a spot on the wall, half-listening. I considered my conversation with Lara, the other cheater. She'd said that our situations were completely different. This type of thinking made me lazy. I just assumed he'd always love me, and I didn't have to work for it. What a terrible mistake I'd made. He hung up and said an officer would be at the house within the next few hours, depending on any emergency calls that came in.

"Why did you do it, Ethan?" I asked.

"Haven't we gone through this? Let's move on, Cass, please."

I bit my bottom lip and considered his proposal. I decided, no, I wasn't ready to move on. "So, you slept with a crazy psychopath because I work too much?"

His jaw clenched and unclenched. He was obviously

annoyed and sick of talking about it. *Too bad*. I leaned forward.

"No." He sighed. "I shouldn't have said that."

"But you see now, don't you?" My heart fluttered in my chest.

"See what?" he asked, and annoyingly looked sincere in his confusion.

"See how crazy she is," I cried, throwing my hands up. *Why is he so slow lately?*

He sighed *again*, as if I was putting him out. As if this load on his back was so heavy, he couldn't stand up straight. But I was the one hunched over so far I was practically touching my toes. I could have punched him right in his perfectly straight nose.

"Yes, Cass, I see. She's crazy. She's a terrible person. Is that what you want? Does that make you feel better?" he said in a voice devoid of emotion.

"It would make me feel better if you actually meant it," I muttered, sitting back and crossing my arms. Pouting like a child. "I need another," I said, extending my hand with my empty glass. Ethan stood obediently and walked to the kitchen.

Perhaps it was the need to win, or perhaps it was my desire for retaliation against Emma. Tit for tat. Or it could be love. Whatever the case, I decided I would stay with Ethan, at least for a bit.

He returned and placed the drink in my hand when the doorbell rang. My stomach turned; surely, the police wouldn't be able to get here so quickly. Was it someone else?

"Evening, I'm Officer Daley," the cop said when we opened the door. "You lucked out, though, your neighbors down the road not so much. Their vehicle was broken into and I was about to leave when the call came through."

"Come in," Ethan said, gesturing him toward the living room.

After we were settled, we explained what happened and showed him the texts and emails. He took a report and told us he'd speak with Emma the next day.

When we were done and he had the folder of evidence, Ethan walked Officer Daley—our false hero—to the door and re-joined me.

"Do you feel better? I think when he goes to her house, it will scare the shit out of her, and she'll knock it off," Ethan said.

"I hope so," I said before gulping down the rest of my drink. Maybe it was the vodka, or maybe I needed a release for my pent-up anger, but I surprised both of us with what I said next. "Want to sleep with me tonight?"

"Really? Are you sure?" Ethan asked. His blue eyes lit up. The desire practically wafted off his skin.

"Yes, I'm sure." I had never been surer of anything in my life.

I started walking up the stairs and called over my shoulder, "Are you coming?"

Ethan followed without a word. The second we entered the bedroom, I tore off his clothes and pushed his rock-solid chest so he was sitting on the side of the bed and leaning back on his hands. I stripped for him. I knew the parts of my body he found irresistible and made sure he drank them all up. Slowly. He was a man who'd been crawling through the desert, and I was his water. He went to say something, and I placed my finger on his mouth to silence him. Stepping back, I finished by shimmying out of my panties and kicking them to the side. Then sidled up to him, making him beg with his eyes. I lifted my tongue to my top lip with my mouth slightly parted, then watched his eyes turn hungrier. Hand on his chest, I pushed him to his back then climbed on top, straddling him with my legs that he couldn't resist. With my head flung back, I rode him, extracting every thought of Emma from his memory with each thrust of my hips and pounding his mistakes in, showing him to never step out on me again, proving that he was mine.

THE NEXT MORNING, I woke up and turned to find Ethan's side of the bed empty. I panicked, then heard the shower. He didn't leave me.

Using sex to control men wasn't something I particularly enjoyed. I grew up watching my mother do it. I instantly felt sick to my stomach for acting like her. My father walked out on us early enough I had no memories of him. My mother claimed he was a deadbeat who never held a job, and we were better off without him. She was probably lying. It's where I got it from. If I had to guess, based on the parade of men she marched through our dilapidated trailer each night, she never had a clue who he was. I didn't care either way. I had enough disappointment from one parent that I had no desire to duplicate that disappointment from another one.

There were a few men who would stick around longer. They were usually at least a decade older than her, and only kept for their money. In those years, when my mother managed to hang on to one of those poor saps longer than a night, we would have food in the fridge. I sometimes ended up with a few outfits that fit and were purchased new and not handed down from some compassionate church group. But those men would eventually catch on to my mother's true intentions when their bank accounts had been depleted in exchange for pills and vodka. They'd leave, and we'd be back to living off scraps and hand-me-downs.

Then one summer day it was too hot to play outside and too hot to move around when inside. I sat in front of the window AC unit begging for mercy. My mother had stepped up her game by then, heroin being her drug of choice. I hadn't heard her stir in her bedroom for hours, so I inched into her room and stood over her. She was disgusting, mouth hanging open, syringe lying next to her on the bed. While I stood and watched, her skin turned paler and grayer. Even my young mind knew something was wrong. I was at a crossroads. There was a very important decision to be made: call for help or go into my room and pretend I didn't see a thing. I tiptoed to bed and watched the changing light move across my ceiling, waiting for the moon to complete its rotation and the sun to light up my room.

The next morning, I listened for signs of my mother shuffling around the trailer. The only sounds coming through the paper-thin walls were the dripping of a faucet and the muffled static from the television. *Had it worked?* I let myself feel hope and crept out of bed then into my mother's room. The lump under the comforter wasn't moving. The hope bloomed. I tentatively inched closer. My mother's unseeing eyes stared at nothing. I let myself breathe. I took four more confident steps, close enough to touch her, and gave her a hard shake. Her head lolled to the side, and those unseeing eyes looked through me. I jerked back, knocking over a lamp on her nightstand. My lips curved up into the biggest grin I'd ever smiled in my whole life, then pinched my arm until the tears came, before running to find a neighbor.

After my mother's death, I was sent to live with my grandmother, whose house was filled with sunshine and the sweet smell of freshly baked cookies. I had never met my grandmother before then. Finally armed with the knowledge that a normal life, one filled with stability and love, had been just out of reach all that time was enough to erase any guilt I'd experienced from letting my mother die and not calling for help.

No one knew this about me. It was a secret I'd kept in the deepest, darkest part of me. I was a phoenix who'd risen from the ashes on air made of lies. My entire life was built on a foundation of untruths. This is why lying came so naturally for me and why I was so good at it.

I didn't like to think about my mother. She deserved everything that happened to her. I shushed the voice in my head and reminded it those were things we don't think about. I walked into the bathroom and joined Ethan in the shower—this time letting him take control.

After the shower, we both dressed and went downstairs. Ethan made us each a cup of coffee and we sat at the kitchen table. So normal. And all the pieces of my life started to slide back into place.

"Should we talk about it, or do you need more time?" he asked.

"Talk about what? The sex?" I asked.

"Well, yeah. The sex. Us. All of it." Such a serious conversation, yet we were sipping our coffee and speaking like we were discussing the weather. The high from sex still tingled under my skin.

"I've decided we can work things out. You don't have to

sleep in the guest room anymore. I don't trust you, and you still have a lot to prove. But we can't move forward and work on us without getting things back to normal."

He looked unsure. It wasn't the reaction I wanted. I expected more fanfare. Jumping up and down, a whoop, something other than just sitting there looking confused. *Is he having doubts?* Was he thinking of *her*, of Emma? Even thoughts of her name made my spine stiffen.

"Well?" I prompted. The morning soured.

"I'm just surprised is all. That's great, really great, it's just—" He hesitated. "I'm in no position to make demands, but I need things from you, too. I need you to try for me. Be more affectionate, show me you love me, and don't spend all your time at work."

I swallowed what I'd like to say and stared through him with my face expressionless. He hated when I did that. He said it made him feel like I was tuning him out. I usually was. The conversation made me uncomfortable. I despised talking about these things. Feelings, our relationship. I preferred to just be. Ethan was the exact opposite. He was perfectly comfortable talking about feelings. I suppressed my instinct to snap back and smiled sweetly. "Well, it's settled, then. And we both have promises to keep."

"Yes, settled," he said. The husky sexiness was back in his voice. It melted me enough to dismiss his demands. Once he was back, I'd decide if my prize was worth keeping or if I'd throw it away later. It was too hard to decide with Emma muddling up my thoughts. I needed her out of the way to figure out my true desires.

Ethan stood and kissed me on the forehead. "I love you, Cass. It's always been you. We'll get us back. I promise." He walked into the bathroom, leaving me alone with my thoughts.

His phone chimed on the table next to his coffee mug.

I can't meet tonight. Come over this afternoon.

It was from Emma.

TWENTY-SEVEN

CASS

"YOU SLUT, I can practically smell the sex on you." Julie shook her head, smiling at me from the other side of my desk. "Should I high five or shake you?"

"Twice. Ugh, I have no self-control," I said, covering my face with my hands.

"Not with Ethan. You never did. I just knew it," she said, slapping her leg. "I was telling Victoria last night; I bet she caves. I still don't trust him. You can get all gooey and smooshy for him, but I'm keeping my eye on him."

I considered telling Julie what I'd seen on Ethan's phone. I was a fool. I believed him, and he was just playing me, playing her too, actually. I wondered what Emma would think if she knew how hard he was working to get me back. He was probably telling her the same things, how much he loved her, that it was only them. She was probably sitting in her apartment holding her breath, waiting on him to leave me and come running into her arms. She could hold it forever, turn blue from it, suffocate.

"I know, I know. I let him move back into our room too," I said. I still wasn't ready to give up and let Emma declare victory.

"I'm not in love with Ethan, so my forgiveness doesn't come so easily. I still think you should kick him out, make him suffer through at least a month of Sandra. But you never listen to my good advice," Julie said.

"I always listen to you, except when you're wrong," I said and let out a strangled laugh. Julie arched an eyebrow. *I should tell her. She can help.* I couldn't bring myself to do it. She'd never forgive Ethan. And just in case I did decide to stay with him, I didn't need the extra drama.

"What do you think people will say?" I asked.

"About what? No offense, but everyone already knows what happened. The toothpaste has been squeezed from the tube—there's no putting it back."

"No, I know. I meant about him living with me. About me staying with him. Will people talk about it?"

"I mean, probably. It's not like he isn't already living there. But people have short memories. They are too wrapped up in their own shit to think about everyone else's all the time. It makes for an interesting story now, but it will be old news soon. I'm going on record to say I'm totally against this, though."

I changed the subject and explained how I finally called the police on Emma, and Officer Daley planned to speak with her today.

"Good. Because I was about to pay her a visit myself," Julie said.

She could visit her, but Ethan was still seeing her; he

knew what she was putting me through and didn't care. All this time, begging me not to leave him, to be with me, and still sneaking around with her, too.

Why was I chasing after a man who was proving again and again he wasn't worth it?

THE PLANS for Blaxten's new brand launch were finally coming along. St. Pete had finished construction on the new pier, and I pulled some strings to rent out the entire thing. With 360° views of downtown St. Petersburg and the bay, it would be one of our best events. We'd start with dinner and speeches at the restaurant at the end of the pier and finish with live music and drinks outside. I read over the night's itinerary for a third time when my phone rang.

"Mrs. Mitchell, hello, it's Officer Daley."

"Hi Officer, how did it go with Emma? Is she going to leave me alone now?"

"I'm hoping so, ma'am. She admitted to sending you the initial email, but she denied sending anything else. That's not a surprise, though. I'm hoping that my visit was enough of a scare and the harassing emails and texts will stop now."

I tapped my lips with my finger, wanting to ask more, like how she looked, what her body language suggested. But I doubted he was looking close enough to observe the small nuances I needed. No, the only person I could count on was me. Emma had declared check, and if she didn't stop, I would be the one declaring checkmate.

Twenty-Eight

ALICE

A WALK around the building to clear my head was in order. Cass was losing her luster. Her heart may be breaking but so was mine. I lost the most important person in my life. She wasn't Cass anymore. Was this a temporary leave of absence? When would she return? If not temporary, the time to move on had arrived, but I wasn't ready to give up yet. Her work was suffering. We were on a sinking ship, and I was running out of fingers to plug the holes. The thought of leaving her was unbearable, but so was the thought of staying. I had time, I'm not sure how much, but a change of plans was in order, and planning was something I did best. There was no one better suited to fix this mess than me. I just needed to get a few obstacles out of my way.

I walked back inside and found Cass sitting in her chair staring at the wall. *Typical.* "I'm going to take a drive to the pier. The events manager and I spoke earlier, and she said she'd be there this afternoon. Do you need me to take care of anything before I leave?"

"Nope. All good here," she said without looking at me.

"I'll be off then. Text if you need anything. I don't think I'll be back in time before you leave. I'll see you in the morning."

She finally turned her head and smiled. "Thank you, Alice. For everything."

I almost confessed everything right then and there. My fickle heart's guilt almost got the best of me. I nodded curtly and turned to leave, then stopped.

Tentatively I walked closer to her. "I'm not sure I've ever shared this with you." I paused, waiting to ensure I had her full attention. "I didn't have a family growing up. Well, not what one would consider a *typical* family. I'm sure it's no surprise that I don't have many friends, or even acquaintances. However, we've grown close over these years, and I consider you the closest thing I have to family. It pains me to see you going through this. I suppose what I'm trying to say is, I'm here for you. As your assistant, but also as a friend."

Her hand lifted to her chest. I imagined her heart beating beneath it. She reached out with both hands and clasped mine tightly. "I appreciate that. And you. You do have friends. At least one very good one. I'm here for you too, I hope you know that." She released her grip on my hands and I left. There were no words to be said. Anything more could have ruined it.

I DIDN'T HAVE plans to drive to Emma's apartment that day, I absolutely was going to go to the pier to speak with the events manager about final preparations. However, the exit to her place was right before the exit to the pier, and an unseen force pulled me off the highway.

I parked in the lot in a spot with a clear view of her front door and pulled a hat low over my face. She lived in one of those two-story complexes where all the apartments' front doors lined up facing the parking lot. Very unsafe if you ask me, as anyone could walk right up to your door or peer in your front window, but it made spying much easier. When Emma's door opened and a familiar girl walked out, I audibly gasped.

What in the world is Aubrey doing here?

I watched her slide down and drop her head to her knees then crawl to the window. I leaned forward to make sense of the scene unfolding before me. She jerked back and fell, scrambled to her feet, and ran away crying. The chances of her recognizing me or my car were slim, but I slouched down in my seat just in case.

I sat in my car debating whether to drive away or try to get a look inside Emma's apartment. I wanted at the very least to understand what had spooked Aubrey. I tried to think of an excuse to explain my presence when another Mitchell pulled into the parking lot and ran up the stairs his daughter had just run down.

Tsk, tsk Ethan. You're not supposed to be here.

I didn't wait to see how long he stayed in his girlfriend's house.

Foregoing the pier, I drove back to the office

"AND YOU ARE ABSOLUTELY certain it was Ethan *and* Aubrey you saw?" Julie asked me.

"Yes. Without a doubt."

Julie stood and walked to her window. Her back stiffened and she turned. "Wait. What were you doing at Emma's apartment?"

I'd prepared for this question and answered with ease. "I just had a feeling. I can't explain it. I was passing by her exit, and something told me, 'Alice, you need to turn there.'" I hoped the information was enough, that Julie wouldn't dig further and ask how I knew it was Emma's exit, for example. I willed her to move on. We held each other's stares.

"Come with me. Let's tell her what you saw."

One down, one to go.

Cass looked up, brows touching, when we entered her office. "What's going on? Alice, I thought you were going to the pier. Why are you two looking at me like that?"

Julie closed the door. We remained standing.

"Go on, Alice. Tell her."

I explained the perplexing scene I'd witnessed.

"That'll be all," Julie interrupted when I'd gotten to the end.

"I'm so sorry, I know this is terrible news—"

"I said, that will be all," Julie repeated, her brown eyes boring into mine.

I resisted the urge to humph. She had quite the nerve. *I come here and give them pertinent information, and this is the thanks I get. I may not be so inclined to share the next time I observe something amiss. Perhaps I'll leave Julie out from now on. Perhaps I'll find a way to get rid of her completely.*

"I already knew," I heard Cass say as I closed the door.

The urge to stay and listen was overwhelming. Knew what? That I was there? Aubrey? Or that Ethan was?

I sat in my cube, drumming my fingers on my keyboard, pretending to work. Standing, I pretended to stretch. Julie looked through the window and our gazes met. Her head tilted to the side, and I collapsed into my chair.

I packed up my things for the second time that day and drove home.

At my kitchen table, I pulled out the folder of recent press featuring the agency and Cass. There had been an uptick due to the Blaxten win and upcoming event. I picked up my scissors and one by one methodically cut Julie out of every image. Once done, I popped the top off the black Sharpie and went through each article, crossing out each mention of Julie or Parker. With my work complete and spread in front of me it became quite obvious what needed to be done. Cass did not need these people in her life. They no longer served her in a positive way. She needed a fresh start.

She needed me.

TWENTY-NINE

CASS

FOR ONCE I was happy to see Ethan's car already in the garage when I got home. I walked into the house and found him in the kitchen. Before I could say anything, he told me about Aubrey's visit to Emma's.

"How exactly did you find out Aubrey went there?" I asked.

"She called me—wait, is that what you're more concerned with? That Emma called me versus the fact our child skipped school and went to confront an adult? One who you *claim* to be terrified of?"

"I'm mad at all of it, Ethan. And I have every right to be terrified of Emma. You've seen the texts and emails. The ones she *claims* she never sent to me. The bathroom, and all my stuff. And frankly, knowing you answered her call is a significant cause for concern."

Ethan steepled his fingers and leaned his forehead at the peak. *Always the victim.*

"She sent me a text saying she had something urgent to talk to me about and it had to do with Aubrey; I couldn't just ignore it. I called Aubrey and she didn't pick up, so I panicked."

Liar.

"Well, if you must know, Alice already told me Aubrey went to see Emma today."

Ethan's face changed from panic to confusion. "How would Alice know?"

"How she knows is unimportant. I don't believe anything Emma says, so we need Aubrey's version."

I called Aubrey's name from the bottom of the stairs. I opened my mouth to call her name again and she appeared at the top.

"What?" she asked. Her shifty eyes didn't match her snippy tone.

"Your dad and I need to talk to you, come down for a minute."

She begrudgingly clomped down the stairs and followed me into the kitchen. Once we'd situated ourselves around the table, I asked where she'd been that afternoon.

She traced the lines of the wood in the table with her finger, refusing to meet our eyes. "At school."

"Aubrey, we know you weren't at school. I'd like to hear exactly what happened. I promise you aren't in trouble."

She looked up and sucked in a deep breath.

"It started with two really bad things. First, I broke into mom's phone. I found out who she was." She met my gaze. I smiled sadly to encourage her to continue

She took another deep breath and dropped her eyes to her lap. "Then I found her address, and it was right near school, an easy walk. So, I forged a doctor's note."

"Oh Aubrey, you didn't."

"I did. I walked to her house. It was hotter than hell. Sorry, heck. I got there and pounded on her door. She finally opened it and asked who I was. I just started screaming at her; I lost it. She started to close the door and I shot my foot forward to block the door from closing. I figured she'd just kick my foot away or something, shut the door, and it would be over. I'd walk back to school and that would be the end of it. But she looked down at my foot, sighed, and let me in! She told me her neighbors didn't need any more reasons to talk about her."

I was horrified at the thought of Aubrey in Emma's house and shot Ethan a look. He refused to meet my gaze.

"What happened next?" I asked.

"Her apartment was a disaster. I mean, it was probably nice at one point. But it was worse than my room when it gets really bad. There were no lights on, and the curtains were closed so it was dark and depressing. And the mess. Dirty dishes everywhere. She was burning a vanilla candle, but it still smelled so nasty. She looked nasty too. She had on wrinkled sweatpants and a sweatshirt, and her unwashed hair was piled on top of her head in a greasy, messy bun. Her face looked all puffy and swollen and her eyes were red."

I smiled despite myself. Aubrey continued.

"She pushed aside this gross blanket on the couch and told me to sit. Then she said 'So, you came here to what? Confront me? Yell at me? Tell me how awful I am?' I had gone there to destroy her, but mom, it was so weird, it was like she was already destroyed."

I nodded slowly; my entire body stiffened.

"I told her you and dad aren't getting divorced, that he regrets everything and he told me so. I told her that he was begging for you to take him back. I told her she was terrible, and our family was fine before she ruined everything. Then she started crying, said she was sorry, she's not that person, that she fell in love, but then dad dumped her, and now she was a wreck and blah, blah, blah—"

"Okay, I think that's enough," Ethan interrupted.

"Let her finish. If you don't want to hear this, leave. But let your daughter finish."

Aubrey's eyes widened. She looked unsure for a second. Her eyes narrowed in her dad's direction. She turned toward me and went on, "Yeah, okay. So, it got all awkward. I was just sitting there watching her cry, not knowing what to do. I stood and told her 'good. I hope you die in here, sad and alone' then ran out. But Mom, this is where it gets super creepy. There was a place in the curtains where I could see in just enough from outside. I squatted down and watched her. She was just sitting in the chair glaring at the door. No tears, nothing. Then she grabbed a glass and chucked it. It hit the wall so hard I heard it from outside. She started slamming her head with her fists, then looked up and screamed. It was totally insane. I didn't know what she'd do next, so I ran all the way back to school."

No one said a word. Ethan and I both stared at her in shock.

"I'm sorry, Mom. I know I should have stayed out of it. I was just so angry. But now I'm scared. She's out of her mind."

"See?" I said to Ethan. "I told you there is something wrong with this girl. Now do you believe me?"

"Aubrey, go back upstairs and let your mother and I discuss this," he said.

She looked back and forth between us. "Am I in trouble?"

"We'll figure that out later," Ethan replied.

We sat in silence until her door slammed closed upstairs.

"Look. I'm not arguing with you that something isn't— off, about Emma. This whole thing whether it's getting fired, or losing me, or all of it, it's made her a little unhinged," Ethan said.

"A little?" I snorted.

"You know what I mean, Cass. If we ignore her, she'll eventually cool off and move on with her life. First the cops, and now Aubrey stopping by. This can't be helping the situation."

"You're the one who wanted to call the cops!"

"I know, I know. But I didn't think Aubrey would show up at her house too!"

I filled my cheeks up with air and swallowed it down. "I can't do this anymore. I've abandoned my entire life for Emma. I want nothing to do with her yet there she is, always. I have a work event right around the corner, and this family is a disaster. This is too much. I'm about to have an absolute meltdown." I leaned my forehead onto the palms of my hands and sucked back tears. "Something has to give," I whispered.

Ethan walked over and put his arm across my back. My body was so dragged down by it all, I couldn't even recoil at his touch. If he knew I wasn't so ignorant to his lies, that I knew his communications with Emma extended well beyond an 'emergency with Aubrey,' what then? How would he wiggle himself out of that situation? I wanted so badly to blurt it out, right then. But information is power, and I didn't want to give mine up.

I stood. "I'm telling Aubrey she's grounded for the weekend for skipping school, and she is to cease all communication with Emma. My advice is you do the same."

THIRTY

ALICE

WE HAD BEEN in Cass's office for two hours now reviewing the mocks for the event. What should have been an easy one-hour meeting was being dragged out by her constant interruptions. Ethan this and Emma that. I considered myself an extremely patient person, but I was ready to snap.

"Can you keep a secret, Alice? Of course, you can." She laughed, looking not at me, but instead gazing out the window.

A flush of giddiness tingled beneath my skin. Could this be my reward for the last two hours of torture?

"Your secrets are always safe with me," I said, a teasing smile crossed my face.

"I think Emma's been following me, but I'm afraid to tell anyone because what if it's all in my head? I knew Ethan had planned to go to her house before you told me. I saw it on his phone. I'm such an idiot. I can't believe I let him move back in."

I pushed my glasses up my nose to hide my rolling eyes. Women are always believing every word that comes from a chiseled face.

"What makes you think Emma is following you?" I asked, my tone very concerned of course.

She filled her chest with air and huffed it out. "I don't know. That's the problem. Everywhere I go I get this feeling like I'm being watched. I've tried to catch her. I almost did in the grocery store the other day. She always has dark clothes on, a hoodie, sometimes a baseball cap. She's very sneaky. I never get my phone out in time to get a picture."

"Oh my," I exclaimed, pressing a hand dramatically to my chest.

"What should I do?" Her eyes seemed to plead for an answer. "I can't talk to Ethan about it. Especially not now that we know he is still doing whatever. What would you do? I sound completely paranoid, don't I?" She laughed nervously.

Not only did she sound paranoid, she looked it too. The fidgeting, darting eyes, and sweat beading her brow were quite unbecoming.

She whispered, "Don't tell anyone, not even Julie, okay?" Then she smiled and said hello. I twisted and saw the reason for her change in tone.

"These look amazing," Julie said, walking up to admire the table centerpiece.

"Don't they?" Cass said. "The team did such a fantastic job. I can't wait to see it come to life."

"Are you bringing what's-his-name?"

I stifled a laugh.

"Ethan will be there, so behave."

"I can't be held responsible for any arsenic that gets

dumped in his drink or sprinkled on his dinner," Julie said, leaning in to inspect another mockup of the exterior designs.

Cass scowled, and I couldn't hold my giggles in any longer.

"Alice gets me," Julie said, winking. "I came to check if you needed any help, but it looks like you ladies have it under control."

"Other than the day-of chaos, I have it covered. It will be an event to remember," I replied.

We wrapped up the meeting shortly after Julie left. I returned to my cubicle.

We were so close to everything I wanted; I'd been waiting for the right moment. A good time. I was getting so absolutely sick of this new overly dramatic Cass, I feared the time would never come. She was losing her mind, being pushed to the edge. I had to finish before she fell off it.

My eyes unfocused and I was pulled back into the dark closet. Those were the good days. When my punishment was fear rather than pain. Cass didn't speak of her mother often, but when she did, I had to bite my tongue until it bled. She had no idea what a terrible childhood entailed. Not a clue. She escaped hers. For some of us, it wasn't so easy. I always hoped some of her goodness would rub off on me, so I could turn my back on my past, too.

"Alice, did you hear me?"

I nearly jumped out of my chair. "I'm sorry, I didn't see you there."

Cass laughed. "Where'd you go? You looked completely zonked out there for a minute."

I waved her suggestion off with a flick of my wrist. "Thinking through any potential problems and how to solve them. You know me. Always two steps ahead."

"That's why you're the best." She grinned. "Would you mind grabbing me some lunch? I'm starving and don't want to take a break."

I took her order. My smile fell when she turned her back to me.

THIRTY-ONE

CASS

UNABLE TO THINK of a good excuse to get out of dinner with Ethan, I sat across from him in the busy restaurant in downtown St. Pete. It had always been one of my favorite places, good food, on the water, and great service, but that night my couch felt like the much better option.

"How's the rebrand and event planning going?" Ethan asked. He gripped one corner of the napkin swaddling his silverware and let its contents clatter chaotically to the table. I picked up my napkin and slowly removed each utensil one by one, placing each in its proper order next to my plate before gently smoothing the napkin across my lap. I looked up to see if he'd learned anything from my exaggerated show. He was too engrossed in the wine list to notice.

"Yes, most of my work is done, the rebrand, media plan, and such. It's all Alice from here. Flowers, band, menu, lighting, all those details she's great at. I'm surprised you care, actually, since I've been accused of being too wrapped up in work."

I was ornery that night, ready to deliver tiny pinches and see how far he'd let me get before his temper flared. It was a game I liked to play. He'd already caught on to it many years ago. But that didn't make it any less fun. I still hadn't found a way to confront Ethan about my suspicions that he was still seeing Emma, which put me in a perpetual state of grumpiness, especially around him. There hadn't been many opportunities to search his phone, but of the few I'd gotten, I hadn't found any more texts. Their entire string had been deleted in fact, including her contact.

"What did that waitress say the fish special was tonight, almond crusted something?" I asked.

He put the wine list on the table and lowered his chin to look at me. I smiled back sweetly.

Shaking his head, he picked it back up and declared he would be drinking scotch tonight. I deflated—it would take a few more pinches. I got such a thrill out of setting him off. I never liked when it happened, but that excitement right before he'd explode made my stomach drop like I was flying down a roller coaster. He'd say something nasty, then I'd be mad at him for days. My mother got high on heroin and painkillers; I got high on anger and drama. I spent my entire life running from my genetics, but they'd always been faster than me.

"Officer Daley called to check-in yesterday," I said.

"Why wouldn't you mention that earlier?" he asked, his tone gruff.

I widened my eyes in surprise. "I have a lot on my mind currently." I waved my hand between us.

He removed the attitude from his words. "What did he say? Did something new come up?"

"No, just wanted to know if the harassment stopped. Which of course I told him it has not. The bitch is still obsessed with me, filling up my phone with the same shit."

"It may not be her. And you don't have to be so callous and vulgar; you're better than that."

"First of all. Fuck you and fuck her. How's that for vulgar? And second, who the fuck else would it be?" I side eyed the tables nearest to us and noticed a few of the diners had stopped talking, their heads were shifted slightly our way. Everyone loves a good public fight, as long as it's not their own.

"Who the hell knows? I'm sure your competitors would love to take you down. Revenge for stealing a client. It could be anyone."

"I don't *steal* clients. I earn them. Because I'm damn good at making them money."

"Whoa, tiger." He chuckled and held up his hands. "It was a compliment. I didn't mean *steal* in a bad way. I just meant I'm sure there are other enemies you have out there based on your success. Chill."

There is nothing that makes me more unchill than being told to chill or being told how I should feel at all. I wrung my napkin in my lap. Twisting, twisting, twisting until it wouldn't twist anymore.

"I have one enemy. And her name is Emma. Period. It was her and has always been her. And if you don't want me to cause a scene and embarrass us both in this restaurant full of all these people" I swooped my arm dramatically around the room "I suggest you keep your incorrect theories to yourself."

He pressed his lips together until they turned white.

"Besides," I said, oozing the honey back onto my words. "This is a celebration for our fresh start. Oh, but first I have something to show you." I retrieved my phone from my purse and unlocked it.

He groaned. "Not more texts from her."

I froze and looked up. "Yeah, how imposing that would be for *you*. No, I was looking on Emma's Instagram, did you know how trashy she is?" I turned my phone around and showed him the photos I'd taken screenshots of. It took hours of scrolling to find the most unflattering one where she was hammered, sloppy, hanging all over boys. Ethan grabbed my wrist of the hand holding the phone and pushed it to the table.

"What's the purpose of this, Cass?"

Undaunted, I returned his look.

"You're so much better than this. Why are you stooping to this level?" he asked.

"Yes, I *am* so much better than this," I said and held up my phone with the photos for him to see again.

He picked his menu up and buried his face in it. "I'm not doing this with you tonight. Don't be crazy."

I squeezed my hands in fists and clenched my teeth.

"I'm going to the bathroom. Can you order me a drink if that waiter ever decides to come back and do his job? Or is that too much to ask? Order some calamari or something for an app, too."

Ethan didn't bother looking up from his menu. I stood and ripped it down, placing my face inches from his. A few more heads turned our way.

"Okay?" I asked.

He pulled it back and sharply muttered okay.

My heels tapped on the marble floor as I weaved my way through the looky-loos to the ladies' room. I ignored all of them. I shut myself in a stall and put the seat down before dropping down on top of it and placing my head between my legs. There were so many tempting sharp objects within reach to funnel my rage into. He's lucky I didn't pick one of them up and cause a real scene. *Call* me *crazy. The nerve.* I should have stabbed his hand to the table and walked out, leaving him stuck there.

When I'd composed myself, I exited the stall and nearly barreled into someone I had no desire to see: Lara.

"Cass! I thought that was you I spotted across the room. So good running into you." She leaned in for a hug. I rolled my eyes when my face was over her shoulder and out of sight. I was in such a foul mood I couldn't even stand myself.

"Lara, hi. Lovely to see you too, are you here with Lucas?" I smiled sweetly.

"Yes." She lowered her chin. "And you?"

"Ethan." I straightened my spine and hitched my chin up. "We've decided to work things out."

"I'd heard rumblings, and glad to hear they are true. I honestly believe you two are meant to be together." She placed her hand on my arm, and I forced myself not to look at it with disgust.

I stepped out of her way and up to the sink as she slid into a stall. To make matters worse, she was a pee talker and thought it appropriate to continue our conversation while she performed her private business. I turned on the water and left it running after I finished washing my hands, using my phone as a distraction while she rambled on. The toilet flushed, I tossed my phone back in my purse and leaned on the counter looking her way, like I'd been sitting there hanging off every word, and not gagging at the fact she was talking to me while she was using the bathroom.

"So, you and Ethan," she said, easing next to me at the sink to wash her hands. She was smiling at me in the mirror, like we were co-conspirators. To busy my hands and not punch the mirror and shatter her face, I dug my lipstick from my purse and applied it, keeping my eyes on my reflection.

"Yep," I said through open, occupied lips. She wanted more, but I refused to give her any. My life wasn't fodder for her and Lucas to gossip about over their cabernet.

Her left eyebrow arched as high as her Botoxed forehead would allow.

I winked at her in the mirror, then walked out to rejoin my shithead husband at our table. Much to my delight, a sweating glass filled with vodka and soda greeted me upon my return.

"Feeling better?" he asked after I sat.

"Yes." *No.*

"Can we move on and have a nice night now, and not talk about her?"

"Fine," I said, picking up my menu.

He followed. "What are you thinking?" he asked, scanning the menu.

That you're a revolting, deceiving, worthless man.

"I think I'll go for a steak. Extra bloody." He studied me with raised eyebrows, and I chuckled. "I ran into Lara in the ladies' room."

"Yeah? She here with Lucas?"

"She is," I said, twirling the lime around my drink with my straw.

"Well then, I guess we don't have to worry about any tables or fists being thrown." He laughed.

"What do you mean by that?" I asked. My clipped tone caught his attention, and he put his menu down.

"You remember her and Mike always fighting, don't you?"

"I do. You can hardly blame Mike, though. Now that her little pussy cat is out of the bag, that she was sleeping with Lucas behind his back, makes you view those fights differently, doesn't it?"

He was inspecting me now. His jaw clenched and unclenched. He was onto my game and deciding whether to take my bait or keep swimming. He shook his head once before burying his face back in the menu.

"I think I'll go with the swordfish tonight," he said. "Something different."

I grabbed my drink and finished the last three-fourths. The waiter was passing by. Perfect timing on his part; he'd finally figured out how to do his job. I held up my glass and smiled, motioning for a refill.

I looked around the restaurant, wondering if any of the other women were as broken as me. If they were also sitting across from their dates, pretending to laugh, pretending to smile, pretending to be alive. Ethan brushed a stray crumb from the table. Was that what I was to him? An annoying crumb to be flicked away? Was he even thinking of me? Or were visions of black hair splayed out on white sheets floating behind his eyes?

I felt my phone vibrating in my purse against my leg and I bent to retrieve it. After unlocking the screen, I handed it to Ethan without a word.

His thumb swiped up through the barrage of messages.

It was another one of her mass assaults. I was accustomed to these. More of the same, just repeated words *'Bitch' 'Cunt' 'Fuck You.'* This night's word was 'Bitch.' Ethan scrolled through the texts, his brow wrinkled. I snatched my phone back.

"You won't find anything different. She just repeats herself, same as all the other ones I've shown you. Who's the crazy one now?"

Ethan's forehead creased even further. His eyes didn't leave the phone. I'm sure she played the innocent victim with him, the same as she had with Officer Daley. He was trying to understand why she'd lied to him. What to make of it all. Trying to connect what she'd told him with the proof I'd shown him, again.

My poor, dumb husband.

Thirty-Two

Cass

ALICE and I walked down the hall to my office while she read from her notebook. "The centerpieces are all set, caterers should be there by noon, and lighting and design crew are already there and well underway. I'm heading to the pier when we finish up. Your makeup and hair team will be at your house by three, so make sure you are home, showered, with face clean and moisturized by two thirty." She looked up as if to check I was listening.

We reached my office and I stopped before entering. "Got it. Be home by two thirty and you're on top of everything else."

"Yes, exactly. Okay I'm off now. I need to get down there and make sure they aren't screwing anything up."

"Have I told you, you're the best?" I called to her retreating back.

She waved a hand above her head in acknowledgement.

Julie popped her head in. "We still riding together tonight?"

"Yes," I said. "But I forgot to ask Alice what time the car service would be at your house. All I know is I'm supposed to be home by two thirty, showered, and face moisturized."

Julie chuckled. "Did you ask Mom if next week's lessons were on oral hygiene?"

"You're just jealous you don't have an Alice."

"I'm much happier without, I assure you. I'll shoot her a text and find out myself, since you are useless. Do I have to be nice to Ethan tonight?"

"I would love to say no, but yes, yes you do."

"Fine. But I'll be saying mean things in my head."

"That is absolutely approved."

Carla walked in, her face tight. "Oh, good. You're both in here."

My stomach lurched and my mind managed to formulate at least one hundred versions of what had happened in the two seconds it took her to step inside the office and close the door. "I just got a call from the caterer. The check for the final payment bounced."

"What?" Julie exclaimed.

"It has to be a mistake," Carla said. "There should be plenty of cash in the account. But I checked, and it's empty."

"Not tonight. Any other night but tonight." I rubbed my temples.

"I gave the caterers a credit card, so that is taken care of. And I have a call in at the bank. The woman on the phone wasn't able to help, but she has a business manager calling me back."

"How much money, Carla? How much was in that bank account?"

Carla looked about to cry. "It was just over three million, and the balance is now zero."

"Fuck, when's payday?" Julie whipped out her phone. "Okay. Okay. Payroll isn't due until when, next Tuesday?"

"Yes, that's correct," Carla replied.

"Carla, call Alice and tell her anything not paid yet for tonight should be put on her Amex, that fraud was detected on the main account and they froze it. Can you make sure her limit is high enough to cover everything? Then make sure we don't have any checks out to ad publishers that haven't been cashed, tell them the same thing, and give them a credit card to charge. We can't have campaigns shutting off because of some bank error. Is there anything else anyone can think of?" Julie looked between Carla and me, we both shook our heads. "It's a mistake, a simple mistake. No one is allowed to worry until we have something to worry about. Understood?"

We nodded.

"We're worrying, right?" I asked when Carla left.

"We are fucking panicking," Julie replied.

"IS EVERYTHING ALRIGHT WITH YOU TWO?" Victoria asked in the limo on the way to the Blaxten event. "You're both unusually quiet."

Julie and I exchanged glances. "We're fine, it's just a big night for the agency," Julie said with a strained smile. She took Victoria's hand and turned her gaze toward the tinted window.

"Anyone want a drink?" Ethan asked cheerfully. He began pulling bottles out and reading labels. When no one answered, he shrugged and scooped a few cubes of ice into a crystal tumbler and poured half a glass of rum over them.

It was clear neither Julie nor myself had filled our significant others in on the missing money. It was a quiet ride to the pier. I was mentally calculating how far in the hole we were, and how long it would take us to dig ourselves out of it without losing every client we had. *It's some sort of bank error. Or insurance will cover it. Or, or, or...*

"We're here," Ethan cried, making me jump. "You are being weird tonight. You sure everything's okay?"

"Yes," I said. "I'm fine."

Walking up the pier was like stepping into another world. The new Blaxten 'B' was everywhere, lit up in the brand's blue. There were fire blowers, contortionists, and stilt walkers lining the sides of the pier giving the guests an exciting entrance. Their blue sequined costumes shimmered in the lights. I smiled at each of the performers. Regardless of what was happening with our bank account and my marriage, this would get us great press. And apparently, we needed that more than ever before.

We joined the cocktail hour which was already in full swing. I looked through the crowd for Alice to compliment her on her good work but couldn't find her among the sea of tuxedos and ball gowns. She was probably bossing the catering staff around to ensure dinner would be ready on time. We spotted Blaxten's CEO and CMO standing by the bar. Julie and I made our way through the crowd, Ethan and Victoria in tow.

"Cass, Julie!" We exchanged air kisses on each cheek with Tara. "Amazing job, just look at this. I'm blown away. The new brand is beyond our expectations—and this event." She gazed around the room. "You've outdone yourselves. I knew we picked the right agency."

"Thank you, we're proud of this one. With such a great company behind the brand, you made our jobs easy," I said.

"And the night is just beginning," Julie chimed in.

"Herb, Tara, this is Victoria, Julie's wife, and my husband, Ethan." I turned to Victoria and Ethan. "Herb is Blaxten's CEO and Tara is their Chief Marketing Officer." They exchanged handshakes and I thought I saw a second of hesitation in Tara's eyes as she reached for Ethan's hand, a slight flicker of disgust flashing across her face. I'm sure I was being paranoid. There is no way Ethan's cheating reached the clients.

"Shall we go inside? Dinner should be ready shortly. The two of you can get situated for speeches. Dinner will be served followed by the band and drinks back out here." The four of us headed inside the restaurant.

Tara let out a gasp and Herb nodded in approval. It *was* gasp-worthy. Everything was bathed in a glow of blue lights, the stage had massive screens with an animated Blaxten logo. Each of the tables had intricate centerpieces of branches dripping in tiny crystals. Everywhere you looked were beautiful details, with just the right touch of branding. Alice was standing on the far side of the room. I motioned her over.

Tara beamed at her. "Alice, I believe you had much to do with tonight's event."

"Team effort as always," Alice replied.

"Well, our compliments to you and the entire team, then," Herb said.

"If you'll follow me, we can do a quick sound test, then

we will be ready to welcome the guests in." Alice ushered them to the stage.

Julie leaned in and whispered, "We are still panicking, but we're doing a hell of a job hiding it." We clinked glasses, split our lips into smiles and joined the group at the stage.

Intros and speeches went smoothly. Herb and Tara were walking from the podium and the waitstaff was passing out salads, as my gaze wandered to the back of the room.

Time slowed. Sounds retreated.

She wore the same red dress she had on in the photo she sent me on the day my life fell apart.

Emma.

From far away she looked stunning. Her black hair hung in loose waves down her back, and the red dress clung to her body in all the right places. She and I locked eyes. She began making her way to the stage and a slight stumble gave her true state away. *Stop her!* My mind screamed. But my mouth and body wouldn't listen. Everyone stared, but no one moved. *Why isn't anyone doing anything?*

As Emma walked up on the stage and started clapping slowly, a hush fell over the room. Her red lips spread into a menacing smile. Her gaze swept the room and she began.

"Good evening, everyone. My name is Emma, I won't be long, don't want to keep you from the lovely dinner Alice and Cass have lined up. That man next to Cass is her husband, Ethan. Everyone, say 'hi Ethan.'" All heads in the room turned in our direction.

"Get her off the fucking stage, Ethan," Julie hissed at him. He started to stand.

"Oh, looks like my time with you will be cut short," Emma continued. "Just one quick thing, and I'll be gone. For those who don't know, Ethan and I were together." Her gaze locked on my husband. "Ethan, before I met you, the guilt of sleeping with a married man would have made me feel awful, totally the worst, but I'm not that girl anymore. Look who you've turned me into? Are you happy? You told me you loved me. And silly me, I believed you. After all we've been through. All I've sacrificed. I'm sure you're thinking you are the one who's done the sacrificing. It's always about him isn't it, Cass?" Our eyes locked. My fist curled around my knife. She turned her attention back to the entire room. It didn't make a difference the imaginary spotlight still lit Ethan and me up. I refused to sink into my chair and show how I truly felt. Julie squeezed my leg under the table.

Emma continued, "But all those sweet nothings you'd whisper to me in bed, they were all lies, weren't they? I was nothing but your plaything, your dirty little secret." Two men had Emma by the elbows and were leading her out. She screamed over her shoulder, "I'm not a doll, something to play with when in the mood, then toss to the side when not. Apparently, you didn't realize this. And now you'll pay. You and that stuck-up wife of yours. Cass. Everyone's beloved Cass. She has *my* life. The only reason she's living it is because she got to it first!"

The screens behind Emma changed from the Blaxten logo to a scene I'd lived a thousand times in my head. The two men dragging Emma stopped and everyone in the room gasped as they watched me scream at a laughing Emma enjoying her iced latte. I looked at Emma, her head tilted to the side and for a second she actually looked confused. The look was quickly replaced by cackling, the security guards remembered their jobs and tore their attention away from the screens and dragged her from the room. Alice had made it to the stage ripping out plugs until the screens turned off.

Whispers reverberated around the room.

"Get up, Cass." Julie grabbed my arm and squeezed. "Fall apart later but get up right this second and say something. You can still save this." I raised my face to her with hollow eyes and like a zombie, walked to the stage.

I cleared my throat, closed my eyes, and took three deep breaths. When I opened them, I was beaming. "Well, that wasn't part of the planned entertainment for the evening, but I hope you all enjoyed your pre-dinner show." Uncomfortable laughter rippled through the crowd. "Unfortunately, we had to let poor Emma go a few weeks back. We pray she gets the help she needs, and I will have our human resources department checking on her tonight. Her safety is, of course, the most important thing. Now, we have the finest chefs in the Bay area, so everyone enjoy your dinner. Bon appétit!"

A smattering of clapping accompanied me back to my table, where the entire Blaxten team looked both horrified and angry. It was an uncomfortable meal, enjoyed by no one.

THIRTY-THREE

CASS

BITCH, Die, I'll Kill U. These were just a few of the words now decorating the walls of my trashed office. Along with the new wall décor, my entire workspace lay in ruins. Desk drawers hung open, and the contents from every piece of furniture lay smashed on the floor. Alice stood next to me, arms crossed and clucking her tongue. After avoiding Ethan successfully for much of the weekend, I'd looked forward to escaping to the office, despite the humiliating event, which turned out to be much worse than being at home.

"You noticed the video?" I pointed to the large TV on the wall. It was the only thing that hadn't been ripped down besides the white board.

"That's not something easily missed," Alice replied.

A man's face filled the television. A woman from off camera told him to smile. Screeching tires and the collision of metal and flesh echoed through the room. The woman holding the phone screamed, and the view changed to the sky. We heard people screaming for help but couldn't see them. The camera wobbled. We listened to the rustling of clothing, which was muffling the sounds of screams and chaos in the background. Someone had picked the phone back up. Right before the video ended, it turned toward the woman who just seconds ago—from the sound of her voice —seemed so happy and full of life. Her leg was twisted the wrong way, blood stained the road below her. The dead woman's face filled the screen. The video ended, then began again, a never-ending loop of horror.

Alice walked to the TV and turned it off. A loud silence hung in the air. The kind so bloated with thoughts you can almost hear them hum.

"This probably isn't the best time to tell you this, but Tara's assistant called. They're canceling the contract," Alice said.

"Of course, they are," I replied flatly.

Small groups of employees started to gather outside my office, craning their necks to get a peek at what was going on. My neck arched and I closed my eyes. *What a shit show.*

"Have you thought about leaving him?"

"Excuse me, what?"

"Ethan, leaving him. I must assume if you left him, she would stop all this."

"I—that's not exactly what—"

"Oh, for fuck's—this bitch. I really will kill her now." Julie had arrived and slammed the door behind her. She was always the one getting to slam doors.

I rubbed my temples; the cushions of my couch had been pulled off and sliced apart so their stuffing bled out around them. Probably for the best, otherwise I may have chosen to lie down and go to sleep, ideally forever.

"Alice, go tell Carla to call the police. Send an email to the staff; we are shutting the office for the day, and they can all work from home. Or go home and watch Netflix. I don't care, I just want everyone out of here while we deal with this," Julie commanded.

Alice scurried out to find Carla. I picked up my toppled chair and collapsed into it. "How do you think she got in?"

"That's a good question. We took her keycard. I should have told Alice to grab IT too; he can check the keycard swipes," Julie said.

"Keep an eye out for her, so she can get him before she sends the staff home; he'll be the first to run for the exit when he hears they all have the day off," I said.

"You know, we probably shouldn't be in here now that I think of it. It's a crime scene."

My body had become glued to the chair. "There was a video, too," I said, pointing to the TV.

She marched over and turned it on. She watched a few loops, her body so still I'd thought she'd turned to stone; the only things moving were her hands by her sides, clenching and unclenching.

"Let's go sit in the boardroom."

I kicked off my shoes and stepped around the rubbish to walk out of my office. Julie trailed with my purse, briefcase, and the discarded heels. Alice and Carla approached from down the hall.

"Alice, call James and have him come to the boardroom before you send the email to all employees. Carla, call the police. Once you two are done, someone grab Cass a coffee and a water and come meet us in there, too. Everyone else, back to your desks. We'll be releasing employees early today and handling this situation." Julie's voice was calm and commanding, but her eyes were on fire; I could practically see the flames flickering in her brown irises.

All the color seemed to have drained from the world. I walked through the black and white hallways ignoring the stares. Once in there, I sat at the table. Julie paced around the room chewing on her thumb's cuticle.

Carla walked in. "The police are on their way." She took a seat. James stood in the doorway with his hands in his pockets, inspecting his Converse sneakers. Alice crossed her arms and leaned against the wall.

"How are you holding up, Cass?" Carla asked.

I looked at each of them, staring at me, waiting for a response. "I'll fucking kill her," I snarled.

Alice quickly covered her mouth to stifle a laugh.

"Try to refrain from saying things like that when the police get here, dear." Carla smiled at me.

"James, have you checked the swipe history of all the employees' keycards yet? Let's get a printout ready for when they show up. As every employee's name is attached to their badge, it should be easy to find out which one let her in," Julie said.

James looked relieved to have something to do. He took his leave without a word.

"You are sure you took her keycard from her when we fired her, right?" I asked Carla.

"I did. I don't know how she'd get in, unless she had somehow—"

She rushed out into the hall and yelled at James's back, "James, be sure to check Emma's requests for replacement badges, go back six months."

"Good thinking," Alice said when Carla came back.

Julie's eyes narrowed. "James is usually pretty good

about remembering to turn off badges. I can't see him making such an irresponsible mistake. My money is on a friend letting her in." She pulled out a chair and sat. "We should check everyone's emails, especially the people we know she's friends with. See if they were dumb enough to plan anything over their work emails."

I leaned forward. "Alice, do you know who she's close with?"

Alice sat at the table and opened her notebook. "I do." She hunched over and began scribbling a list of names, then ripped off the paper and slid it across the table in my direction. "I'd start with that group." She pointed a finger at the list with a haughty look on her face.

The fluorescent lights made the room too bright. A headache sat on my skull like a helmet. I picked up the paper and read down the list, trying very hard not to hate the people behind the names. Sliding the paper back to Alice, I told her to give it to James.

"Carla, why don't you go up front and greet the police when they get here," Julie said. Marching orders assigned, the two women stood and scurried off to complete their tasks.

Pricks of static had entered my bloodstream, flowing uncomfortably through my veins, but I was calm, eerily calm. I couldn't help but wonder if I had caused this. If the fit I'd thrown had antagonized Emma in some way and set off the chain of events leading us to this moment.

"What are you smirking about? Thinking of all the ways you're going to get revenge?" Julie asked. I reminded myself to pay closer attention to my face.

"I need to call Ethan, but I can't lose my shit until we deal with the cops. His voice will trigger me."

"Strange, isn't it?"

"That she trashed my office? Yeah, strange, crazy, beyond comprehension."

"No, how she got in. I hope we don't end up having to fire the entire company. I don't trust anyone right now. The money too, it's all happening at the same time. There's no one else it would be, but these events somehow feel disconnected," Julie said.

A flash of anger shot through my ribcage. "That's ridiculous. They all fit perfectly together! There's literally no other logical explanation."

Julie stood and walked to the glass wall, gazing at the office. "Right." She turned around. "It's almost too perfect though, you know?"

"No, I don't know. You sound like Ethan." My flesh was on fire. Tiny flames licked at every inch of it.

Carla opened the door with two uniformed officers. My skin cooled enough for me to remember to behave.

Emma wasn't the only one with things to hide.

Thirty-Four

Cass

The police had come and gone, fingerprints, photographs, and statements taken. A cleaning crew worked on restoring my office back to proper order while Julie and I waited in the boardroom. We sent James, Alice, and Carla home. The badge used to access the building had been a guest badge. There was no way to trace who used it, or when it had been swiped from James's desk. He felt terrible. I wanted to blame him, to have a target for my anger, but there were plenty of other directions to throw that rage. The emails also proved a dead end. There was no evidence that Emma had been in the building or anywhere near my office. Our only hope was her fingerprints, but we had to wait on those results, or the second interview they planned on having with her.

The lights in most of the building were off, giving it an eerie abandoned feeling. I looked at my best friend wondering how much worse things could get.

"I'm going to grab my things from my office, then let's get out of here 'kay?"

I nodded.

A few moments later she returned with a piece of paper.

Her face was unreadable. She placed it in front of me and walked around the table and sat.

I picked it up confused. My hands started shaking as I read the typed note.

"Tell me it isn't true, Cass."

I shook my head, but without much conviction. "Who —Where did you get this?"

"Tell me!" she screamed.

"I'm so sorry."

She shook her head. "No, this can't be true. We supported you. All of us."

"Emma hasn't been sending me texts or emails." I filled my chest with a large gulp of air and clasped my hands together in my lap. "It was me. I sent them to myself."

Her stare sent a wave of hot needle pricks across my skin.

"I've been using an app. Emma hasn't sent me anything, other than that first email. I programmed them into the app to send them to myself."

She continued staring at me. Had she even blinked? I fidgeted in my seat and glanced at the door wanting to bolt.

"And why in the actual fuck would you do that, Cass?" The way she said my name made my stomach lurch. In all the years we'd known each other, even during our worst fights, she never sounded so cold, so angry, or so full of hate. I swallowed back tears and tried to keep the quiver from my voice.

"I—Ethan wasn't seeing my side, so I had to show him," I said.

She slammed her hands on the boardroom table and my body lurched back, banging into the back of my chair. "And what about us, Cass? What weren't you getting that gave you the right to lie to me?"

"I wasn't thinking. I just—my head wasn't right. I was so angry, and hurt, and sad. I wanted everyone to feel the same, not just say they did. It doesn't make sense. I know it doesn't."

Julie's face was fury personified. "Not good enough. Not even close. This is our business, our life. I was on your side. Me, Victoria, Carla, Alice. All of us. We would have walked through fire for you. And this is how you repay us? With this —this game? I'm going to ask you a question. And don't you dare lie to me. I swear to God, Cass. Did you steal the money and trash your office?"

"No! I promise. None of those things were me." I was whipping my head side to side, pleading with my eyes for her to believe me. "The only thing I did was send the emails and texts to myself. Everything else is Emma. I swear Julie, I swear on everything. On my kids! If I'd known she would have done all this, I wouldn't have sent them. I didn't think she would actually start harassing me. I fucked up. Help me, tell me what to do."

She folded her hands and leaned forward. Given her expression, I wasn't her Cass anymore. I was the enemy. She was all business. I shouldn't have been shocked by what she said next, but I was. To end like this was unthinkable. We were unbreakable. Our bond was deeper than family, because we weren't bound by blood; we didn't have to be loyal. We stood by each other out of love, no matter what.

Or at least that's what I'd thought.

"The police are involved, and these are *real* crimes. They

are going to dig through everything and find that stupid app. It makes Emma look innocent. And worse, it makes you look guilty. But that's not even the worst part. Not even close. You've completely demolished my trust. I am sorry this happened to you but I *was* on your side, and this little stunt you pulled was reckless and selfish. You need professional help, Cass. You also need to sign over your rights and remove yourself from this business. We're losing clients, money is disappearing, and if this gets out this agency will never recover. I love you, but I can't be there for you right now. And it kills me to say that."

Julie was quiet for a moment. I waited for some magical solution to save me from myself. She stared through me, into the darkest parts of my anatomy. She finally saw it, the monster that lurked within me, the one I had tried to hide, even run from. I desperately wanted to escape its clutches, but it held my body hostage. I always knew if it was ever unleashed those who loved me would abandon me. I was right.

Her face matched her cool voice. "I need you to leave."

"I understand," I said. "You're right. I'm sorry. It was a stupid mistake."

"Just go."

I wasn't entirely sure what did it, the abandonment, not knowing what would happen next, or her forgetting me, like our history was meaningless and non-existent, but something in me, a thing that had become so fragile, snapped.

"What did you expect?" I screamed, Julie didn't even flinch. "My husband fucked one of our employees, he continues to defend her, and continues to *see* her all while living in my house begging me to take him back. She ruined everything. Am I supposed to just smile and pretend like none of this is happening? Like everything is fine? Like I'm just great. Always unflappable Cass."

The room felt like it was washed in hues of red. We both stared at each other with our chests heaving.

"How do you know he's still seeing her?" Julie finally asked.

"I saw a text," I whimpered. "He never stopped. It was all a show."

Julie wove her fingers together on top of her head and tipped her face to the tiled ceiling. "Fuck," she said, barely above a whisper.

"I know I need therapy, and I agree it's probably best for me to take some time off in case any of this gets out. It's already causing enough trouble for the agency. But Julie, I can't lose you, too. I'm going to Emma's house tonight. Ethan supposedly has a work dinner, but I'm going to catch him there and put an end to this mess."

"So now you're graduating from fake stalker to real stalker?"

My face burned, and I lowered my eyes.

"I'll think about it," she said.

It was all I could ask from her at that point.

THIRTY-FIVE

CASS

A BOY SAT on the bench. I narrowed my eyes, no not a boy; a woman with a baseball cap pulled down over her face and her hair tucked under it. Her intense stare focused on the apartment building I came here to watch. I walked closer.

"Julie?" I asked, sighing with relief.

She grabbed my wrist and pulled me down next to her, hushing me.

"He's in there," she said. Her eyes slid in the direction of what I assumed was Emma's apartment. She pointed toward a door. I knew the building but hadn't had the chance to figure out which unit was hers. This revelation completely froze me. The little ball of hope I was clasping onto so tightly started to slide from my grip.

"He's been in there about an hour. You were right," she whispered.

"An hour."

She shushed me again.

I would kill him. And her. My surroundings turned crimson. I had the urge to run into the parking lot and start flipping cars. I clasped my hands in fists and my body shook uncontrollably.

I finally looked at Julie and could tell she was having similar thoughts. Her breathing was rapid, and her eyes were practically shooting flames.

We sat in silence. Time lost all meaning. I didn't take my eyes off the door. Finally, it started to open. I went to stand, ready to run up the stairs and start stabbing people. Julie pulled me down. Ethan's hair was a disaster. Sex hair. He glanced back at Emma's door, then jogged down the stairs. I wished he would fall and break his neck.

Before getting in his car, he looked around. I swear we made eye contact. I grabbed hold of Julie's hand while slumping in my seat.

"Shit, he looked right at us," I said.

"Sit up and act natural," she chastised.

His tires screeched on the pavement, and he peeled out of the parking lot. The ocean raging in my ears drowned out all other sounds.

"You came," I said when I finally got my voice back.

"I'm so mad at you I could strangle you, but I couldn't let you come here by yourself. I knew there was no stopping you, but I can't let you get in more trouble than you already are."

I nodded in agreement. She was right. Going there wouldn't change anything. It wouldn't make Ethan stop seeing her. It wouldn't put my marriage back together. It wouldn't erase what I'd done, and it certainly wouldn't bring back the stolen money.

"Come on, let's go. No more of this, Cass. It ends tonight."

I promised her, hoping I'd be able to keep it and it wasn't another of my lies. I walked away with tears blurring my vision, leaving her on the bench.

When I got home, I went straight to my room and flung myself on the bed. I curled into a fetal position and sobbed. Emma still had her nails hooked in my husband's heart. She was a liar, a thief, and a criminal, and because of my stupid mistake I'd be blamed. I'd thought I'd lost everything before, but I was still falling, with no idea when I'd reach the bottom.

"Stupid bitch!" I screamed. My throat was raw, snot poured from my nose, and my stomach roiled with nausea. After a few moments, my sobs reduced to sniffles. Rolling on my back, I pounded my chest with my fist. The ache in my heart was worse than ever; I wanted to rip my heart out and tear it in half with my hands. The doorbell rang, followed by footsteps pounding down the stairs. *Oh, the kids are home.* I hadn't even remembered to get in the shower to cry. The thought of them sitting in their rooms listening to me sob sent more silent tears streaming down my face.

A soft knocking on my door was followed by Ben's voice, "Mom? There's someone here to see you."

"Who is it?" I asked with as much normalcy to my voice I could muster.

"It's a cop," he answered. He sounded nervous.

I rubbed my eyes and hauled myself out of bed. A quick check in the mirror above my dresser confirmed my thoughts. I looked like shit. I shrugged a shoulder and went downstairs to find Officer Daley in my entryway.

"Mrs. Mitchell, I've been trying to get ahold of you all

day. Have you received any of my voicemails?" he asked. Ben stood behind me and could practically hear the gears whirring in his head.

"Ben, go upstairs and let me speak with Officer Daley," I said to him, smiling, assuring him that all was okay.

"Uh, yeah, sure," he said.

I turned back to Officer Daley and widened my smile. "Apologies. I've had a really long day. I must have missed your calls."

"Are you okay, ma'am? You look...." He cleared his throat. "You look upset."

"I'm fine," I sang. "Totally fine. How can I help you?"

"I went and visited Emma this morning, Ms.—" He reached into his back pocket, pulled out a little notebook, and flipped to a page scribbled with notes. "Ms. Wallace." He lifted his head. I smiled, waiting for him to continue. My cheeks were starting to hurt, and I felt more serial killer than happy homemaker. He cleared his throat again. He must be one of those men uncomfortable around emotional women. I hoped for his sake he didn't have a daughter. If he couldn't handle the aftermath of a crying middle-aged woman, a teenage girl would make him run for the hills.

"Yes, well. I spoke with Ms. Wallace. As with the emails and texts, she denied any involvement in the office break-in or the stolen money. We have asked her to come down to the station tomorrow for formal questioning and fingerprinting. The team will compare the fingerprints found in your office and see if there is a match. As far as the money, that's been passed onto the proper department. They'll begin their digital forensics investigation and go from there." He looked down at his notebook. My smile slipped off and was right back in place when his gaze lifted to mine again.

"*Of course,* she would deny it. Who wouldn't?"

"Yes, you're probably right. I asked if I could search her phone and she said no. Without a warrant or permission, unfortunately there's not much I can do at this point, but we're working on getting one. For her apartment and electronics." The sudden urge to vomit clutched my stomach.

"So, what do I do from here? She showed up at my private event—isn't that enough to arrest her?"

"My advice is to block her number from your phone. If you have social media, find and block all your accounts from her there too. Refrain from any contact digitally or in-person." His gaze dropped. "I would also recommend your husband do the same." His awkwardness was making me angry. He was supposed to be the professional here. I was cheated on. Shouldn't I be the uncomfortable one? "We'll speak with her tomorrow, and once we have collected enough evidence, move forward with charges."

Two bright beams backlit Officer Daley as Ethan's Porsche pulled into the driveway.

"That's Ethan, do you need to talk to him as well?"

"No, I'll be in touch tomorrow after we've completed our official interview." He dipped his head and made his way to the police cruiser parked on the street.

"Thank you," I called to his back. *Smile, smile, smile.* I squeezed the doorframe and welcomed Ethan home.

THIRTY-SIX

ETHAN

IT HAD BEEN two days since I'd learned about Cass's unexpected unemployment so hiding my own had become much more difficult. I was waking up every morning, getting dressed, and finding places to search and apply for jobs. After the stunt she pulled, I'm not sure why I even bothered hiding my secret. I was fired for being bad at my job. What she did was much worse. I still wanted to be with her, and I wasn't ready for her to find out I was still seeing Emma, or about the other women. Staying quiet seemed like the safest option. I think deep down thoughts of what Cass might do when she found out scared me.

"What are you going to do with your day?" I asked before turning to hang a pair of slacks in the closet.

"Is that some sort of dig?" she snapped.

My back stiffened. Now that she had me to blame for losing her job, there was no winning with her. I considered leaving, but still couldn't fathom life without her.

I shook my head and walked around her to grab another pile of clean laundry. I wasn't going swimming in her toxic pool, not this time.

"I'll get coffee started," she declared.

I should leave. Why did I beg to come back?

"Everything okay?" I asked.

"Everything's fine," she said in a much more cheerful tone. Keeping up with her swinging moods gave me whiplash.

"It will be okay, Cass. I'm sorry you're going through all this." I was trying my damnedest to feel sorry for her. I knew my lousy choices led us here, but faking her own stalking? What had she been thinking? Her moods weren't the only things causing whiplash. One second, I felt guilty, the next furious, and the next scared of what she'd do next.

She opened the door and walked out.

Seriously, Emma, fucking return my texts. If you stole the money and broke into her office you've gotten yourself in deep shit here.

I watched my phone, waiting for a reply I knew wouldn't come. I had been texting her since Cass confessed, with no answer. I scrolled through the endless unanswered texts. She was quick to respond when she needed money, but now there was radio silence. There was no way she knew what Cass had done. Julie and I were the only ones, and I knew for a fact Julie wouldn't have told her—I wasn't going to be the one.

It didn't seem like something Emma would do, the stalking. But after what Emma pulled by blackmailing me for money, it was hard to deny she was the one who stole from the agency. I stuffed my phone in my pocket and went downstairs.

"Heading to work?" Cass asked.

"Yep, see you tonight."

The way she looked at me was unnerving, like her eyes were peeling off my skin, like she knew I still had things to hide. I shook off the feeling, got in my car, and drove to Emma's.

I pounded on Emma's front door. No answer. With my hands cupped around my eyes I tried to see through her front window, but the curtains were pulled tight. The door next to hers opened and a couple walked out.

"Hey, have you seen Emma?"

"Naw man, haven't seen that chick in a while."

"Thankfully," the girl with him said. They looked at each other and laughed before walking away.

I called her phone with my ear pressed against the door. She rarely had her ringer on, but my stomach was twisting with worry. She had changed, but not speaking to me for so long was more out of character than showing up at an event and giving a speech about what a dick I am.

"Mr. Mitchell? What are you doing here?"

Shit, shit, shit.

I turned, lowering the phone from my ear and came face to face with Officer Daley.

THIRTY-SEVEN

CASS

I STOOD in our front hall screaming Ethan's name. His footsteps pounded down the stairs.

"Cass, what is it?" he cried when he reached me. I turned around and moved out of the way. "What is that?" he asked quietly, stepping closer. "What the fuck!"

A dead blue jay had been placed on our front porch. It looked so peaceful it could be sleeping. Its wings had been folded across its front like a blanket.

"I was cooking dinner," I said, out of breath, "and the doorbell rang—"

"That's weird, I didn't hear it ring," Ethan interrupted.

A flash of annoyance spiked through my stomach. "What does that have to do with anything? Let me finish. I was cooking dinner, and the doorbell rang. My hands were covered in ground beef, so it took me a bit to get them washed. By the time I got to the door no one was there, so I stepped outside. And look!" I pointed to the door.

Ethan's mouth dropped open. He reached up to touch the red paint on our front door. When he pulled his two fingers away, they were covered in red. Still wet. He rubbed them against his thumb, his eyes not leaving the word: DIE. The red paint dripping from each letter was almost comical in its effect. Like a horror B-Movie. Only this was my house, and my life, not some movie.

"It's her. This is the same thing she did to my office. The same exact thing. And now she's coming to our house. Threatening me. I'm calling Officer Daley."

"Wait. Do you think that's a good idea?" he asked.

My eyes bulged. "You don't think he'll find out what I did, do you?"

I had to think, but my head was filled with noise. I couldn't live like this. Constantly looking over my shoulder. Wondering what she'd do next.

"I should confess. If the police see I'm being honest, then surely they'll believe me."

"That's a terrible idea," Ethan said. "Let's just clean this up and forget about it."

I stomped past Ethan to retrieve my phone from the kitchen. I wasn't ready to confess my sins, but no way was I going to let her get away with this. Everything she had done was a crime. My actions weren't illegal—at least, I didn't think so. Thankfully, Daley picked up on the first ring and told me he would swing by later.

I walked into the living room and Ethan was staring intently at his phone with his eyebrows drawn together. He looked up when he heard me.

"Look at this," he said, holding his phone up.

"What am I looking at?" I asked, walking closer to him so I could see the screen. "Oh, the cameras! Did you find anything? Let me see, I didn't even think to check there." I reached out to grab his phone from his hands and he pulled it away out of my reach.

"There's nothing to see," he said, momentarily flustered. I narrowed my eyes. I'm positive there was something I'd like to see on his phone, and it had nothing to do with the door camera app.

"What do you mean?" I asked. "Surely the cameras caught the person who did this. They would have had to be standing right in front of it to write Die on the door. This will be the proof we need. Enough for them to arrest her, enough for a warrant. They'll find the stolen money. There's no way she's smart enough to hide millions. Finally, she'll be punished."

"That's exactly what I'm saying," he replied. "All the cameras have their motion detection turned off. It didn't record anything." He was still looking at his phone, shaking his head. He paused and lifted his eyes to me. "Did you turn the cameras off?"

My eyes widened and my mouth formed an *oh*. "Why would I do that? I've been a prisoner in my own home, terrified to leave the house because of her. The last thing I would do is turn the cameras off. Unless—" I paused, and looked off to the side, contemplating. Chewing on my situation like a rare, bloody hunk of meat. I looked back at him pointedly. "Unless you turned them off." I waited and watched. His eyes widened.

"What? No. What are you saying?" he asked. "Do you honestly find it so far-fetched that I'd question you after what you did?"

"Perhaps you had a reason to turn them off?"

"I wouldn't vandalize my home. You're not making any sense."

"You would if you were working with her."

"I wasn't accusing you of writing 'Die' on our front door. I was asking if you turned them off accidentally. You're being awfully defensive, though. Do you have something to hide? I know for a fact I do not. My secrets are all out, Cass, there's nothing more to learn. No matter how many stories you conjure in your head to further justify your bad behavior. It doesn't make them any less fictional."

"Are you sure about that, Ethan? Because you have proven to be an exceptional liar."

His jaw clenched. I pictured my hand reaching into his throat and snatching the truth from it.

"I'll be upstairs. Text me when the police are here," Ethan said. "You better hope they don't find out what you did. You're so concerned with Emma getting in trouble, I recommend stepping back and thinking about how much trouble you may be in."

"Hello," Officer Daley said when I opened the door.

I shot Ethan a text and showed Daley to the living room.

"Mr. Mitchell, good evening." He nodded his head at Ethan when he joined us. "Nice to see you again." My head turned sharply in Ethan's direction at that. "I assume you called me about the graffiti?" he asked, turning and pointing toward the defaced door.

"Yeah, thanks for coming. Again." Ethan said.

"Yes," I whimpered and wiped a tear from my right eye. "I'm scared she's going to *kill* me."

I refused to look at Ethan; I didn't have time to bother with him disagreeing with me. And if he defended Emma, tried to deny it was her, or explain it away as no big deal, well, then I'd just be forced to pull Officer Daley to the side and tell him my theory about the two of them working together. It was Ethan's moment. Time to pick sides. He could stand there and shut the hell up, or I'd make his life a lot harder than it needed to be. I'd worry about what Daley meant by seeing Ethan again later.

"Yes, she may be escalating. As you know we haven't had much luck getting any evidence from the other crime scenes or getting ahold of her as a matter of fact. Have the two of you spoken to her or actually seen her recently?"

We both silently shook our heads. "I'll be reporting this as a direct threat to your life. Between the money, the office, and now this, Emma has certainly gotten herself in some trouble."

My shoulders relaxed.

"Good, because that's exactly what it is. A threat to my life. And conveniently," I looked at Ethan "our cameras didn't record any of it, as the motion detection was turned off. So of course, we have no video of her doing it."

Officer Daley's head swiveled looking at each of us. He could sense the tension, I'm sure of it. It was so thick you could have scooped it with a spoon and taken a mouthful.

"How does the motion detection get turned off? Is there some sort of switch on the cameras?" he asked.

"No. It's within the app." I opened the app on my phone and showed him how the slider worked. "It's a built-in feature, so when you're at home the cameras aren't constantly recording every time you walk past them. It helps the batteries last longer."

"Who has access to this application?" he asked.

"Only myself and Cass," Ethan replied, looking at me.

"Interesting. I'll put the call in, and we'll fingerprint the entire area. I would suggest changing your password to the app, just in case. Avoid the door until they get here. I'll take a drive over to Emma's house and see if she's there. I'll also have some officers canvass the neighborhood and ask if anyone saw anything."

"Okay, thank you," I said, my voice cracking. "I appreciate your help."

"We'll get to the bottom of this." He nodded and left.

I angrily wiped the tears from my eyes, looked at Ethan and smirked. "Look who's the one in trouble."

He huffed out a laugh. "You really are an amazing actress, aren't you?"

I gasped. "Excuse me, *what*?"

"That little act you put on. Enter police officer from stage left. Cue the waterworks. Were those even real tears? *I'm so scared.* What the hell is going on with you, Cass?"

"Funny, because I have the same question for *you*."

"Cass," he said, his tone dejected. "There is nothing else I can tell you. At some point you're going to have to believe me or this is never going to work. This is so unhealthy. All the accusations. All the anger. It's time to let it go. You're only hurting yourself at this point. Emma is clearly having some sort of mental crisis, between showing up at the event, all of this. It can't continue forever. She'll get sick of it or will get help. Because that's what she needs, a psychiatrist. Frankly, you do, too."

"Screw you, Ethan. What she needs is to be put in jail. And I'll stop accusing you of things when either Emma disappears or you stop coming across as suspicious. It's in your hands. And not my job to prove anything to you. You started this. Not me."

We stared each other down like two dogs with hunched backs and hair standing on end, snarling and circling each other, waiting to see who would pounce first. Ethan's shoulders slumped, then he rubbed his face with his hands. His back started convulsing. I thought he was crying. When he moved his hands away, I saw there were no tears, but he was laughing maniacally. I took two steps back and sucked in my breath.

What the hell?

"We're all fucked up, aren't we? You, me, Emma. All of us."

"Don't you dare compare me to—"

"*Stop.* Just stop. I'm too tired for this. One day I hope we can all be honest. Or better yet, I hope you and I can be honest with each other." He walked upstairs. I was too shocked to say anything, so I just watched his retreating back, letting him go.

When I heard our bedroom door shut, I backed up to the wall and slid down until I was sitting on the floor. *What have I done?* Just when I thought I was getting somewhere, it became evident I was getting nowhere at all. Everything would be so much easier if I could just stop loving him. I slammed my head against the wall until the headlights from the police cruiser in the driveway lit up the hallway through the front windows.

I stood, smoothed my hair, straightened my mask, and went to greet them.

THIRTY-EIGHT

CASS

THERE WERE TOO many versions of the truth floating around. That's the problem with lying. You can never tell just one. Because when people ask questions, they become more curious. And you end up piling on the lies. I had so many versions of the truth: one for Julie, one for Ethan, one for the police, one for my kids ... too many to keep straight. I was choking on them, always afraid to open my mouth, terrified I'd slip up, and worried I'd then have to come up with another lie to cover that lie, to cover the other lies. But the truth was no better.

I was so sure I'd broken free from the prison of my past. Had shed that life, my mother, and my childhood like a snake slithering out of its skin. Or like a twenty-year-old husband stealer wiggling out of a tight dress before crawling into bed with a married man. I hadn't. I was selfish, deceiving, and vengeful. I'd spent a lifetime pushing all the things I hated about my mother deep within the confines of my soul. Emma and Ethan cracked me open. If only I'd known the shell was so thin. I wasn't free. I was still being held in a prison lined with bars made of my lies.

A cloud of hopelessness engulfed me, fogging my vision. What was the point in even trying? My fate was out of my control. Ethan would never choose me. Even if he said it, he'd never mean it. He'd already shown me I wasn't enough. Had I ever been? There were probably ten, twenty, one hundred Emmas before me. This was just the time I'd caught him.

Alice's voice sliced through my thoughts, bringing me back to the present. We were out to lunch. My secrets were still secrets.

"I think you should get revenge. On both of them," Alice said between bites of her quinoa chicken bowl. She said it so matter-of-factly, I almost convinced myself my evil thoughts were normal, innocent, justified even. I'd sit at the next charity dinner event laughing over my champagne glass with the rest of society. *Yes, Martha, I did kill my husband. Stabbing is such a messy affair, all that blood. A gun, too. Too much brain matter, it would never clean off the marble. But strangling. Now that is a murder that doesn't leave a mess. And how did you say you killed your Andrew?* I giggled, and Alice seemed to think I was laughing at her comment, so she joined in.

"Emma has ruined your professional and personal life; it's not right. People shouldn't be allowed to get away with these things."

"How would I even get revenge?" I asked. "I thought him finally seeing her for who she was would be enough. Apparently not. She's harassed me, humiliated me at a client event, destroyed my office, vandalized my home, stolen a significant amount of money from us, lied about it, and he *still* goes crawling back to her."

"He's a fool. He has no idea what he's tossing away. You're beautiful, smart, and so fun to be around. And he goes and ruins it. Twice!" Alice shook her head and looked at me bug-eyed. "Emma is nasty and so boring," she spat her name out like it tasted sour.

"I just feel so terrible that you lost your job over this, too. I can't believe Julie wasn't able to find you something else."

A darkness passed over her face like a cloud floating in front of the sun. I blinked, and it was gone.

"No, don't worry about me. With the Blaxten account being canceled and the theft, the agency is struggling to pay bills. It wasn't a surprise at all."

"I could talk to Julie. Ask her to reconsider."

"I appreciate that, but I didn't plan on staying. Not with you gone. I have some money saved, and that second property, I could always sell it if something doesn't come up soon."

"A second house?"

Her eyes narrowed. I felt terrible, Alice made it a point to memorize every detail of my life and I couldn't be bothered to know even the big stuff about hers. She smiled. "A woman I used to care for had no family when she passed. Left the place to me. It's old and in dire need of repairs, but I'm sure I could get enough to live off for a few years if needed. I don't require much."

I glanced down at my phone and noticed a missed call from Officer Daley. "Oh! Give me one second, this is the police officer investigating her. Let me just call him back and see what Emma had to say about the vandalism."

"Sure, no problem." She barely hid the excitement in her

voice, but it was written all over her face. Another front row ticket to the next episode of my very own trashy reality TV show. I put it on speaker to reward her for her loyalty.

"Officer Daley," I said toward the phone.

"Cass, hello," his voice came through mixed with what sounded like road noise. He must have been in the car. "I'm just leaving Emma's house for the third time today. Unfortunately, I haven't been able to catch her at home, or by phone—for many days. It seems her cell phone is turned off, as it just goes straight to voicemail."

"Are you sure she's not in her apartment hiding from you? Just kick down the door and search her apartment. I'm sure she's in there."

He chuckled. "This isn't a TV show." He missed the memo, apparently. This *was* a television show, I was the star, there just weren't any cameras. "I can't forcibly enter her home without a warrant."

"Then get one," I demanded.

"It's not that simple. I will continue to drop by and keep you posted when I'm able to speak to her. She could have gotten a job and is at work. I'll call you when I have more information." I ended the call.

"What are you smiling about?" I asked Alice.

"Just picturing Emma on the run. A fugitive. I wonder if she's scared?" She started cackling.

"Surely, they will track her down. How far could she have gone? Should be interesting to hear what she has to say for herself."

"Interesting indeed." Alice smirked.

AFTER LUNCH, I returned home with a strange feeling flipping my stomach. With Emma gone Ethan wouldn't be sneaking off to her house. It also lessened my chances of getting caught faking the texts. Perhaps Ethan knew exactly where she was, and he was in on it, helping her avoid the police. I scoured the credit card statements daily, looking for hotel bills or any out-of-state charges.

"How was everyone's day?" Ethan asked us when he arrived home that evening, eagerly looking around the dinner table at the kids and me. He seemed desperate to regain a sense of normalcy, to pretend all was well. A real-life Norman Rockwell painting. I should have changed into a poodle skirt, donned an apron, and served my family a steaming roasted chicken to really set the mood.

I stared at him, wondering why I'd fought so hard to get him back. If I'm being honest with myself, which I rarely am, I didn't understand why I hadn't just walked away.

"Fine," both kids replied. Aubrey still held a grudge. Ben didn't seem to know how to act. Yet, Ethan was barreling through conversations unperturbed. He appeared to be the only one completely fine.

"I'm not hungry. Can I be excused?" Aubrey asked me.

"Sure, Aubs, why don't you get some homework done?" I said, smiling. I wanted to hug them both, gather them in my arms and rock them. Tell them how sorry I was. Turn back the clocks and erase their memories of the whole, horrid ordeal.

"Well," Ethan said cheerfully. "Ben, how about you bud, do you have any homework tonight?"

"Yeah, a bit," Ben grumbled and pushed the food around his plate.

"Happy to help if you need any," Ethan replied.

I took a bite of my dinner, despite having no appetite at all. Sitting across from me was a man still in love with a runaway girl. I sighed and stood to clear my plate and busy my hands with the dishes at the sink.

"Ben, you done?" I asked.

"Yeah," he said, setting his plate on the counter and running in the direction his sister had a few moments before.

My phone vibrated and Ethan's eyes lit up with hope. He tried to hide it, but it was impossible not to notice. I had been reading his face for too many years. I had every movement, even the slightest ones, memorized. I knew what he was hoping for. She could have been texting me and telling me she was on her way to murder me and cut my body up and he still would have been happy to learn she was safe.

"You seem more interested in who that is than I do, so go ahead and look at it." I said flatly.

"What?" Confusion spread across his face. "You criticize everything I do. I can't breathe without you yelling at me."

I stopped rinsing the dishes and turned around. I could ignore him, finish the dishes, make myself a drink, and spend the evening silently watching television, like we'd done the last three nights. Or I could tell him exactly what I thought of his stupid looks every time my phone made a noise. I wiped my hands and grabbed my phone.

"It's a call from Daley," I said.

He perked up. "Are you going to call him back?"

"Yes, maybe they found her body." I laughed and walked out with my phone before he had a chance to react.

They didn't find her body. There were no new or interesting developments at all. Her friends and family hadn't heard from her, and people were starting to worry.

The most popular theory remained that she was upset about Ethan leaving her, went a bit mad, and took off after taking that insanity out on me. Daley still seemed to think she'd come slinking back to town, and we'd all just carry on. Everyone else may be able to move on with their lives, but not me. There were zero leads on the missing three million dollars. It was transferred to some offshore account, untraceable they said. Still under investigation, Daley said.

My guess was, Emma was still around, and close. She was hiding, biding her time, and she wasn't going to stop at destroying my career, office, and front door. It was obvious Ethan and Officer Daley thought I was being dramatic whenever I shared my theory. It was ridiculous, really. What would it take for these men to realize what an evil, awful human she was?

"Your girlfriend is still missing," I said to Ethan and enjoyed his grimace. If I couldn't make him love me the way he used to, as if I was the only woman in the world, then I'd make him hate me. Maybe when I finally decided to lock away my costumes for good, we'd all find how fucked up the real me is.

"Do they have any idea what's happened? Is she listed as a missing person now?"

"Do you care?" I asked, narrowing my eyes at him.

"Of course I care, Cass. I don't want anything bad to happen to her. I get you're angry at her, and I am too. But surely you don't wish her dead?"

I considered my answer. "I don't care what happens to her, if I'm being honest. As long as she stays out of my life."

He inhaled sharply. "I hate what I did. But what I hate more is what my actions have turned you into. Even more bitter and cold. All I ever wanted was for you to be warm, loving, and caring. To show me you love me. And I've screwed up so badly; you're nastier than you've ever been. I thought I was the broken one, but I've broken you, possibly beyond repair. And I hate that. I'm going to bed. I love you."

"You *and* Emma broke me. Both of you," I yelled at his back. He paused briefly, shook his head, and left me alone. He was always leaving me. Physically and emotionally.

I stopped breathing completely. A scream was lodged in my throat. A tremor started in my hands then seeped through my entire body. Rage was lighting up every nerve, setting my entire body on fire.

Thirty-Nine

Cass

A SIREN BLARED in my dream, a hand tugged at me, trying to tell me something, but I couldn't understand what. I sat up in bed and smelled smoke. It wasn't a dream.

"Get up!" I ran, shrieking down the hallway, pounding on doors. Ethan flew into the hallway in his boxers, his face frozen in terror. Aubrey and Ben walked out of their rooms, rubbing the sleep from their eyes, confused, then began screaming. The sounds of my family's terror blended with the blare of the smoke detectors. I covered my ears with my hands, trying to think of what to do. Black plumes of smoke billowed up the stairs, filling the hallway and swirling around us.

"Drop," Ethan demanded. "Everybody on the ground now. Try not to breathe in the smoke."

We followed without a word, all of us slamming onto the floor on our bellies. He motioned for us to follow him to the stairs.

"I'll go downstairs to find a way out," he yelled over the alarms.

I pulled my shirt over my mouth and nose, indicating for the kids to do the same. We were all coughing, and my eyes burned. I put an arm over each of their backs and held on tight. Ethan came crawling back up the stairs a few seconds later, coughing.

"There's a path ... to the door ... move fast. The entire ... living room is on fire. Turn around .... crawl down the stairs ... backward and head ... for the door." His coughs broke through his words as he struggled to deliver the instructions.

I let the kids go before me. We mostly slid down the stairs. Ethan motioned for them to stay down and crawled to the front door. He crouched down between them and pulled them toward the door. He dragged them much faster than they would have been able to crawl on their own. My heart lurched watching him save his children. And in a split second all the hate was gone, I loved him fully and freely. A love that burned as brilliant as the flames consuming my house. I looked back over my shoulder at the angry blaze engulfing my living room one more time before running outside. All four of us fell on the front lawn coughing, spitting, and crying. I drank in the faces of my children, covered in ash except for the streaks from their eyes where their tears had cleared a path, and I broke down into sobs. I was so close to losing them, and the pain was worse than any pain I'd felt from losing Ethan.

The alarms woke the neighborhood. I was huddled on the grass with my arms draped around Aubrey and Ben; I couldn't move, I couldn't let go. Someone placed a blanket over our shoulders. It was a hot, muggy evening, but we were shaking like we were sitting in the snow. Ethan was talking to someone, a neighbor I recognized from his daily runs, but who I'd never spoken to other than a wave and hello. I heard a siren in the distance. Someone must have called 9-1-1. We watched the flames light up the front windows. They were hypnotizing, almost beautiful. I used to love the smell of campfire. It was one of my favorite smells. I can't stand it now.

The fire truck arrived in what felt like seconds. The firefighters pulled a long hose into the house to save what was left of our home. I sat and watched in shock. The kids' sobs had calmed to whimpers. Finally, ambulances pulled onto the street behind the fire truck and the paramedics moved us, working fast and with precision to check our vitals. Ensuring we were safe.

My throat was raw from the smoke and it sent me into a fit of coughs. The paramedic had a tough look, her brown hair pulled back in a tight bun and her face was all angles, sharp and serious. But she had kind eyes.

"You're all very lucky." She smiled. I imagined what horror those eyes had seen. How could they still be so kind?

"Emma," I whispered.

"What was that? Is there someone else in there?" She turned to yell and alert someone. I gripped her wrist, digging my nails into her flesh.

"No," I said. "This was Emma. She did this. She tried to kill us."

"I don't understand," she stammered. "You know who set the fire?" She looked at me, those kind eyes now terror-stricken. I released my grip and started screaming.

"Emma. Emmmmmmaaaaaaa." The small crowd that had gathered on our lawn and the surrounding street turned and silently gaped at me. I screamed her name until it became inaudible. Until the noise leaving my lips was reduced to animal-like shrieks. I started kicking my legs and ripping out my hair.

Hands pushed my chest. I was lying on my back, staring at the roof of the ambulance. A needle slid into my arm, then I was falling down, down, down. Into darkness.

I WOKE TO BEEPING, the sharp smells of antiseptic and bleach, and faint hints of smoke. My eyes were heavy. I blinked lazily, trying to open them and bring the bright room into focus. Ethan must have sensed my movement because he jumped from the chair next to my bed and his face filled my vision.

"Cass? Cass, can you hear me? Are you awake?"

I groaned and let my gaze wander around the room, taking in my surroundings. A hospital room. *How did I get here?* Gravity took over and when my eyelids shut, I saw flames. *Fire!* I fought to sit up, but my body was too heavy.

"The kids?" I asked. My hoarse voice sounded husky and strained. I was barely able to speak above a whisper.

"The kids are fine, everyone is fine. Julie and Victoria came and got them. They were able to put the fire out, and most of the damage was contained to the first floor. We are lucky." Someone else had said we were lucky. Who was that? I remembered the kind eyes. The paramedic. Then I remembered how I got there.

"It was her," I murmured.

"What was that?" Ethan asked, moving his face closer to hear me.

"It was Emma," I growled. "She tried to kill us."

He sat back in the chair and clutched my hand between both of his and brought it to his lips. His watery eyes searched my face.

"Was it an accident?" he said with his voice trailing off.

I could have shaken him, but my limbs seemed to be filled with lead, and I was tethered to the machines surrounding me.

"This was no accident. She wanted us all dead. How can you defend her when your children almost died?"

His shoulders slumped. He brought our hands to his forehead, his head bowed like he was praying. When he looked back up, he was crying. "I'm so sorry."

PRESENT

CASS

MY ENERGY IS DRAINED. Recalling everything we've been through in one sitting, while simultaneously picking and choosing which parts to share with Daley and which to leave out has left me craving my bed. I want *my* bed, in *my* home. However, Emma took care of that when she burned the entire first story of our house. We are currently piled into the first rental we found. It works, for now.

"There was no evidence Emma had anything to do with the fire. In fact, she had been missing for days prior to the fire being set. Why are you so convinced she's responsible, Cass?" Officer Daley asks.

"Are you serious? What more evidence is needed? You said so yourself, the investigation found the fire wasn't an accident. They found evidence that lighter fluid had been poured all over the room before the fire was set. It had to be her," I say. He wasn't questioning her guilt when he came and saw me in the hospital. He visited me the night I was admitted. He had told me they'd increase resources and he'd find her. We had agreed all our lives were in grave danger. I knew something had changed the second he sat down. My instincts were right. *What's changed?* I asked myself again. *Why is he questioning her involvement now?*

"But it couldn't have been her," he says.

"That's ridiculous. How can *you* be so sure it wasn't her?" My voice is shrill. *How dare he?* My mouth is about to get me in trouble again. But I don't care. I don't like where this is going, and I'm about to stand and kick him out. Tell him exactly what I think of his shoddy detective work. He leans forward with a strange smile on his face. All the blood in my body turns to ice.

"Because, Cass, we found Emma's body this morning. From the looks of it, she's been dead for quite some time. The autopsy will give us an exact time of death, but based on the initial reports, she wasn't the person who set that fire. She couldn't have been."

I laugh. Inappropriate reaction? Probably. I couldn't help myself, it slipped through my lips as easy as the lies had slipped through Ethan's—and mine. Of course, she's dead. Even in death she found ways to continue to fuck up my life. I find nothing funny about her death, I'm not that evil. I simply have no clue how to act anymore. All heads in the room turn in my direction.

"We won't be saying another word without our attorney," Ethan says as he stands and points his finger to the front of the house.

"Why do we need an attorney? We didn't kill her!"

"Shut. Up. Cass." Ethan looks at me, his face is twisted in fury. He looks demonic; I've never seen his face like this.

It's enough to make me swallow any other questions I may have.

Officer Daley stands and nods. "Understood. I think that's a good idea. Calling an attorney, that is. For both of you." He looks between my husband and me. I'm wringing my hands and rocking. Everything is moving too fast, and my mind can't keep up. So much information to process and ponder. There's no time. I need the roaring in my ears to subside so I can think, so I can understand what's happening to me. "We'd like to speak with both of you at the station tomorrow. It would be in your best interest if you cooperate now that this is a murder investigation. Feel free to bring your attorney with you."

He goes to leave and stops. "Oh yes, one more thing. Here is a warrant for this house and your primary residence. My partners will be coming tonight. Again, I ask that you both cooperate. It will be much easier for all involved, including you. Have a nice evening."

Two police officers come through the door after he leaves. I see their mouths moving but I can't make sense of what they are saying over the buzzing in my ears. I put my head between my legs and try to stay conscious. Black spots dot my eyes. I sit up and see Ethan handing them my phone and computer. I know it's over. I know I've been caught. My secrets are about to be exposed.

FORTY-ONE

CASS

THE POLICE HAVE SEPARATED US. They must be talking to Ethan first, because I've been sitting alone in this concrete box for hours. I look up in the corner at the camera and the angry red light that's been staring at me the whole time I've been in here. I can visualize the grainy images it's capturing. The aerial view of the chipped, stained linoleum floor, the white concrete walls, the uncomfortable plastic blue chair I'm sitting in, the small table, and the empty plastic blue chairs awaiting my captors. It's a view shown on every whodunnit documentary. I used to love binging those types of shows. I never expected to be starring in one. They always show this as part of the episode, the accused criminal in the interview room. I'm sure my story will be juicy, strange, and despicable enough to warrant a *Dateline* special. I'm sure the footage that stalking camera is capturing will be part of their B-roll.

I put my arms on the table and rest my head on them. I

want to fall asleep or be somewhere else. I didn't kill Emma. The police think I did. Or they think Ethan did. Maybe they think we did it together. I did very bad things, but murder isn't one of them. I wonder if Ethan is guilty. And if he is, is he in a cinderblock room like this one confessing? Or worse, is he using me as his scapegoat? His sacrificial lamb?

"Mrs. Mitchell?" My head jerks up. Two men I've never met walk in.

"I'm Detective Brooks and this is Detective Sanchez," the overweight, balding one introduces himself and his partner. Everything about Brooks looks used and worn. Detective Sanchez looks shinier and new. Sanchez takes off his blazer and drapes it on his chair, then proceeds to roll up the sleeves of his white button-up shirt revealing a skull forearm tattoo. This surprises me, as it doesn't fit with the rest of his clean-cut look. As they both take their seats, the scraping of their chairs on the linoleum makes an awful ear-piercing screech.

I notice the folder Brooks holds for the first time when he slams it down on the table. I want to reach out and grab it, flip through every paper, know what they know, and what Ethan said. I sit on my hands to avoid temptation.

"Mrs. Mitchell, before we begin, I need you to understand your rights." Brooks proceeds to read me my Miranda rights, his voice is flat and bored, as if he's done this many times before. Sanchez leans back in his chair, fiddling with a pen, barely looking at me. He hasn't said anything yet.

"I want an attorney," I rush out. "I'm not speaking without my—"

As if she's a mind reader, my attorney, Felicity O'Connor comes barging through the door.

"Don't say one word," she says to me. She wags a finger

tipped with a red lacquered nail at the detectives. "Really, boys. Are we going to play these games? I told you both I needed a few minutes with Ethan before we started with Cass." She clicks her tongue and pulls a chair from the corner of the room and takes a seat next to me.

The two detectives watch her with smug smiles. Like the Miranda rights, this is a game they've all played many times before. I'm completely in over my head. The detectives have the confidence of men who win. But Felicity has the confidence of a woman who wins, too. Her dark auburn hair is expertly swept into a French twist, and she has dark brown eyes, alert and conniving, the eyes you want your attorney to have. She purses her red-stained lips and opens her briefcase, producing her own file and a yellow legal pad. She flips to a blank page too fast for me to read the notes from what I assume is Ethan's interview.

"I didn't kill Emma," I proclaim confidently. Felicity's head whips toward me. I've done something she doesn't like. I don't care. I need everyone in this room, and that damn nosy camera to listen to me. I'm not a murderer. I'm a lot of things, but I'm not a murderer.

"Why don't you let the detectives ask the questions before you say anything more," Felicity says.

I nod in compliance. I doubt I'll be able to follow her directive; I've never been good at keeping my mouth shut, especially in high-stress situations.

Brooks and Sanchez chuckle. *Assholes.*

"Now Cass," Brooks says. "I understand you had an ongoing case open with Officer Daley. You accused Ms. Emma Wallace of harassing you. Text messages, emails."

"And the break-ins, stealing, and fire," I add. "She set fire to my home. My entire family was almost killed. Did he tell you that? Surely, he's told you everything she's done to us."

I'm panicking. I look at Felicity, and she has one eyebrow arched. I look back at the detectives and their smirks curl higher. *Shit. Shit. Shit.* I break out in a cold sweat. I can hear my heart pounding in my ears, a drum beating the tune of my death march.

"Yes. And the fire," Brooks says, almost to himself.

"The thing that's most interesting, Cass...." Sanchez speaks for the first time. He drops his pen, and it clatters on the table, then he sits forward. The smile is now gone. "... is that we have searched through Emma's phone and computer, and we found one email to you." He flips through the folder and slides a copy of the email that started this whole thing across the table. I turn my head, as I can't read those words again. If he pulls out the photos of her and Ethan, I'll vomit. "This was very strange to us, as you can imagine, especially after looking through the endless pages of text messages and emails she's been allegedly sending you. But it's not unheard of for people to use other devices when they're doing things like this. A friend's computer, a burner phone ... criminals can get quite creative." He chuckles. I stare back at him. The color has drained from my face and I'm sure my lips are white from pressing them together. Felicity sucks in a breath next to me. She knows. They all know. I'm sure this was already discussed during Ethan's interview. I grip the seat of the chair with both hands.

Brooks takes over. "We did however, find an application on your phone. Care to tell us what you were using AutoSender for?"

"Don't answer that," Felicity says.

Why not? My secret is already out.

The entire room shifts, the floor has turned into liquid, my vision blurs. I'm about to pass out. I ask for water.

I take a sip of the room temperature water Detective Brooks hands me in a clear plastic cup. I contemplate my options. Lying. Lies would only get me in more trouble. I may as well come clean. It's time. Then I can figure out how to pick up the pieces and get myself out of this much bigger mess. Julie was right, but I already knew that, didn't I?

I explain what I did. How I used the application on my phone to send myself all the texts and all the other emails besides the first one. I pre-programmed the delivery for when I knew I'd be with Ethan or someone else. I explain why I did it. Not that it mattered to them. I'm guilty of one crime, so that makes me guilty of everything.

Felicity's shoulders slump. I feel sorry for her. She was a winner and with me, she knows she doesn't stand a chance. But I need her. I'm in big trouble, more trouble than I've ever been in. I made up the stalking, but I did *not* kill Emma.

"But the event. She crashed my event, made a big speech. There are hundreds of witnesses. It wasn't just me. She did things too. I wouldn't have destroyed my office or my own home or stolen from my own company. I faked the texts, but I would never have done it if I'd known how far she'd end up taking it."

Brooks rubs the space between his eyes with a finger. "Yes, there are a lot of layers to this. And look, I get it. Emma worked for you, you trusted her, and you trusted your husband. Finding out about the affair changed you. It made you do things and act differently than you normally would have."

Yes, exactly. I sit back and my muscles relax. They understand it wasn't me. The fake texting was so out of character. I was out of my mind. It was the anger, hurt, and rage acting; it wasn't me, it wasn't Cass.

Brooks snickers to himself. "I mean, if my old lady cheated on me. Oooooweeee. I'd be angry, that's for sure. I would probably want to kill the poor sap she had sex with."

I narrow my eyes at him. He doesn't get it. He thinks I'm a fool stupid enough to believe his nice guy act. Stupid enough to think he is my friend. Another liar.

"I didn't kill Emma," I say again.

"See, that's hard to believe, Cass," Sanchez jumps in. He's not even trying to pretend he's on my side. The good cop, bad cop routine. I roll my eyes and instantly regret it. The camera is watching. The detectives are watching.

"What's hard to believe? My husband cheated on me. I wanted everyone to hate her, so I faked some text messages and emails. Surely that's not illegal. But everything she did *is* illegal," I say.

"Gray area for sure," Sanchez says. "But the stalking isn't really what I'm concerned with."

"What exactly are you concerned with?" I ask.

Felicity glares at me. She's angry. I can't blame her.

"I can see exactly why you would hate Emma. What's hard to believe is that you didn't kill her. In fact, I think you did a lot more than 'just send some texts and emails.'" He holds up his fingers in quotes. He's mocking me. He picks up his pen and leans back in his chair, his gaze seemed to pass over me. "I think you killed Emma, and I think you set that fire in your house, vandalized your office, and stole money from your company. See, I think you weren't getting everything you wanted. What did you say? Sympathy, understanding? Everyone to hate Emma? So, you had to step it up. Make her *really* evil."

"But the event," I whisper. "She did that, so why do you think she's so innocent and wouldn't do anything else?"

I can feel the burn of their stares. I instantly regret everything and wish Emma was alive so I could kill her myself. Even in death, she's ruining my life. I stand and sweep my arms across the table so the papers fly around the room. I scream. This part will for sure be used in every story ever run on me on every television station.

Felicity stands so quickly her chair clatters to the ground. "Interview's over."

I WAKE UP IN A CELL. There is just me, concrete walls, a toilet, and a bed attached to the wall with a plastic mattress on top. On one wall there is a door with a frosted window, and on the other a window to outside, where freedom is, the window is covered in metal bars. The walls are grimy; blood, dirt, and other bodily fluids stain the concrete, a sick painting telling the stories of the prisoners who have passed through this room before me. I can practically touch both walls with my hands if I stand in the middle. I'm lying on the bed with my arm draped over my face. The red light from the camera floats behind my eyes. I picture all the people at home watching me from the comfort of their living rooms. The newscaster proclaims my guilt then cuts to the grainy image of me in the interview room, hurling the contents of the table to the floor, evidence of the guilt they've already stamped me with. Hammering the nails into my coffin, one showing at a time. I am fucked.

I stand and walk, two steps to the back wall, two steps toward the door, two steps to the back wall, two steps to the door. What's next? Am I arrested? I can't remember what happened or what was said after I screamed. This is all Emma's fault. And Ethan's. I didn't think it possible to hate them more until they stole my freedom. I worry about where my kids are. Whether they've been told what I did. If they hate me. I hope Ethan is here in this building with me. Locked up in his own cell.

Who killed Emma?

Was it Ethan? He may have been truthful when he said he'd do anything to get me back. Did he kill her because of the stalking? I look up at the barred window. *I've gone too far.* Someone killed Emma, and I probably had something to do with it. But it wasn't my hands that wrapped around her throat, as much as I'd dreamed of all the ways I'd take her life.

I turn around at the screeching of metal and my cell door opens.

"Dinner," a solemn policewoman says, before sliding a tray into the small room.

I grab the tray and place it on the bed. A slab of unidentifiable meat drenched in gravy, a hard roll, and a side of limp green beans sit in the individual indents on the tray. I push around the food. I'm hungry, but not enough to eat this food. I look at the silver toilet with no lid and grimace thinking about what happens after you eat. Is this my life now? If it is, I suppose I better try to acclimate myself. I take a tentative bite of the meat— generous description—and gag. The roll will have to do for tonight.

I have no idea how any of this works. Do I just sit here? What am I waiting for? I stand on my tiptoes to peer out the window. Too high. I place my hands on the windowsill and try to lift myself up. Too weak. I plop down on the bed and chew on my thumb's cuticle.

I fall asleep. When I open my eyes the same policewoman who brought my dinner is opening my cage door. She has another tray. Orange juice, a hunk of what I believe is eggs, and a slice of plain toast. She tells me to eat fast because I'm to meet with the detectives again after I'm finished. I nibble on the disgusting food and try not to puke. A few minutes later the police officer is back, asking me to stand. I put my hands behind my back so she can put my wrists in handcuffs. I've never been in handcuffs. No, that is a lie. I was arrested once for drunk driving. I was young and dumb and drove home tipsy after a happy hour. Not my finest moment. I'd thought that night was the end of my life. If only I'd known what was coming, where my life was eventually heading, and the night in the drunk tank would have felt like a luxury vacation.

I follow her down the dimly lit hall, trying not to fall. Walking with your hands pinned behind your back turns out to be harder than walking in four-inch heels. With no way to stop myself if I fall, I picture my face smashing into the floor, all my bones shattering, starting with my nose. I concentrate harder on each step. She leads me into the same room as yesterday. Or one that looks the same. After she removes the handcuffs, I sit down and rub my wrists.

Peeking at the red eye of the camera, I see it's still watching, still recording every movement. It's just waiting for me to create another scene for my documentary. I sit up straight and force myself not to fidget. Must look innocent. The door opens and Felicity walks in.

"Oh thank god. Are you here to take me home?"

She sits and puts her hand on mine. She doesn't have to

speak for me to know I'm not going to like what she's about to say. "The detectives are coming in for another interview. Answer their questions unless I tell you not to. Today can go two ways, you'll be formally charged, and I'll begin the steps to request a bond hearing. Or they'll let you go."

"So you'll be able to get me out of here?"

She shakes her head. "It's not guaranteed. Especially with murder charges, but I will try."

Sweat drenches my skin. I look at the door and imagine myself running through it. My dreams of escape evaporate when it opens and Brooks and Sanchez walk in looking clean and rested. It must be nice. I'm still in the same wrinkled clothes, day old makeup, and would kill for a shower. My hands instinctively lift to my hair, smoothing it behind my ears.

"Are you feeling better, Mrs. Mitchell?" Brooks asks.

I glance at Felicity, afraid to speak. She gives a curt nod.

"Yes. A bit tired," I reply.

"Sorry our accommodations weren't up to your standards." Sanchez sneers. I hate him.

"Let's pick up where we left off," Brooks continues. "You, according to your own admission, created fake text messages and emails to garner sympathy from your husband and friends. You also filed a false police report. Are you aware that's a crime?"

"First-degree misdemeanor," Felicity jumps in. "Hardly murder."

"A first-degree misdemeanor that carries up to twelve months in prison," Sanchez says.

I wasn't thinking of the ramifications of my actions when I did it, I was just thinking of the reactions I'd get. I wasn't thinking about anything but Emma. That was the problem.

"I wish it were as easy as slapping you on the wrist with a false police report charge, Cass, but you must know that's not what concerns us."

"That's all I did," I whimper. Tears slip down my cheeks. I didn't even have to fake them.

Sanchez chuckles and I glare at him. "It's hard to believe anything you say, knowing everything we do now," he says.

"An unfortunate situation indeed," Brooks adds.

"Stop talking in circles, let's get to the reason why we're here, if it isn't about the texts or emails. I'd like to work on getting my client bonded out so she can be home with her children," Felicity says.

"There's the matter of the fire," Brooks says.

I wince, remembering the smoke burning my lungs with each breath and the flames so hot and so loud. And my children's faces. Covered in ash, coughing, their expressions terrified.

Sanchez opens the same folder they had yesterday. He flips through the pages and pushes a photo across the table. Felicity and I lean in to see what he's showing us. I jerk back. Emma's death mask is frozen in a look of horror. She is not floating amongst the beautiful Everglades, a porcelain doll silently spinning in a watery grave. She has been discarded in what looks like a desolate alley. Her mangled body is surrounded by filth and trash.

"We are most interested in who murdered Emma Wallace," Sanchez says.

Felicity is unfazed by the gruesome photo. Her eyes flick to it then back to the detectives. "You have no evidence my client is involved in either the fire or the homicide. She and her children almost died in the fire. It's ridiculous, and, furthermore, you have no evidence to corroborate these false accusations," she says.

"*Ridiculous*," Sanchez says. He's back to leaning in his chair and fiddling with his pen. I wish I could rip it out of his hands and jam it into his ear. "Sending yourself text messages and emails and pretending they are from your husband's mistress, that's certainly ridiculous. Bludgeoning that same mistress until her skull was crushed, then proceeding to stab her twenty-four times..." He begins taking out more photographs, flipping them over, one by one. Macro images of Emma's body. Her head so disfigured you can see skull fragments and brain matter amongst the gore. And her body, so covered in blood, it almost looks fake. My mouth fills with warm saliva and I swallow it down to keep from vomiting. "...I think we can all agree that 'ridiculous' isn't the word any of us would use to describe what happened to Ms. Wallace. Disturbing, disgusting perhaps. Both better words."

"You know that's not what I meant." Felicity glowers at him. "It's *ridiculous* that you think my client had anything to do with this." She waves her hand over the grisly images. "There is no evidence linking Cass to this murder."

"Unfortunately," Brooks says and frowns with his lips comically low, "that isn't the case. We have evidence that not only places Mrs. Mitchell at Emma's home the night of the murder, but we also have acquired additional forensic evidence connecting her to the body and murder."

I slam my hands on the table and shake my head. *No, no, no, no!* I whip my head toward Felicity, begging her to do something with my panicked eyes. Tiny orbs of white dance in my vision. Her gaze remains locked on the detectives.

"Explain," she says.

Brooks clears his throat, takes a sip of coffee, then continues. "On the evening of Emma's murder, Mrs. Mitchell was at Emma's apartment. We have surveillance video showing her pulling into the high school parking lot near the victim's residence at 1:42 p.m. Additional surveillance footage shows her walking in the direction of the apartment building. Also, cell phone records show her phone being in that same vicinity between the hours of three and four p.m. Her vehicle is then shown leaving the high school at 6:08 that evening. Interestingly this is all on the same day Cass's office was vandalized. You had quite a busy day it seems. I've read through Officer Daley's report from that evening. He said you seemed very distressed. It had been obvious you'd been crying."

Felicity is furiously scribbling notes on her yellow legal pad.

Sanchez sits forward and clasps his hands. "We also found several strands of blonde hair in Emma's hands. Looks like she put up a bit of a fight for you."

"What? No!" I yell. "I didn't—"

There were others there that night too, one person close to me. So close she would do anything for me, someone just as angry as me, because she was wronged too: Julie. Ethan as well. But the hair. I couldn't imagine either of them setting me up for murder. I'm not ready to share that information with these two cops. Not until I've worked out what happened to Emma. Who the real murderer is.

I shut my mouth and refuse to answer any further questions.

FORTY-TWO

CASS

I'VE BECOME A RECLUSE. A troll hidden away in my cave not fit for society. By some miracle, I'm out on bond, a bond that took a good chunk of our life savings, awaiting trial for the murder of Emma Wallace. Even in death, she is the winner. I'd protect Julie no matter what, even if she placed my hair in Emma's hands. I owe her that. It's safer if the confession never passes through her lips, even to me. I vowed to never ask her. There's still a chance Ethan could be guilty, but not one I'm willing to risk. I've thought a lot about the blonde hair found on Emma. Why Julie or even Ethan would try to frame me. It's the only piece that doesn't make sense. I have nowhere else to go, so I don't dare ask Julie about Emma's murder. If she did try to frame me, I'd rather go to my grave not knowing. Nothing makes sense, but it hasn't for a while. I suppose I've given up.

As the prosecutor's evidence made its way to Felicity, I learned more about just how gone my marriage was before

Emma even entered the picture. Felicity couldn't share what she learned during Ethan's interview, bound by attorney client privilege. But when Emma's phone records became evidence, she sat me down and showed me everything. The blackmail, the other women. With everything out, it was enough to dissolve the thin layer of gossamer fabric binding us. I moved into Julie and Victoria's, while Ethan and the kids stayed at the rental house. I'm not sure I can trust Ethan with the kids yet, but I've been left with no choice, as the entire country is convinced of my guilt. The depression and desperation are making my mind slip away. Some days I doubt my own innocence.

The hair. It's the only reasonable explanation.

Julie and Victoria go to work every day. The agency is dying due to departing clients and lack of cash. Everything we worked so hard for is disappearing. Julie's not giving up, and if anyone can save it, she can. And me, I roam their halls day after day, night after night. I'm not sure what to do with all the free time I've recently been gifted, though. I'm avoiding the windows so the media vultures can't see me. I am free from my cinder block prison cell, but I am still locked up.

I'm painfully aware I'll be going to prison after my trial. I've already been convicted in the court of public opinion, so why should the actual court be any different? The fear of the unknown, the life that isn't a life; I can't do it much longer. I don't have to, though. My trial is set for one week from today. It's been a long four-month wait, and I'm running out of time.

I stand at the window hidden behind the curtain and pull it aside to peek out at the swarming predators. Their numbers have tripled in the last few days. All of them frothing at the mouth, hoping to get a shot of the dead woman walking. They know these are my last days of freedom too. I want to run outside and scream 'I'm innocent!' and beg them to believe me. I want to tell them my story. They don't see a woman scorned, a woman whose heart was ripped out and snipped apart, bit by bit. They see an evil monster, a killer, a woman who doesn't deserve to walk among them, to breathe the same air. They wouldn't listen, they wouldn't take my side. They would plaster my face on their newspapers, run Breaking Specials on their television shows: 'The Liar Lies.'

I begged Felicity to let me tell my story. If they could just see me and hear my words. Not the words of the people trying to put me in jail. If they would just listen. She refused. Told me it would be worse than suicide. So instead, when the vultures call, or become brazen enough to knock on the door, I send the calls to voicemail or ignore their insistent pounding. If I have to leave the house to meet with Felicity or for some other unavoidable reason, I hide my face and say, 'no comment.' My lips are sewn shut with clumsy stitches. Felicity thinks I'm guilty, too. I'm sure of it.

There are only three people in this world who know I'm innocent. One is dead. One is me. And the other is the murderer.

I eat dinner with Julie and Victoria, studying Julie, trying to figure out if she has something to hide. I do the same with Ethan when he brings the kids to visit. I don't accuse either of them. I know what it's like to have your innocence questioned unfairly.

THREE DAYS REMAIN until the trial. I'm losing my mind. I'm starting to further question myself. I could have done it. I hated her enough to do it. Did I black out? My rage finally took over. The monster living within my soul fully woke up, slid on my skin like a silk bathrobe, committed this act of revenge, then crawled back to the shadows. It's impossible. I couldn't have forgotten something so big, so bad. I was so fully convinced I'd been protecting Julie, but I'm not so sure anymore.

If it weren't for the hair ...

I'm standing at the window in my hiding spot behind the curtain when I see her. I gasp. My Aubrey. No, not Aubrey. I take a risk and lean closer to the window. It's a reporter I've never seen before. I have all their evil faces memorized. She's new. She looks like an older version of Aubrey.

I walk to the front door, swing it open and march right through the swarm toward her. I ignore the flashing of bulbs, the barrage of questions, 'Cass, did you do it? Why did you do it? Do you feel bad? Do you have anything to say to Emma's family?' I swat at my face. They are buzzing, lethal hornets.

"Would you like an interview?" I ask Aubrey who isn't Aubrey. She's so surprised her microphone clatters to the ground.

"What?" she asks. I can see a full circle of white around her blue irises. Blue, the color of the bay.

"Yes," her cameraman answers for her. He's already hauling his equipment onto his shoulder and walking toward the house. "Amber, come on!" he prods. Even their names are similar. Felicity will be mad, but what choice do I have? I refuse to be silenced. Not anymore.

Before I can question my decision, we are in the living room, the coffee table has been removed, and two chairs are pulled in its place. Two men run around setting up lights.

"Do you mind if I go change and put on some makeup?" I ask Amber.

"Yes, whatever you need." The hint of a southern accent rings off her words, an accent I can tell she's trying to hide. We all have parts of our past we'd prefer to leave behind, I suppose. By the time I'm ready and back downstairs, the living room has been transformed into a television set. Amber is sitting in one of the chairs testing her mic's audio. Another man straps a mic around my waist and clips it onto my blazer's lapel. I take a seat across from Amber, and I tell her my story.

Previews of the interview are splashed across the television before we've even finished. If I had time to be amazed at the efficiency of it all, I would be. I'll be the talk of every household in Florida—maybe even the country. I wonder if anyone will believe me. Some women out there, women whose husbands did the same thing to them, will comprehend the state I was forced into. Women who have felt the deep level of betrayal I've felt. Or, will they think I'm guilty too? Because they've walked in my shoes, and can understand how the need for revenge can turn anyone into a murderer? Will they be watching and wishing they had the courage to do the same to the woman who stole their safety, their comfort, their life?

I tell the truth. I'm aware this is hard to believe from a liar like me. But I do. Every question I answer with the sincerest honesty. At first it feels uncomfortable. My throat is so used to deceit it doesn't know how to form these sounds of truth. As the story tumbles out into Amber's waiting lap, it becomes easier. I wonder why it took me so long to rip off my mask. To be me. By the end I feel free, weightless, like wings will rip through my back and carry me off. My body will soon be shackled, but my mind is free. That's okay. I'm okay with that. The last shot, the one that's splashed all over the newspapers the next day, is of me smiling. If only they knew what was behind that smile. If only they knew it was honest and virtuous. It was a smile lifted by the weightlessness from no longer being burdened by my lies.

But no one ever believes a liar, not even when they've finally decided to speak the truth.

"WHAT THE FUCK? WHAT. THE. FUCK?" Felicity says even before she's fully sitting across from me at the kitchen table. Julie is pacing around us. Victoria is busying herself by making a tray of cheese and crackers and drinks. "All you had to do was keep your mouth shut for three more days. Was it so hard?"

"I wanted to tell the truth," I whisper to my lap. The high of truth telling is wearing off, and I'm realizing the gravity of my mistake.

"Nobody gives a shit about the truth, Cass, especially not them." She jabs her finger toward the front of the house where the media is camped outside. "All they care about is ratings and viewers. And a murdering suburban wife and mother brings all those. They don't want you to be innocent. They want your head! And you gave it to them. Served it to them at a dinner party. They're all sitting around your table, toasting each other and laughing at their good luck. Fuck. Three days."

"I'm sorry," I say. My bottom lip quivers. I can smell the musty stench of the jail cell and hear the clanging of the metal as the door shuts forever.

"Okay, okay. She fucked up. What do we do now? There has to be a way to fix this," Julie says.

Victoria comes over and gives my shoulder a squeeze before placing an ice water in my trembling hand. "It will be okay. Don't lose hope," she whispers in my ear.

Felicity pinches the bridge of her nose. Thinking. We all watch her in silence, hoping she has the answers.

"Okay," she says. "We can figure this out. What time is it? We need to watch the interview. See what everyone else is seeing. An edit can change everything."

"6:15," Julie says, checking her watch. "It should be on in fifteen minutes."

"Good, excellent," Felicity says. "Let's watch and we'll go from there."

The four of us pile into the same room that, only hours before, had been a television studio. Everything is back in place. How different I feel sitting here now with a stone in my stomach and a lump in my throat.

The news anchor begins, "Tonight, we speak with Cass Mitchell. Once a prominent local business owner, she now sits accused of murdering her husband's mistress. But first, Tom is going to give us our weekend forecast. How are things looking out there, Tom?" We release a collective breath and listen to Tom tell us what beautiful weather we have to look forward to, perfect beach and boating conditions. I imagine my children huddled around their television waiting to see what their monster of a mother has to say. From the moment I delivered Aubrey, then Ben, I promised myself I wouldn't disappoint them, not like my mother had disappointed me. Yet here I am. History repeating itself. I choke on a sob and Victoria gives me a supportive smile. Julie and Felicity's eyes don't leave Tom and his overenthusiastic report of the weather.

The newscaster comes back on the screen, her expression solemn. "And now, after the commercial break, our exclusive interview with the accused murderer, Cass Mitchell."

"Quite the introduction," Julie snorts. Victoria shoots her a disapproving look.

I sit on my hands and try to remain calm. I told the truth, finally. Everyone has to believe me.

My face fills the screen, I cringe as the camera zooms in close enough to see every pore and wrinkle. I inwardly thank myself for having the foresight to have brushed my hair and put on makeup. We watch in silence while I tell the world my story. How Ethan and I met, fell in love, our family. How blindsided I was by the affair. Add to it the devastation when I learned it was with one of my employees. I admitted I went too far, that I concocted the entire stalking fallacy out of desperation and hurt. I wasn't thinking, I was wrong. And I was sorry. Amber shifts the interview to the real question everyone is wondering. The reason so many people are staring at their television with hunger in their eyes. Millions of people leaning toward their televisions, ready to hear me admit my guilt and take responsibility for my crimes. I don't give them what they want. I look directly in the camera, the shake from my voice gone, and I tell the world.

"I wanted her dead, I wanted everything bad the most heinous parts of our brains can imagine to happen to her. But I didn't kill her. The night I was at Emma's house I was there because I knew Ethan, my husband, was there. I saw a text message on his phone, and I went there to catch him.

After I saw him coming out of her apartment, I was distraught. I had agreed to let him back into my life and I thought we were moving forward. Seeing him there shattered me all over again. I was right back where I started. So, I walked and cried and walked some more. I had to compose myself before I returned home to my children. That's what I did. I drove home to my children. I was there that night, but I didn't kill anyone. But my husband, Ethan, did."

The interview ends and the television fills with the news desk and the smiling man and woman behind it. They move on, discussing the next item of news. Julie flips off the television and the three of us watch Felicity. Waiting.

"I can work with that," Felicity says, nodding. She stands and repeats herself, "yes, I can work with that. Let's meet tomorrow. I have work to do tonight."

Victoria, Julie, and I sit, deep in our thoughts. I study Julie, attempt to rifle through her mind and see if she is thankful for what I've done for her. I wonder if she feels any guilt. Ethan will be taking the fall for it if I'm let off and she's the actual guilty one.

Does she care? Because I don't.

FORTY-THREE

CASS

MY TRIAL IS NOW a day away, one more sleep. I'm saying my goodbyes like a terminal patient breathing their last breaths.

"Hi Cass, it's Alice. I called to check how you're doing."

"It's so good to hear from you."

"I saw the interview. I believe you. I'll be at the trial every day supporting you. Is there anything I can do?"

"I don't even know—" My voice cracks, I knew saying goodbye to her would be emotional. We'd worked together for so many years, Alice had become like family. "I'm sorry, it's a lot right now."

"No need to apologize, I can only imagine."

I thank her through tears for her support as a friend and an employee. By the time I'm done we're both crying.

"What are you doing now?" she asks. "Why don't you come over, have a cup of coffee. Forget about everything for an hour."

I think of the circus outside the house and what it would take to even get to my car and drive there. I'm about to decline, but these are my last few hours of freedom. I'll never be able to drive to a friend's house for coffee again. I say I'll be there in twenty minutes.

I ease out of the driveway and slowly make my way through the crowd. None of them follow me out of the neighborhood. I take in the scenery beyond my windows, looking out at the glassy water as I drive over the bridge to Tampa, until I pull into the driveway at Alice's small bungalow.

She opens the door and pulls me into a hug. "Let's go sit in the kitchen. I'll get that coffee started."

Despite knowing Alice for years, this is my first time in her home. It's exactly as I would have pictured it: meticulously clean, with minimalistic décor and every piece of furniture having a functional purpose. There are no photographs, and very few knickknacks. I follow her to the cramped kitchen and take a seat at the round wood table tucked in the corner. Alice busies herself fixing a pot of coffee. When she's done, she brings two steaming mugs to the table and places mine in front of me. I go to take a sip but hesitate. She watches me over the brim of hers and giggles before taking a long gulp. The laugh is cold, and it feels like the temperature of the room drops. I wrap my arms around myself and shiver.

"Have you figured it out yet, Cass?"

The hairs on my arms rise. I want to be anywhere but here. Alice isn't acting like Alice.

"Figured what out?"

"Who killed Emma, of course."

"No, have you?"

She throws her head back and laughs.

"I don't understand," I say as the room starts to spin and sweat trickles down my back.

"Me. I killed her. I did it for you."

I shake my head. "For me?" I stand and go to leave. She places a gun on the table. So casually. As if she's offering a plate of macaroons to go with our coffee.

"Sit."

I comply.

She sighs dramatically. "So many chances," she says almost to herself. "I gave Julie so many reasons to kick you to the curb. *You* so many reasons to kick Ethan to the curb. I've put so much work into this Cass. Can't you see?"

"Why, why would you do any of this?" If I can keep her talking, I'll have a chance to escape.

She looks hurt. "For us of course. So we could be together. You and me. How it was meant to be."

Click. Click. Click. Slowly it all clicks into place.

The money, the woman I kept seeing, the house, the fire, the office, the letter given to Julie. None of it was Emma. My enemy was much closer than I'd ever imagined. Standing right in front of me the entire time. And I opened the door for her and invited her in.

"What do you want from me?"

"I've told you. Just now, before, a thousand times. You don't listen, do you?"

My mind spins, two hands clasping for reason but grabbing nothing but air.

She shakes her head. "I want you, Cass. I've always wanted you. But without all those other people." Her face looks as if she's sucked a lemon. "Everything has been set up. The money, the location. We can start over again. You and me. There's no turning back now. I planted your hair. The evidence. It all points to you. You can come with me, or you can rot in jail."

I have to choose my words carefully. "I have children. You must know I can't leave Aubrey and Ben..."

"Shut up, just shut up!" She clasps her hands in her head and shakes her head back and forth. Now is my chance, I stand, and she grabs the gun. "Please sit." Her voice is too calm, eerie. She's two different people in one body. Maybe more.

I slowly lower myself back into the chair.

"Okay." I hold my hands out in front of me. "Let's talk. We can talk. Alice, it's me. Cass. Your friend, your *family*. You remember saying that don't you? Don't do anything you'll regret. Whatever it is, help, support, I'm here for you. I've always been here for you."

A smile slits her face that burns my throat with bile.

"You must think I'm a fool."

Before I have a chance to figure out what to do, Alice lunges across the table. There's a prick in my neck and the room blurs. My head cracks on the tile.

Then there is nothing.

FORTY-FOUR

CASS

I WAKE up in an unfamiliar twin bed. Pain beats within my
skull to the tempo of my heartbeat. I moan and lift my
hand to my head, but it flops back down; the effort is too
much. My voice reverberates through my mind, screaming
at me to move, to run, to get away. My body won't listen.
Groaning, I roll over on my side. A glass of water sits on the
otherwise empty nightstand. I don't trust its contents, but
my body's relentless thirst is too much to bear. I lift a heavy
limb to grab the glass and manage to prop myself up on my
elbow. The water slides down my throat. My breathing is
heavy and raspy, and it takes me a few moments before I'm
able to hoist myself into a sitting position. I catch my
breath then lift my head to take in my surroundings. The
room is small, barely large enough for the twin bed I'm
sitting on, the nightstand, and the rocking chair in the
corner.

I look toward the door. A piece of paper rests on the

floor. Can I trust my legs to stand? I push myself up and take two shaky steps before collapsing to my knees.

Don't scream, don't try to escape. If you do either, I will kill you. Obey and you'll get the answers you're looking for.

Alice signed her name in her familiar script. Whatever poison she'd injected me with begins to take its leave. The cotton balls stuffed in my head, softening my thoughts, disintegrate. I sit on the floor for a few moments catching my breath and sweep my gaze around the room. The single window is covered in wood planks. A pile of sawdust coating the floor below indicates they were a recent addition. I stand and stumble to the door, trying the handle. Locked. Not a surprise. Just as I've managed to get myself back on the bed the door opens. My head whips up and Alice walks in carrying a tray of food.

"Wonderful to see you awake," she chirps. "The headache should wear off soon. Eating will help. We have plans to make, so let's get you back in working order, shall we?"

"People know I'm here, they'll come looking for me," I croak.

"They've already come to my house. Unfortunately for you, that is not where we are. I've had ten years to plan this, Cass. I'm a very patient woman. This is my *other* house." She rolls her eyes and I remember our lunch. I'd felt guilty for forgetting about this house.

What the fuck is happening?

After placing the tray on the nightstand, she takes a seat next to me on the bed. "I'm sure this is all very confusing for you. But not to worry, you'll have all the answers your little mind is frantically searching for very soon." She taps the side of my head and smiles at me.

I glare at the food with distrust, but I'm famished. What's worse: starving to death or death by poison?

As if reading my mind, she adds, "It's just food, nothing that will harm you."

Alice stands and intertwines her fingers at her waist. "Go on, eat. You need your strength." She turns and leaves me in the room alone with the suspicious food. The lock engages and I'm a prisoner again.

I pick up a slice of toast from the plate and turn it over, then take a whiff. It looks innocent enough. A piece of toast with some jam slathered across it. My stomach groans, making the decision for me. After a few small nibbles, my mouth takes over and I finish every bite of the breakfast Alice has provided. My energy begins to return, and with it, the sudden urge to use the bathroom.

My fist pounds on the door calling her name.

She finally comes and opens the door. "What is it?" she huffs.

"I need to use the bathroom."

She sighs and produces a pair of handcuffs. "Hold out your hands." I stumble back, the sight of them bringing back memories of jail. Not that this room is much different from my cell, other than slightly more palatable food, and a slightly more comfortable bed. The fear of the unknown, of what happens next, is very much the same.

"These are the rules, Cass. If you want your answers, and more importantly, if you want to stay alive, I suggest you follow them without complaint."

I honestly don't know what I want more, whether that's life or answers. I hold out my hands and she fastens the cuffs to my wrists.

"I can't have privacy?" I ask when Alice follows me into

the small bathroom. There's a shower, toilet, and pedestal sink. She simply looks at me, so I break eye contact and continue with the humiliating experience of peeing under her watchful stare.

"Can I take a shower?" I'm not sure what plan I'm trying to formulate, but a shower means feeling better, or even escape. I'd take either at this point.

"No. But you can brush your teeth and hair, and wash your face at the sink." She points to the brush, toothbrush, toothpaste, and face wash lined up on the chipped counter.

Afterward, I'm shuffled back to my cell of a bedroom.

"They'll figure it out, find this place ... wherever it is. They'll all show up looking for me. Any minute now."

She smiles from the hallway, hand on the door handle. "I'm not sure who 'they' are, but the media is reporting you've run off with the money you stole from you and your partner's business. Apparently, some new evidence emerged linking you to that whole messy ordeal. Tsk, tsk, Cass, stealing from your best friend like that." Her smile morphs into an exaggerated frown then curves right back up again. "I'm happy to show you some of the clips if you don't believe me. Oh, and the police have already searched my house; I gave them full access. They thought I may be your accomplice, hiding you away. You aren't the only one capable of fooling people."

I USE meals to track time. It could be worse, I suppose. She could slowly starve me to death. Breakfast, lunch, dinner, sleep; another day gone. It's been four days and I've missed my trial. I'm sure that's another slew of charges. I have so much time to think yet I still can't figure out why this is happening. It doesn't help that my mind softens more each day. I think, and I think, and I think, but it's like screaming into an endless void, with no answer and no one to hear you.

Is Ethan looking for me? Julie? The kids? Or is this easier for them? No lengthy trial to sit through, no obligatory visits to jail to be burdened by. Do they believe what the police and media are saying? That I am guilty and have run away? It's what I had been accusing Emma of doing.

Alice places breakfast on the nightstand. There's a change, something additional added to the tray. Does this mean answers are close?

I pick up the photo and study it intently. It's a grainy Polaroid of a mother and newborn. The colors have faded with time, and the edges of it curl in on itself. It's a snapshot from the hospital. The mother's dirty blonde hair hangs in tangled strands falling in her face, hiding it, and pooling on the baby's belly.

"Who are these people?"

"You wanted answers. I'm giving you what you want. This should please you."

She closes the door and leaves.

I hurl the tray across the room. The tray's contents clatter against the space she occupied and fall to the floor. I'll regret throwing it in a few hours when my stomach is crying for food. I stare at the photo, holding it far away then up close. I flip it over and search the back for writing, anything to explain why Alice gave it to me.

There is no lunch, as punishment for the thrown breakfast I assume. Dinner comes with more extras. This time photos of a young girl—perhaps five or six—and a newspaper article. The photos look like they were taken at a hospital as well. Each one is from a different angle to highlight the child's injuries, some fresh and some scars possibly years old. There are circular burn marks, scratches, bruises, older white scars, and fresh, angry new red ones. The girl's ribcage protrudes through her skin, and her cheeks are sunken, clearly malnourished. I flip through them, silently crying for the child in them.

HOUSE OF HORRORS: LOCAL FOSTER HOME RAIDED, HUSBAND AND WIFE ARRESTED

FAIRFAX, VA –A local couple has been charged with multiple counts of child abuse and neglect after a raid conducted on their home uncovered a house of horrors following an anonymous tip. Respected pastor Charles Donavan and his wife Tonya are currently in custody facing multiple felony charges. According to court documents, the couple's four foster children were being raised in deplorable conditions, deprived of food and basic care, and physically and mentally abused while in their care.

According to Virginia Police Chief Peter Williams, "These children have su!ered egregious abuse including being locked in dog kennels, and starved for days, possibly longer. Injuries found seem to date back years. Broken bones that never healed properly, and evidence of cigarette burns covering their entire bodies. I've been with the force for over twenty years, and have never seen anything so evil."

Neighbors and members of Donavan's congregation were equally shocked. "I would have never expected this from them. They were always so kind and giving. I've never seen either of them so much as lose their temper," said a neighbor who requested to remain anonymous.

Both Charles and Tonya are currently being held at the Fairfax County Detention Center awaiting trial dates.

The newspaper article and photos are sprawled on the bed. The longer I stare at them the less I understand.

"You're wondering what this has to do with you, aren't you?"

I start at the sound of Alice's voice. She leans against the doorjamb with her arms crossed and a smirk playing at the corners of her mouth. I consider running at her, barreling through her and taking off. But I don't trust my atrophied muscles. I've been locked in this room eating barely enough calories for days.

"Yes. None of this makes sense."

"Well, little sister. Those are photos of me," she says, stepping into the room.

There is too much information packed into that small sentence. My mouth flaps open and closed trying to keep up with my thoughts.

"Why did you just call me sister?" I ask tentatively.

"Because that's exactly what we are, sisters. Surprise. Quite the family reunion, don't you think? Mother would be so proud."

I shake my head. "No. I have no siblings. I have no sister."

"None that you knew of. And technically we're half-sisters. But half is still blood. Mommy dearest gave me up as a baby, long before you were born. Threw me out like trash. And that's who I ended up with." She points to the newspaper article. House of Horrors seems to glow from the faded, yellowed page. "It took forever to hunt down that piece of shit who birthed us. And imagine my surprise when I found out she had another daughter, one she kept. Mom was dead by the time I found her. Probably for the best, but delighted by the prospects of a little sister, I had to find her. To find you and save you from whatever horrors you were being forced to endure. That wasn't the case for you, was it? You weren't sent off to live with monsters. Quite the opposite, in fact. You were sent to a grandmother, a perfect, wonderful grandmother. And how unfair is that? She was mine too. Why wasn't I sent there? What made you so special that you got to have her but not me? Alas, we grew so close over the years. I just knew I could move past this awful jealousy. If only you'd see. Accept me. Love me."

Her fisted hands punch the sides of her head. Her mind is gone. Alice is broken. My sister. Another life my mother ruined.

FORTY-FIVE

CASS

THE FEELINGS ENTANGLE themselves within my heart, vines growing and twisting across themselves. How different would my life have been if I'd known this? How different would hers have been? This is all my mother's fault. I've been lying on the small bed, on top of the faded flower comforter for hours, a day, a week, who knows? I've been reduced to an animal having to use the bathroom in the corner of the room.

With nothing to do, I'm transformed from this room of torture to my grandmother's warm, sun-bathed kitchen, only it's not just the two of us. A second, older girl is there too. We're baking cookies, laughing. We're happy. The life that could have been. But no, my mother stole that life from Alice, from all of us. For no good reason. She didn't want any of us, but she was so selfish she couldn't even give us up the right way. The way that would have afforded us the opportunity to experience love. For me not to grow into a lonely and bitter adult. And for Alice not to grow into a jealous murderer.

I hate Alice. But I also feel incredibly sorry for her. I get it. I understand where her hate was bred.

"Eat and drink these. I want to show you something." Alice hands me a glass of water and a slice of bread. I greedily snatch them from her.

"Stand, wrists out," she commands when I'm finished eating.

I slowly push myself so I'm standing. I wish I had the strength to kill her. Push her on the bed and smother her face with a pillow until the life leaks from her body.

We shuffle down the dim hallway to another door. This one is not fitted with locks on the exterior. My legs feel like they've lost the ability to hold me up when I walk into the room.

FORTY-SIX

ALICE

I LEARNED about my past by pure accident. Well, I didn't accidentally go searching through my foster mother's things, the house I'd been sent to after The House of Horrors, but I knew she snuck into her room to read romance novels while her husband worked. I dug through her drawers, hoping to get my hands on one of them to read, but stumbled on a box with my name on it instead. A few faded papers, yellow with age and the photo of my mother and I as a baby in the hospital filled the box.

Another thing stuck out to me: *No known living relatives.* My birth mother lied. She had to have known her own mother was still alive. She chose my life for me, and she chose wrong. I asked my foster mother that evening, with tears in her eyes she explained she didn't know much, but information wasn't so secret back then, not if you had gossipy church friends in the right jobs. That was when I learned about Cass. I pictured the dark closet, the years of abuse. I had to find my little sister.

I didn't have much, but I had a name and the next year I aged out of the system. It took a few years, but I was finally able to fill in the rest, including Cass, my little sister, living her perfect life at college, while I slaved away standing on my feet for nine-hour shifts for minimum wage, barely earning enough to keep a roof over my head and food on my table. I quit my job and moved to Florida to watch, observe, and plan. I moved in with an elderly woman with no family, and left Bethany Moore, my real name, behind. I became a caretaker to the dying. She left me her house, a very convenient location to imprison a person. I'm so glad I never sold it.

Cass was everything I could never be. I wanted to be her, I wanted to be a family, I wanted her for myself. An article about the agency opening finally told me it was time. I read the article at least ten times, then traced her face in the black-and-white photo that accompanied the article with my finger. Her perfect face. Her perfect smile. Her perfect life.

I carefully cut out the photo of her from that article, keeping only her; I didn't need Julie. I dug through my junk drawer in the kitchen and found a thumbtack. Back in my bedroom, I ripped down the poster above my bed, a replica of Van Gogh's *The Starry Night*. I'd thought myself so clever and cultured when I'd hung it up. I placed the thumbtack through the photo of Cass, careful not to pierce through any part of her, and hung her smiling face above my bed.

Getting a job at the agency had been a lot easier than anticipated. I spent years watching Cass, but her career had never held much interest to me. A goal in mind, I spent a month learning everything about the industry, about online, print, and television advertising. How it all worked from media planning to media optimization. I learned more watching YouTube videos and reading articles and blogs than any four-year degree. I was a sponge, sucking up every drop of knowledge. I was ready. I applied for an assistant position.

My cover letter was assertive, well researched, and professional. It worked, as I received a call for an interview two days after applying. The listing had over two hundred applicants. I had something those applicants didn't have. I knew Cass, and I knew the agency. She liked my enthusiasm, she told me during the interview.

I got the job. By then, my little Cass shrine over my bed had grown. Photos and articles I'd collected from my online research, a few I had taken myself from my in-person research. Some would call it stalking, I consider it research. With my new job, I now had more access to Cass. I was no longer watching from afar. I was part of her life, interacting with her. I worked my way into earning her trust, proving my loyalty. We grew closer and I learned more about her life, including how after our mother died, she wasn't sent to foster care. She never needed saving. I feared she may end up at my house one day and stumble on my collection. I purchased a second house, and moved into that one full time. Only returning to lie on the bed and visit Cass whenever I felt her slipping away.

Then it happened. It was as if the universe finally answered every prayer I'd ever whispered into its winds. The account managers all went out to lunch. It was a Friday, so I knew they'd take longer than our allowed hour lunch break. They always did on Fridays. I walked past Emma's desk and noticed her phone sitting there. I knew her passcode. I knew everyone's passcode. People are so brazen with that type of information. You only have to watch someone's fingers once and you have access to their entire life through their phone. People are on their phones so often they are bound to unlock it at least one time within view. You just have to be watching and pay attention. It's so simple. At least for the observant like me.

I expected to find something embarrassing. Some raunchy texts or photos I'd allude to in a conversation with her later. Enough to unnerve her, something to provide a bit of amusement on a slow day. It would be fun to watch her pretty face sweat. I never expected to find what I did. Texts, emails, photos. Thousands of them. Between her and Ethan. Their entire love story at my fingertips. I got my phone out and took photos of everything. By the time they all returned, giggling and chatting, I was long gone, Emma's phone back where she left it, all fingerprints wiped off just in case. You can never be too careful.

I spent several nights sitting on my bed, staring at Cass, asking her what to do, what to do.

I DIDN'T EXPECT everything to go so perfectly. Even the most devious crevasses of my mind could have never divined a more perfectly orchestrated symphony. I was good, but I wasn't *that* good. But then Cass fell apart. It was repulsive. She redeemed herself, though. Oh, my, did she redeem herself. The fake stalking. Brilliant. I wish I had come up with it myself, but it gave me an idea. Push Cass farther off the edge, and everyone away. I'd have Cass all to myself. We could start over, have the life we both deserved. A fresh start.

Imagine my surprise when Emma played right into my hand as well. The little show at the event—the perfect diversion. A few more Emma misbehaviors manufactured, and no one would ever suspect me.

I followed Cass to Emma's house that night, waiting in my hot car watching Julie and Cass watching Ethan. By then I had access to Cass's entire life. I even had her phone sharing its location with mine. I'm not even sure if she knew it. I had an emergency collection of her hair, just in case. A backup plan is imperative. Cass could comply or she could go down for Emma's murder. The choice was entirely up to her. Cass and Julie left soon after watching Ethan leave. So cowardly those two; I wasn't the only one whose personality was a lie.

Once sure they were gone for good, I was ready. I retrieved my backpack and strutted up to Emma's apartment, knocking three times on the door. She didn't recognize me. Not when I said a cheerful hello. Not when I pushed her back into the apartment. And not when I took out the hammer and bashed in that perfectly shaped head of hers.

I did manage to get some more information from her between the blows while she begged for her life. Turns out Ethan wasn't there for sex. He was Cass's white knight, galloping up on his stallion to stop the evil witch from harassing his poor, fair wife. Hilarious. That would be a piece of information I didn't share with Cass. The time for sharing was over. Her thinking Ethan was still cheating would do nothing but benefit my cause. I laughed hysterically at my good luck. When she was done convulsing and making funny grunting and gurgling noises, I went into the kitchen and found the biggest knife she owned and stabbed her, twenty-four times according to the news reports. I didn't keep track at the time. The quantity surprised even me. It explains the amount of blood. When done, I stepped back to admire my work. Poor, pretty Emma. Now a lifeless, bloody, pulpy mess. Oh boy, I had my work cut out for me. *This could take all night,* I thought while observing the wreckage.

It's okay. I had all night. And I had a plan. I began cleaning with the supplies Emma had available. I brought my own, but they were in my car which was not parked anywhere near CCTV cameras. Another rookie mistake from Cass.

When it got late enough, but not too late, I found hair extensions in Emma's room, the most Emma looking outfit, a pair of leggings, and a cold shoulder T-shirt I tied in a knot to make a crop top. With the baseball cap back on, my long black ponytail, and under the poorly lit lights of the apartment complex, any nosey neighbors wouldn't know the difference. From my car, I retrieved a large suitcase and filled it with the necessary items. Back in the apartment, suitcase emptied, I stuffed her body in. After testing it, I stepped back and considered its weight. It would be a struggle but with enough concentration I'd be able to wheel her out unseen.

I finished cleaning my mess, well Emma's mess, and placed the new throw rug I'd brought in over the spot her body had bled out. Eventually the police would find the evidence and know she had been killed there. But I had time. With my Emma costume back on, I rolled the suitcase out of her apartment and made my way to her car. If anyone saw me, it would only help the narrative. Emma ran away. Afraid to get in trouble for 'stalking' poor, sweet Cass.

I dumped the body behind a dumpster in a seedy area

where I knew it would be a while before anyone would find her. I drove toward Fort De Soto, pulled off in a kayak launch, and threw the hammer and knife as far into the water as my tired arms would allow. Pleased with my work, I went home and waited. I began to question Cass. She'd never agree to my plan. In an act of desperation, quite unlike my typical modus operandi, I went to Cass's house and set the fire.

I didn't expect them to survive. My goal was for them to die, the police to find Emma, and Cass's memory to be tarnished as a murderer. I'd be sad about my niece and nephew dying, though. A necessary evil, I convinced myself. Imagine my relief when I learned they survived, and Cass was charged with Emma's' murder. The fire had been a light misstep, but not a complete stumble. Cass still had the opportunity to make the right choice.

According to my research, the Maldives don't have extradition to the US. I didn't plan on getting caught, but that was important. It's beautiful, and three million dollars will go a long way there. I have two tourist visas with new identities and plane tickets for two days from now.

Cass has one more opportunity to choose sides. I hate her, but she's the only family I have. And if she won't see what's right and help me restore the proper order, I'll kill her.

FORTY-SEVEN

ALICE

"WHAT IS ALL OF THIS?" Cass asks. She's staring slack jawed at my wall of Cass. I've been adding to it for so many years I forget what an impact it may have on new eyes.

"That's you, Cass. Don't families hang photos of each other on their walls?"

She looks at me with confusion.

I sigh. The crystal-clear waters of the Maldives call to me. Away from all of this, and away from the scars left by the Donavans and our mother.

"Why didn't you just reach out? Tell me who you were? Everything could have been so different. We could have been a real family." She cries, but she's not sad for me. She's sad for herself. I know her probably better than she knows herself.

"No Cass, that was never possible."

She shakes her head. "Of course it would be. Alice how

long have you known me? I would have welcomed you into the family. You're practically family already!"

"I'm giving you a choice. Life or death. You can come with me to the Maldives, where we can start over. Or you die here."

"I have children! I can't leave them—"

My eyes dull and face becomes lifeless. I'm bored with this game. "I've changed my mind. Invite revoked."

Before she has a chance to respond, I grab the lamp from the bedside table and slam it into the back of her skull. She crumples to the floor. I'm not in the mood to clean another bloody mess, so I grab a towel from the bathroom and place it under her head. She looks so peaceful, like she's sleeping. I've never strangled anyone so I pause and consider which would be easier. Rope, pillow, or hands. My hands aren't very strong, and with a pillow you can't see what you're doing, I think of the tie-down straps I use to secure my paddleboard to the roof of my car and jog to the garage to retrieve them.

I walk back into the room. The bloody towel is on the floor where I've left Cass, but she's not.

I was only gone seconds, where is she?

Staring at the bloody towel, clutching the rope, anger vibrates through my body.

FORTY-EIGHT

CASS

"CASS!" Alice calls my name, singing it like a twisted nursery rhyme. I grab my head and rock; the agony, it's too much. I look at my blood-covered hands. I'm so sleepy, my body begs to lie down, to close my eyes for just one second.

No! A voice screams in my head. I widen my eyes. I must stay awake.

"Casssss." She's taunting me. My eyes frantically search the dim closet. I need protection. Something. Anything. An object on the shelf catches the light. I stand, trying to make as little noise as possible. I reach up and my hand closes around it. When I bring it toward my face I almost laugh. It's the employee of the year award we gave Alice two years ago. The floor seems to shift, and orbs of sparkling light dance in the room that I know aren't there. I don't have much time before I pass out. Her footsteps are getting closer.

She flings open the door. I lunge. I smash her face, her head, anything I can with the glass statue. Her nails rake the sides of my face. My head flies back when she grabs a chunk of my hair and pulls.

She falls, bringing me down with her, but I'm on top. I have the advantage. I straddle her stomach up on my knees. The glass award is slippery. I lift it above my head with both hands and bring it down on her face. Her head lolls to one side, and I scramble off her. Her hand reaches out and grabs my ankle, but her grip is feeble, and I kick myself free. I'm running, through the house, out the door, down the street. Blood covers me, mine and hers.

I stand in the middle of the street and shield my eyes from the blinding headlights and whisper, *"help"* as I collapse.

FORTY-NINE

CASS

I CAN HEAR Aubrey's voice calling, but she's so far away. Memories of Alice and her house flood my mind. *Oh my God, she got Aubrey!*

I struggle to sit up but am tethered to the bed. Has she used the handcuffs?

"Cass, can you hear me?" It's Ethan. I strain to open my eyes, but it's so bright. Their faces hover above mine. Their beautiful, safe, and healthy faces. "You're in the hospital."

"Where—Alice." Words are too hard.

"She's dead, you're safe. She can't hurt you."

I relax, relieved, and let myself fall back into a dreamless sleep.

When I wake up again, I'm more alert. I roll my head to the right. Julie is next to my bed flipping through a magazine. She looks up.

"You, my friend, are a fucking badass."

I laugh but end up coughing.

"Here, take a sip of this." She stands and holds the straw between my chapped lips. I sip the cold water greedily. "The doctor was just here. She said you took some hefty blows, but nothing permanent. You should be out of here in a week or so."

"I had no idea," I say. "That she was my sister, that she killed Emma. I was going there for coffee. To say goodbye."

"She had us all fooled. They kept telling us you ran away to avoid the trial. It never felt right. Even Ethan didn't believe it. But they wouldn't listen to us. We just didn't put the pieces together fast enough. Looks like you didn't need us to. I was so scared we lost you."

"You can't get rid of me that easily." We both laugh, and she holds the water up again to help me drink.

"Some other good news. The police found the stolen money. We lost a lot of clients, but I think we may have a chance. Now that the full story has come out, people are at least returning my calls. We can start over. Get everything back."

I shake my head as much as my aching neck allows. "I don't think so, Julie. I think I'm calling it quits. I'll be cheering you on from the sidelines this time."

"I thought you might say that. But had to ask. It won't be the same without you, you know? Definitely not as much fun."

I smile and reach for her hand. She squeezes it then sits and goes back to reading her magazine.

When I wake up again, Julie is gone and Ethan occupies the chair. I look around the sterile room.

"The kids are at Julie's, just me today. How are you feeling?"

"My head is killing me. But could be worse."

"I forgive you for accusing me. We've both screwed up, but we'll get through this, we're still a team."

My head turns to him. I'm more alert than I've felt in days. I gaze at him a few moments. "I want a divorce, and I want you to leave."

Fifteen Years Later

Cass

I STOP HALFWAY across the Belaire Bridge walking path to look down the intercoastal. Luna, my rottweiler, sits obediently by my side. She's used to this. I stop in the same spot every day. I watch the water, looking for dolphins and manatees, and enjoy the salty breeze on my skin. Life is much slower these days. I have time for things like walks, and salty air. An anhinga sits on a pile sunning itself, then takes flight. I don't talk about Alice or Emma anymore. Their names have flown away, like the anhinga.

It took a lot of therapy and a lot of sleepless nights for me to recover and get to this point though. For so many years, I'd been wading in murky waters, my feet sunk in the sludge and pulled down by my past. After Alice died, I had two choices. Wade further out and drown, or walk to shore.

I chose the shore.

I stayed with Julie and Victoria for a year. Ethan and I were done the moment I opened that email, if only I'd realized that then. Another crossroads where I chose the wrong turn. I try not to think back on what could have been if I'd walked left instead of right. There's just too many of those moments. Dwelling on them leads to nothing.

I have my own condo now, right off Sand Key beach. My new life is a simple life. I'm no longer hounded by the media vultures. It took them a while to get bored with me, to move on to the next sensational murder case. Occasionally, I'll get a call or a knock on my door on the anniversary of Emma's death, sometimes Alice's. I always ignore them. Aubrey has married a nice boy named Dylan, and they are expecting their first child, a boy; he's due in August. I'll be a grandmother. I'm so excited I can hardly contain myself. I'm already getting lectured on spoiling him, and he isn't even born yet. Ben has moved to Miami, where he's living the single life and loving it. I consider Ethan a friend, no more, no less. I hear he's dating a nice woman. I don't know much about her, and I don't ask. I want him to be happy, to be loved, but knowing too much would be too painful.

I did a few interviews and wrote a book when I was first cleared of all charges. The money I made from them supports me, along with some spending money I get from the occasional freelance gig. Parker Advertising Agency is thriving. I had no doubt Julie would get it back.

I read a lot, take walks on the beach, and enjoy four-course meals at Victoria and Julie's house. No more lies, no more masks. I have discovered who the real me is, and I love her.

"We better get going. Aubrey and Dylan will be here soon," Bryant says, approaching me.

I smile at him and take his hand. They always say love finds you when you aren't looking, and that's what happened with me. Bryant and I met on one of these very walks. Luna introduced us; she fell in love with him first. He is kind and loving and perfect in every way. It took me years to believe I deserve him. But I do. And I wake up every morning, roll over, and study every bit of him, thinking I am so unbelievably thankful for him, for my kids, for my life, for all of it. I smile every day while I wait for him to wake up.

My heart could break, only this time from being too full of love.

The End

WE'RE ALL *LYING*

BOOK CLUB DISCUSSION

1. Alice is a complex character whose motivations changed throughout the course of the book. When learning about her past, did you feel empathy for her? Or were her actions inexcusable?

2. Did Cass's "big reveal" surprise you? Did you understand why she did what she did?

3. Jealousy is a resounding theme throughout the book. How do you think jealousy impacted the course of the characters' lives?

4. Cass and Ethan's relationship play a large role in the overall plot. Besides Ethan not cheating, how could Ethan and Cass have changed the trajectory of their lives?

5. What impact does Julie's friendship have on Cass?

6. Cass has several traumatic events happen in her past; what part do you think these played on the person she became?

7. Emma, in many instances, acted uncaring and selfish, do you think she was acting out from being hurt, immature, or something else?

8. Why do you think Cass initially stayed with Ethan?

9. Cass publicly accuses Ethan of murdering Emma; do you think she does this to protect Julie or for revenge?

10. What twist was most surprising?

Acknowledgments

Am I ugly face crying while writing this, probably. Because holy shit, I'm writing acknowledgments for my first book... what a dream. First and foremost, I want to thank my emotional support person, friend, and editor Alexandria Brown (I'm calling you Alexandria, does that mean I'm mad at you?). Without you I wouldn't be a published author, or even close to the writer I am today. You're stuck with me forever babe, and it's gonna be a wild ride. I'd also thank the other half of Rising Action Publishing's ownership team, Tina Beier, who 'gets' the mom work life, cracks me up, and is a scary good editor. Seriously, how do you find these things? A special thanks to Natasha MacKenzie for designing a cover I'd be proud of readers judging my book by.

Mom and Dad, I was a pain in the ass to raise, now that I have kids, I totally get it, but you have believed in me from the start and you are amazing, they don't make parents better. I know how lucky I am to have you both. A special thanks to my mom for always buying me books...so many books. And when ten-year-old Marie told you she wanted to grow up and be the female Stephen King, you didn't laugh, instead, you signed me up for every writing class and contest.

Laura, my baby sister, I'd like to formally apologize for telling you, "It's easy, figure it out yourself." When you asked me to teach you how to put on eyeliner. It's been 30 years and the guilt is still there. Forgive and forget? Thank you for being an amazing auntie and sister. You're brilliant, I want to be you when I grow up.

Lyric, Braelynn, Blakely, Austin (Stefan, whose idea was it to have all these kids?) I know it doesn't always feel like it, especially when my face is in my computer writing and reading, but you are my whole entire world. You are all meant for big, amazing things. I'm so lucky to be your mom.

Stefan, you annoy the fuck out of me, you crack me up, you make me feel heard, special, and all the good things. Thank you.

Kathy and Bobby aka Hannah and Gramps, you opened your arms to Lyric and me the minute we met, instant family, I love you for that, and for all the love and support I've received from both of you, along with Shelly, Chuck, Kristen, and Davis.

A big giant virtual hug to all my writing pals, especially the Moms Who Write crew. Coy your early feedback is always so motivating, but you also push me to be better. Natalie thank you for being one of my first readers and believing in this book. And to all the other ladies for being the best support.

My AAMP family, you have put up with listening to me talk about this book (and all my other ones) for the last two years, and with just me in general for the last seven. What an honor it is to know all of you. A special thanks to Katie, Herb, Scott, Steven, Phyliss, and Delaney. What a long, strange trip it's been, cheers to more years together.

My BFF J9 not Demmie (but sometimes still Demmie) Mitchell, I love you, I love you, I love you.

Shout out to my Instagram and TikTok friends, readers

and writers, I have a blast with y'all. Thanks for all the support and book recos.

To every Uber Eats driver who delivered Starbucks (sometimes multiple times a day), you are the real MVPs of this acknowledgment section, thanks for the caffeine and for not judging me.

Thank you to every reader who took a chance on me and picked up this book. Words can't express how eternally grateful I am for every single one of you.

And finally, thank you to every teacher out there encouraging reading and opening the magical world of books to children. A special thank you to every teacher who has inspired my children, spent extra time with them when they were struggling, and encouraged them when they were frustrated. I appreciate you every day.

With Love,

ABOUT THE AUTHOR

Marie Still grew up obsessed with words and the dark and complex characters authors bring to life with them. Now she creates her own while living in Tampa with her husband, four kids, two dogs, and a very grumpy hedgehog.

Her debut novel *We're All Lying* released in March 2023, and her forthcoming novel *My Darlings* will be released in 2024. She also writes suspenseful women's fiction under Kristen Seeley with Beverly *Bonnefinche is Dead* available September 2023.

She loves connecting with readers online, so give her a follow on Instagram or TikTok @mariestillwrites and say hello.

9 781990 253317